11

Tsutomu Sato

Illustration Kana Ishida
Illustration assistants Jimmy Stone,
Yasuko Suenaga
Design BEE-PEE

The Irregular at Magic High School

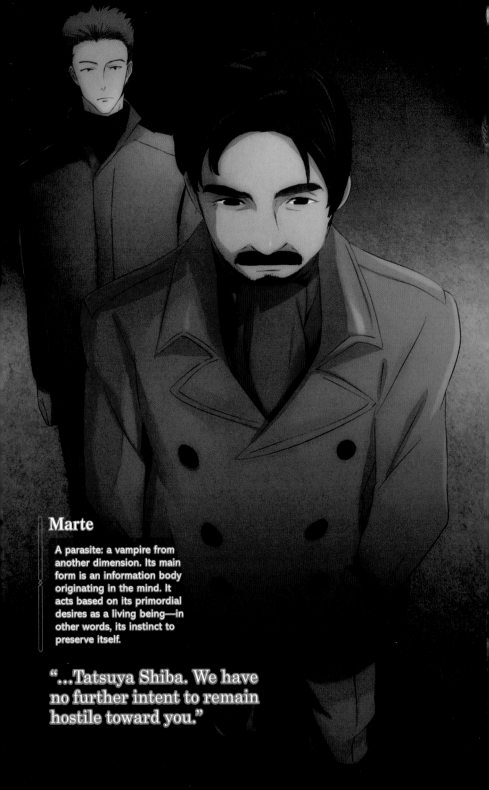

Marte

A parasite: a vampire from another dimension. Its main form is an information body originating in the mind. It acts based on its primordial desires as a living being—in other words, its instinct to preserve itself.

"...Tatsuya Shiba. We have no further intent to remain hostile toward you."

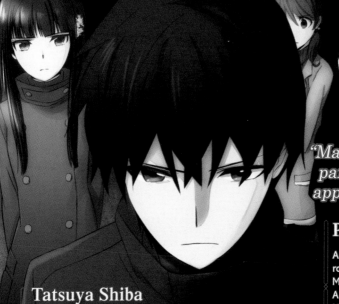

"Master, three parasites are approaching."

Pixie

A home-helper robot belonging to Magic High School. A parasite that copied Honoka Mitsui's brain wave patterns and currently dwells within the robot.

Tatsuya Shiba

The older brother of the Shiba siblings. A student of the National Magic University Affiliated First High School. Part of Class 1-E. He's considered one of the second-rate students, mockingly called "Weeds," but there was a reason why he scored poorly on the practical exams.

"What should I call you?"

Miyuki Shiba

The younger sister of the Shiba siblings. Part of Class 1-A. An elite who entered Magic High School as the top student. A Course 1 student, called a "Bloom," whose specialty is cooling magic. Her lovable only flaw is a severe case of a brother complex.

"...Will... will you hold my hand?"

"Until you
go to sleep…
shall I stay
by your side?"

Angelina
Kudou Shields

A USNA (United States of North America) student who came to Magic High as part of a foreign-exchange program, switching places with Shizuku Kitayama. A blond-haired, blue-eyed girl with unequaled magical abilities.

"Nobody asked for your help!"

What Are Vampires/Parasites?

• Origin

Parasites are considered to be data-based organisms originating in the mind. Originally information bodies of energy that coalesced in another dimension, they are thought to have intruded upon our plane of existence when the dimensional wall weakened during a micro black hole generation-and-evaporation experiment conducted on the outskirts of Dallas, Texas, in the United States of North America.

• Naming

Their name comes from the pattern discovered during the incident where the bodies of victims were all found missing large amounts of blood despite no notable external wounds. This is not because the parasites suck their blood like the vampires of legend but rather a side effect of their failure to replicate themselves.

• Replication Process

Parasites reproduce by splitting off a portion of themselves and sending it into a human body that has been recognized as a potential host. The detachment spreads through blood vessels while absorbing the psions and psycheons in the blood, permeating the victim's physical body by replacing the blood with copies of itself. Upon completion of this process, the parasite can supposedly gain control of the body's spirit, which is purported to be an information body in its own right...but there has yet to be any record of success.

• Objective

Without anything resembling a traditional leader, each of the parasites has the ability to think independently, but all share one consciousness. They can communicate among themselves and also locate their kin within a certain distance. When any of them inhabit an organism, it becomes influenced by that organism's most basic desires. In other words, it has been primal instinct that has driven them to survive and increase their numbers.

• Total Number

Twelve parasites are estimated to have arrived in this world. Their fluctuations in number are as follows:

Three were eliminated by Lina in the USNA proper (although she only destroyed their host bodies; the parasites themselves simply escaped as mental bodies). The remaining nine, including those residing within Sullivan and Mia, fled to Japan. After coming to Japan for a separate investigation, Lina eliminated the parasite Sullivan, and Mia self-destructed on the Magic High campus. Subsequently, Mitsugu Kuroba and his subordinates eliminated all seven of the others.

Meanwhile, the three eliminated in the USNA found new host bodies and traveled to Japan. They attempted to revive the nine eliminated in Japan and successfully revived eight, excluding Pixie. After that, Tatsuya and his friends successfully sealed three of the parasites during a fight. The remaining eight, along with three host bodies, were all stolen by counterintelligence Section Three, who then revived three of the parasites. There is currently a total of eleven remaining.

The Irregular at Magic High School

VISITOR ARC ③

11

Tsutomu Sato

Illustration Kana Ishida

YEN ON

NEW YORK

THE IRREGULAR AT MAGIC HIGH SCHOOL
TSUTOMU SATO

Translation by Andrew Prowse
Cover art by Kana Ishida

MAHOUKA KOUKOU NO RETTOUSEI Vol. 11
© TSUTOMU SATO 2013
First published in Japan in 2013 by KADOKAWA CORPORATION, Tokyo.
English translation rights arranged with KADOKAWA CORPORATION, Tokyo, through Tuttle-Mori Agency, Inc., Tokyo.

English translation © 2019 by Yen Press, LLC

Yen On
1290 Avenue of the Americas
New York, NY 10104

Visit us at yenpress.com
facebook.com/yenpress
twitter.com/yenpress
yenpress.tumblr.com
instagram.com/yenpress

First Yen On Edition: March 2019

Yen On is an imprint of Yen Press, LLC.
The Yen On name and logo are trademarks of Yen Press, LLC.

Library of Congress Cataloging-in-Publication Data
Names: Satou, Tsutomu. | Ishida, Kana, illustrator.
Title: The irregular at Magic High School / Tsutomu Satou ; Illustrations by Kana Ishida.
Other titles: Mahōka kōkō no rettosei. English
Description: First Yen On edition. | New York, NY : Yen On, 2016—
Identifiers: LCCN 2015042401 | ISBN 9780316348805 (v 1 : pbk.) | ISBN 9780316390293 (v. 2 : pbk.) |
    ISBN 9780316390309 (v. 3 : pbk.) | ISBN 9780316390316 (v. 4 : pbk.) |
    ISBN 9780316390323 (v. 5 : pbk.) | ISBN 9780316390330 (v. 6 : pbk.) |
    ISBN 9781975300074 (v. 7 : pbk.) | ISBN 9781975327125 (v. 8 : pbk.) |
    ISBN 9781975327149 (v. 9 : pbk.) | ISBN 9781975327163 (v. 10 : pbk.) |
    ISBN 9781975327187 (v. 11 : pbk.)
Subjects: CYAC: Brothers and sisters—Fiction. | Magic—Fiction. | High schools—Fiction. |
    Schools—Fiction. | Japan—Fiction. | Science fiction.
Classification: LCC PZ7.1.S265 Ir 2016 | DDC [Fic]—dc23
LC record available at http://lccn.loc.gov/2015042401

ISBNs: 978-1-9753-2718-7 (paperback)
       978-1-9753-2719-4 (ebook)

10 9 8 7 6 5 4 3 2 1

LSC-C

Printed in the United States of America

The Irregular at Magic High School

VISITOR ARC ③

An irregular older brother with a certain flaw.
An honor roll younger sister who is perfectly flawless.

When the two siblings enrolled in Magic High School,
a dramatic life unfolded—

Character

Tatsuya Shiba

Class 1-E. One of the Course 2 (irregular) students, who are mockingly called Weeds. Sees right to the core of everything.

Miyuki Shiba

Class 1-A. Tatsuya's younger sister; enrolled as the top student. Specializes in freezing magic. Dotes on her older brother.

Leonhard Saijou

Class 1-E. Tatsuya's classmate. Specializes in hardening magic. Has a bright personality.

Erika Chiba

Class 1-E. Tatsuya's classmate. Specializes in *kenjutsu*. A charming troublemaker.

Mizuki Shibata

Class 1-E. Tatsuya's classmate. Has pushion radiation sensitivity. Serious and a bit of an airhead.

Mikihiko Yoshida

Class 1-E. Tatsuya's classmate. From a famous family that uses ancient magic. Has known Erika since they were children.

Honoka Mitsui

Class 1-A. Miyuki's classmate. Specializes in light-wave vibration magic. Impulsive when emotional.

Shizuku Kitayama

Class 1-A. Miyuki's classmate. Specializes in vibration and acceleration magic. Doesn't show emotional ups and downs very much.

Eimi Akechi

Class 1-B. A quarter-blood. Full name is Amelia Eimi Akechi Goldie.

Akaha Sakurakouji

Class 1-B. Friends with Subaru and Amy. Wears gothic Lolita clothes and loves theme parks.

Subaru Satomi

Class 1-D. Frequently mistaken for a pretty boy. Cheerful and easy to get along with.

Azusa Nakajou

A junior and is student council president after Mayumi stepped down. Shy and has trouble expressing herself.

Hanzou Gyoubu-Shoujou Hattori

A junior and the former student council vice president. Is the head of the club committee after Katsuto stepped down.

Katsuto Juumonji

A senior and the former head of the club committee.

Shun Morisaki

Class 1-A. Miyuki's classmate. Specializes in CAD quick-draw. Takes great pride in being a Course 1 student.

Hagane Tomitsuka

Class 1-B. A magic martial arts user with the nickname "Range Zero."

Mayumi Saegusa

A senior and the former student council president. One of the strongest magicians ever to grace a magical high school.

Suzune Ichihara

A senior and the former student council treasurer. Calm, collected, and book smart. Mayumi's right hand.

Mari Watanabe

A senior and the former chairwoman of the disciplinary committee. Mayumi's good friend. Good all-around and likes a sporting fight.

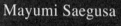

Takeaki Kirihara

A junior. Member of the *kenjutsu* club. Kanto Junior High Kenjutsu Tournament champion.

Sayaka Mibu

A junior. Member of the kendo club. Placed second in the nation at the girls' junior high kendo tournament.

Kei Isori

A junior and the student council treasurer. Top grades in his class in magical theory. Engaged to Kanon Chiyoda.

Kanon Chiyoda

A junior and the chairwoman of the disciplinary committee after Mari stepped down. Engaged to Kei Isori.

Masaki Ichijou

A freshman at Third High. Participates in the Nine School Competition. Direct heir to the Ichijou family, one of the Ten Master Clans.

Shinkurou Kichijouji

A freshman at Third High. Participates in the Nine School Competition. Also known as Cardinal George.

Koutarou Tatsumi

A senior and a former member of the disciplinary committee. Has a heroic personality.

Isao Sekimoto

A senior. Member of the disciplinary committee. Wasn't chosen for the Thesis Competition.

Midori Sawaki

A junior and a member of the disciplinary committee. Has a complex about his girlish name.

Koharu Hirakawa

Senior. Engineer during the Nine School Competition. Withdrew from the Thesis Competition.

Chiaki Hirakawa

Class 1-G. Holds enmity toward Tatsuya.

Midori Ichijou

Masaki's mother. Warm and good at cooking.

Akane Ichijou

Eldest daughter of the Ichijou. Masaki's younger sister. Mature despite being in elementary school.

Ruri Ichijou

Second daughter of the Ichijou. Masaki's younger sister. Stable and does things her own way.

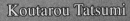

Satomi Asuka

Nurse. Gentle, calm, and warm.
Smile popular among male students.

Kazuo Tsuzura

Teacher. Main field is magic geometry.
Manager of the Thesis Competition team.

Haruka Ono

A general counselor of Class 1-E.
Tends to get bullied but has another
side to her.

Yakumo Kokonoe

A user of an ancient magic called
ninjutsu. Tatsuya's martial arts master.

Toshikazu Chiba

Erika Chiba's oldest brother. Has
a career in the Ministry of Police.
A playboy at first glance.

Naotsugu Chiba

Erika Chiba's second-oldest
brother. Possesses full mastery
of the Chiba (thousand blades)
style of *kenjutsu*. Nicknamed
"Kirin Child of the Chiba."

Anna Rosen Katori

Erika's mother. Half-Japanese and
half-German, was the mistress of Erika's
father, the current leader of the Chiba.

Harunobu Kazama

Commanding officer of the 101st
Brigade of the Independent
Magic Battalion. Ranked major.

Shigeru Sanada

Executive officer of the 101st
Brigade of the Independent
Magic Battalion. Ranked captain.

Muraji Yanagi

Executive officer of the 101st Brigade of the
Independent Magic Battalion. Ranked captain.

Kousuke Yamanaka

Executive officer of the 101st Brigade of the
Independent Magic Battalion. Physician ranked
major. First-rate healing magician.

Kyouko Fujibayashi

Female officer serving as
Kazama's aide. Ranked
second lieutenant.

Ushiyama

Manager of Four Leaves Technology's
CAD R & D Section 3. A person in
whom Tatsuya places his trust.

Retsu Kudou

Renowned as the strongest magician in the
world. Given the honorary title of Sage.

Rin

A girl Morisaki saved.
Her full name is Meiling Sun.
The new leader of the
Hong Kong–based international
crime syndicate No-Head Dragon.

Zhou

A handsome young man who
brought Lu and Chen to Japan.

Xiangshan Chen

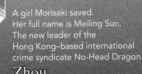

Leader of the Great
Asian Alliance Army's
Special Covert Forces.
Has a heartless
personality.

Ganghu Lu

The ace magician of the
Great Asian Alliance Army's
Special Covert Forces.
Also known as the
Man-Eating Tiger.

Miya Shiba

Tatsuya and Miyuki's
actual mother. Deceased.
The only magician skilled
in mental construction
interference magic.

Honami Sakurai

Miya's Guardian. Deceased.
Part of the first generation of
the Sakura series, engineered
magicians with magical capacity
strengthened through genetic
modification.

Sayuri Shiba

Tatsuya and Miyuki's
stepmother.
Hates them both.

Maya Yotsuba

Tatsuya and Miyuki's aunt. Miya's younger twin
sister. The current head of the Yotsuba.

Hayama

An elderly butler employed by Maya.

Mitsugu Kuroba

Miya Shiba and Maya Yotsuba's cousin.
Father of Ayako and Fumiya.

Ayako Kuroba

Tatsuya and Miyuki's second
cousin. Has a younger twin
brother named Fumiya.

Fumiya Kuroba

A candidate for next head of
the Yotsuba. Tatsuya and Miyuki's
second cousin. Has an older
twin sister named Ayako.

Angelina Kudou Shields

Commander of the USNA's magician unit, the Stars. Rank is major. Nickname is Lina. Also one of the Thirteen Apostles, strategic magicians.

Virginia Balance

First deputy commissioner of the USNA Joint Chiefs of Staff Internal Investigation Office within the Information Bureau. Ranked colonel. Came to Japan in order to support Lina.

Silvia Mercury First

A planet-class magician in the USNA's magician unit, the Stars. Rank is warrant officer. Her nickname is Silvie, and Mercury First is her code name. During their mission in Japan, she serves as Major Sirius's aide.

Benjamin Canopus

Number two in the USNA's magician unit, the Stars. Rank is major. Takes command when Major Sirius is absent.

Mikaela Hongou

An agent sent to Japan by the USNA (although her real job is magic scientist for the Department of Defense). Nicknamed Mia.

Claire

Hunter Q—a female soldier in the magician unit Stardust (for those who couldn't be Stars). The code name Q refers to the seventeenth of the pursuit unit.

Alfred Fomalhaut

A first-degree starred magician in the USNA's magician unit, the Stars. Rank is first lieutenant. Nicknamed Freddy. Currently on the run.

Rachel

Hunter R—a female soldier in the magician unit Stardust (for those who couldn't be Stars). The code name R refers to the eighteenth of the pursuit unit.

Charles Sullivan

A satellite-class magician in the USNA's magician unit, the Stars. Called by the code name Deimos second. Currently on the run.

Raymond S. Clark

A first-year student at the high school in Berkeley, USNA, where Shizuku studies abroad. A Caucasian boy who wastes no time making advances on Shizuku.

Pixie

A home-helper robot belonging to the magic high school. Official name 3H (Humanoid Home Helper: a human-shaped chore-assisting robot) type P-94.

Glossary

Course 1 student emblem

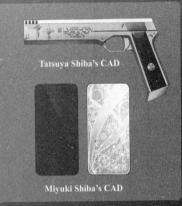

Tatsuya Shiba's CAD

Miyuki Shiba's CAD

Magic High School

Nickname for high schools affiliated with the National Magic University. There are nine schools throughout the nation. Of them, First High through Third High each adopt a system of Course 1 and Course 2 students to split up its two hundred incoming freshmen.

Blooms, Weeds

Slang terms used at First High to display the gap between Course 1 and Course 2 students. Course 1 student uniforms feature an eight-petaled emblem embroidered on the left breast, but Course 2 student uniforms do not.

CAD (Casting Assistant Device)

A device that simplifies magic casting. Magical programming is recorded within. There are many types and forms, some specialized and others multipurpose.

Four Leaves Technology (FLT)

A domestic CAD manufacturer. Originally more famous for magical-product engineering than for developing finished products, the development of the Silver model has made them much more widely known as a maker of CADs.

Taurus Silver

A genius engineer said to have advanced specialized CAD software by a decade in just a single year.

Eidos (individual information bodies)

Originally a term from Greek philosophy. In modern magic, *eidos* refers to the information bodies that accompany events. They form a so-called record of those events existing in the world, and can be considered the footprints of an object's state of being in the universe, be that active or passive. The definition of *magic* in its modern form is that of a technology that alters events by altering the information bodies composing them.

Idea (information body dimension)

Originally a term from Greek philosophy; pronounced "ee-dee-ah." In modern magic, *Idea* refers to the *platform* upon which information bodies are recorded—a spell, object, or energy's *dimension*. Magic is primarily a technology that outputs a magic program (a spell sequence) to affect the Idea (the dimension), which then rewrites the eidos (the individual bodies) recorded there.

Activation Sequence

The blueprints of magic, and the programming that constructs it. Activation sequences are stored in a compressed format in CADs. The magician sends a psionic wave into the CAD, which then expands the data and uses it to convert the activation sequence into a signal. This signal returns to the magician with the unpacked magic program.

Psions (thought particles)

Massless particles belonging to the dimension of spirit phenomena. These information particles record awareness and thought results. Eidos are considered the theoretical basis for modern magic, while activation sequences and magic programs are the technology forming its practical basis. All of these are bodies of information made up of psions.

Pushions (spirit particles)

Massless particles belonging to the dimension of spirit phenomena. Their existence has been confirmed, but their true form and function have yet to be elucidated. In general, magicians are only able to sense energized pushions. The technical term for them is *psycheons*.

Magician

An abbreviation of *magic technician*. *Magic technician* is the term for those with the skills to use magic at a practical level.

Magic program

An information body used to temporarily alter information attached to events. Constructed from psions possessed by the magician. Sometimes shortened to *magigram*.

Magic-calculation region

A mental region that constructs magic programs. The essential core of the talent of magic. Exists within the magician's unconscious regions, and though he or she can normally consciously use the magic-calculation region, they cannot perceive the processing happening within. The magic-calculation region may be called a black box, even for the magician performing the task.

Magic program output process

❶ Transmit an activation sequence to a CAD. This is called "reading in an activation sequence."

❷ Add variables to the activation sequence and send them to the magic-calculation region.

❸ Construct a magic program from the activation sequence and its variables.

❹ Send the constructed magic program along the "route"—between the lowest part of the conscious mind and highest part of the unconscious mind—then send it out the "gate" between conscious and unconscious, to output it onto the Idea.

❺ The magic program outputted onto the Idea interferes with the eidos at designated coordinates and overwrites them.

With a single-type, single-process spell, this five-stage process can be completed in under half a second. This is the bar for practical-level use with magicians.

Magic evaluation standards

The speed with which one constructs psionic information bodies is one's magical throughput, or processing speed. The scale and scope of the information bodies one can construct is one's magical capacity. The strength with which one can overwrite eidos with magic programs is one's influence. These three together are referred to as a person's magical power.

Cardinal Code hypothesis

A school of thought claiming that within the four families and eight types of magic, there exist foundational "plus" and "minus" magic programs that number sixteen in total, and that by combin-ing these sixteen, one can construct every possible typed spell.

Typed magic

Any magic belonging to the four families and eight types.

Exotyped magic

A term for spells that control mental phenomena rather than physical ones. Encompasses many fields, from divine magic and spirit magic—which employs spiritual presences—to mind reading, astral form separation, and consciousness control.

Ten Master Clans

The most powerful magician organization in Japan. The ten families are chosen every four years from among twenty-eight: Ichijou, Ichinokura, Isshiki, Futatsugi, Nikaidou, Nihei, Mitsuya, Mikazuki, Yotsuba, Itsuwa, Gotou, Itsumi, Mutsuzuka, Rokkaku, Rokugou, Roppongi, Saegusa, Shippou, Tanabata, Nanase, Yatsushiro, Hassaku, Hachiman, Kudou, Kuki, Kuzumi, Juumonji, and Tooyama.

Numbers

Just like the Ten Master Clans contain a number from one to ten in their surname, well-known families in the Hundred Families use numbers eleven or greater, such as Chiyoda (thousand), Isori (fifty), and Chiba (thousand). The value isn't an indicator of strength, but the fact that it is present in the surname is one measure to broadly judge the capacity of a magic family by their bloodline.

Non-numbers

Also called Extra Numbers, or simply Extras. Magician families who have been stripped of their number. Once, when magicians were weapons and experimental samples, this was a stigma between the success cases, who were given numbers, and the failure cases, who didn't display good enough results.

Various Spells

• Cocytus

Outer magic that freezes the mind. A frozen mind cannot order the flesh to die, so anyone subject to this magic enters a state of mental stasis, causing their body to stop. Partial crystallization of the flesh is sometimes observed because of the interaction between mind and body.

• Rumbling

An old spell that vibrates the ground as a medium for a spirit, an independent information body.

• Program Dispersion

A spell that dismantles a magic program, the main component of a spell, into a group of psionic particles with no meaningful structure. Since magic programs affect the information bodies associated with events, it is necessary for the information structure to be exposed, leaving no way to prevent interference against the magic program itself.

• Program Demolition

A typeless spell that rams a mass of compressed psionic particles directly into an object without going through the Idea, causing it to explode and blow away the psion information bodies recorded in magic, such as activation sequences and magic programs. It may be called magic, but because it is a psionic bullet without any structure as a magic program for altering events, it isn't affected by Information Boost or Area Interference. The pressure of the bullet itself will also repel any Cast Jamming effects. Because it has zero physical effect, no obstacle can block it.

• Mine Origin

A magic that imparts strong vibrations to anything with a connotation of "ground"—such as dirt, crag, sand, or concrete—regardless of material.

• Fissure

A spell that uses spirits, independent information bodies, as a medium to push a line into the ground, creating the appearance of a fissure opening in the earth.

• Dry Blizzard

A spell that gathers carbon dioxide from the air, creates dry-ice particles, then converts the extra heat energy from the freezing process to kinetic energy to launch the dry-ice particles at a high speed.

• Slithering Thunders

In addition to condensing the water vapor from Dry Blizzard's dry-ice evaporation and creating a highly conductive mist with the evaporated carbon dioxide in it, this spell creates static electricity with vibration-type magic and emission-type magic. A combination spell, it also fires an electric attack at an enemy using the carbon gas-filled mist and water droplets as a conductor.

• Niflheim

A vibration- and deceleration-type area-of-effect spell. It chills a large volume of air, then moves it to freeze a wide range. In blunt terms, it creates a super-large refrigerator. The white mist that appears upon activation is the particles of frozen ice and dry ice, but at higher levels, a mist of frozen liquid nitrogen occurs.

• Burst

A dispersion-type spell that vaporizes the liquid inside a target object. When used on a creature, the spell will vaporize bodily fluids and cause the body to rupture. When used on a machine powered by internal combustion, the spell vaporizes the fuel and makes it explode. Fuel cells see the same result, and even if no burnable fuel is on board, there is no machine that does not contain some liquid, such as battery fluid, hydraulic fluid, coolant, or lubricant; once Burst activates, virtually any machine will be destroyed.

• Disheveled Hair

An old spell that, instead of specifying a direction and changing the wind's direction to that, uses air current control to bring about the vague result of "tangling" it, causing currents along the ground that entangle an opponent's feet in the grass. Only usable on plains with grass of a certain height.

Magic Swords

Aside from fighting techniques that use magic itself as a weapon, another method of magical combat involves techniques for using magic to strengthen and control weapons. The majority of these spells combine magic with projectile weapons such as guns and bows, but the art of the sword, known as *kenjutsu*, has developed in Japan as well as a way to link magic with sword techniques. This has led to magic technicians formulating personal-use magic techniques known as magic swords, which can be said to be both modern magic and old magic.

1. High-Frequency Blade

A spell that locally liquefies a solid body and cleaves it by causing a blade to vibrate at a high speed, then propagate the vibration that exceeds the molecular cohesive force of matter it comes in contact with. Used as a set with a spell to prevent the blade from breaking.

2. Pressure Cut

A spell that generates left-right perpendicular repulsive force relative to the angle of a slashing blade edge, causing the blade to force apart any object it touches and thereby cleave it. The size of the repulsive field is less than a millimeter, but it has the strength to interfere with light, so when seen from the front, the blade edge becomes a black line.

3. Douji-Giri (Simultaneous Cut)

An old-magic spell passed down as a secret sword art of the Genji. It is a magic sword technique wherein the user remotely manipulates two blades through a third in their hands in order to have the swords surround an opponent and slash simultaneously. *Douji* is the Japanese pronunciation for both "simultaneous" and "child," so this ambiguity was used to keep the inherited nature of the technique a secret.

4. Zantetsu (Iron Cleaver)

A secret sword art of the Chiba clan. Rather than defining a katana as a hulk of steel and iron, this movement spell defines it as a single concept, then the spell moves the katana along a slashing path set by the magic program. The result is that the katana is defined as a mono-molecular blade, never breaking, bending, or chipping as it slices through any objects in its path.

5. Jinrai Zantetsu (Lightning Iron Cleaver)

An expanded version of Zantetsu that makes use of the Ikazuchi-Maru, a personal-armament device. By defining the katana and its wielder as one collective concept, the spell executes the entire series of actions, from enemy contact to slash, incredibly quickly and with faultless precision.

6. Mountain Tsunami

A secret sword art of the Chiba clan that makes use of the Orochi-Maru, a giant personal weapon six feet long. The user minimizes their own inertia and that of their katana while approaching an enemy at a high speed and, at the moment of impact, adds the neutralized inertia to the blade's inertia and slams the target with it. The longer the approach run, the greater the false inertial mass, reaching a maximum of ten tons.

7. Usuba Kagerou (Antlion)

A spell that uses hardening magic to anchor a five-nanometer-thick sheet of woven carbon nanotube to a perfect surface and make it a blade. The blade that *Usuba Kagerou* creates is sharper than any sword or razor, but the spell contains no functions to support moving the blade, demanding technical sword skill and ability from the user.

Strategic Magicians: The Thirteen Apostles

Because modern magic was born into a highly technological world, only a few nations were able to develop strong magic for military purposes. As a result, only a handful were able to develop "strategic magic," which rivaled weapons of mass destruction. However, these nations shared the magic they developed with their allies, and certain magicians of allied nations with high aptitudes for strategic magic came to be known as strategic magicians. As of April 2095, there are thirteen magicians publicly recognized as strategic magicians by their nations. They are called the Thirteen Apostles and are seen as important factors in the world's military balance. The Thirteen Apostles' nations, names, and their strategic-spell names are listed below.

USNA

Angie Sirius: Heavy Metal Burst
Elliott Miller: Leviathan
Laurent Barthes: Leviathan
* The only one belonging to the Stars is Angie Sirius. Elliott Miller is stationed at Alaska Base, and Laurent Barthes outside the country at Gibraltar Base, and for the most part, they don't move.

New Soviet Union

Igor Andreivich Bezobrazov: Tuman Bomba
Leonid Kondratenko: Zemlja Armija
* As Kondratenko is of advanced age, he generally stays at the Black Sea Base.

Great Asian Alliance

Yunde Liu: Pilita (Thunderclap Tower)
* Yunde Liu died in the October 31, 2095, battle against Japan.

Indo-Persian Federation

Barat Chandra Khan: Agni Downburst

Japan

Mio Itsuwa: Abyss

Brazil

Miguel Diez: Synchroliner Fusion
* This magic program was named by the USNA.

England

William MacLeod: Ozone Circle

Germany

Karla Schmidt: Ozone Circle
* Ozone Circle is based on a spell co-developed by nations in the EU before its split as a means to fix the hole in the ozone layer. The magic program was perfected by England and then publicized to the old EU through a convention.

Turkey

Ali Sahin: Bahamut
* This magic program was developed in cooperation with the USNA and Japan, then provided to Turkey by Japan.

Thailand

Somchai Bunnag: Agni Downburst
* This magic program was provided by Indo-Persia.

[13]

"…Don't you think that's awful? I'm telling you, it's like I got put on public display!" The girl's high-pitched voice was audibly agitated.

The only response she got was a "…*This is the fourth time*," from another girl, sounding very tired.

The difference in mental states between the two talking over the phone was like summer and winter.

But maybe that was unavoidable. Honoka had a good reason to be this excited, while Shizuku had an equally good reason to stress a need for sleep.

The reason Honoka was so worked up: Her secret, intimate affections had been exposed, and it wasn't just that she liked someone. Details about how she wanted to dedicate everything she had to that person, a thought that seemed *maybe just a little* too serious even to Honoka. It was already embarrassing to hear about her yearnings coming from the mouth of someone else; on top of all that, her secret had been revealed not only to the object of her affections but to a large audience as well. It was only natural that she was agonizing over it.

The fact that it had been not a person who had acted as her mouthpiece but a maid robot possessed by a parasite didn't make her feel any better, either.

"Well, it was embarrassing enough to say it four times," she insisted, her need for reassurance seeping into her sullen voice.

As Honoka sulked, Shizuku, on the screen, breathed a light sigh. *"I get it, so I wish you'd take my situation into consideration, too. What time do you think it is right now?"*

Meanwhile, the reason Shizuku emphasized that she was sleepy: It was a simple matter of the time…or rather, the time difference. As Shizuku spoke, a three-handed clock appeared over the whole display. The short hand on the classic, arabesque design pointed between the IV and the V on the face. The time difference between Tokyo and Berkeley, California, was seven hours. If it was 9:30 PM in Tokyo, it was 4:30 AM in Berkeley.

"I would have appreciated it if you'd waited at least another two hours."

Shizuku's grumblings were also quite natural. Her eyelids seemed ready to close at any moment. Noticing that finally put an apologetic look on Honoka's face, and she shrugged her shoulders.

"I did actually wait one hour, but…"

Shizuku blinked her tired eyes at the excuse and sighed again, this time in resignation. *"That part about you never changes…"*

"I'm sorry for always bothering you…"

"You're not bothering me…as long as you consider the time."

Honoka mumbled, "Sorry…"

Seeing from across the screen that her conversation partner couldn't give any more excuses, Shizuku sighed once more. This time, she appeared to expel her drowsiness along with it. Aside from her half-opened eyelids, her expression settled into a fairly steadfast one.

"But maybe it was good for you, in hindsight."

Shizuku's voice didn't carry much intonation—but it never did, and her pronunciation was clearer now.

"What? What was good? There was nothing good about it!"

Shizuku's words had sounded pretty detached as an attempt at comfort, and Honoka lashed out, completely forgetting how down-hearted she'd been a second ago.

"But you couldn't tell him your feelings, could you?"

Shizuku hadn't claimed that what had happened might be good without thinking it through first. Whether it was because of her friend's tone of voice or the suggestive words themselves, Honoka's argument ended with that one shot.

"You know about your habit of dependence, right?"

"No, that's..."

Honoka reflexively tried to deny it, but she couldn't even fully convince herself. Her argument faded out partway through, and she averted her eyes as Shizuku stared directly at her—albeit sleepily—from across the screen.

"Honoka, how long have we known each other?"

Shizuku admonished her gently to emphasize her point.

"...But it's not like I can help acting that way," admitted Honoka, her voice resigned but also defiant. "I'm part of an Elements bloodline."

Shizuku always doubted that genetics played much of a role in personality, but arguing the point here wouldn't accomplish anything.

"It's not about whether being dependent is good or bad. If everyone was a natural-born leader who didn't need to rely on anyone and always wanted to take the initiative, I don't think the world would be running this smoothly."

Honoka knew her friend wasn't trying to criticize her. She hesitantly returned her gaze to the screen.

"What I'm trying to say is that Tatsuya is a good person for you to lean on."

Their eyes met through their cameras as Shizuku spoke each word as though giving careful instructions.

"You...you think?" asked Honoka nervously.

"Mmhmm." Shizuku nodded without even a second's hesitation. *"I think Tatsuya's the kind of person who won't respond to anything unless*

it's explicitly asked. In exchange, he'll always respond to things people need of him."

"So if I don't say it clearly, he won't understand?"

"Yeah, I think so. And I'm sure he's not the insistent type."

"Umm, what do you mean...?" Honoka asked back.

"I mean that even if you're at his beck and call, he won't force you to do something indecent or anything like that."

Shizuku's answer was truly honest—or blunt.

Honoka's face turned red immediately. But even then, there was a visible glimpse of a slightly disappointed expression.

"Maybe you should be a little bit more forceful in your advances."

"Shizuku!"

Honoka raised her voice and glared at the screen. But the only thing displayed on it was Shizuku's face, looking at her as if to say *Well, it's true.*

"Hmph!" Sullenly, she turned her face to the side.

"......"

"......Shizuku?"

But the next one to make a sound was still Honoka.

"What...should I do?"

"Your only choice is to be aggressive."

It wasn't as though Shizuku had much romantic experience. In fact, some would argue she had even less experience than the average teenage girl in Japan in this day and age. Still, to put it simply, her friend was thinking too much and needed a push forward to get her out of the dead end she was in.

"I've been trying to be as aggressive as I can..."

"You need to try harder. Your rival is too strong."

"My rival...?"

"It's going to be very hard to beat Miyuki."

"Miyuki? But she and Tatsuya are—"

"—*Siblings, yes. And?"*

Shizuku rejected Honoka's commonsense argument with only a

few words, packing into her response the nuance of *You're saying this now? You should understand at this point.*

"But that's—that's not…" With a shocked expression, Honoka shook her head at the camera.

But Shizuku had known her for a long time, and to her eyes, it only seemed like she *wanted* to be shocked.

"Tell me, Honoka, are you sticking around Tatsuya because you want to have sex with him?"

"O-of course not! Which isn't to say I'm not interested at all, but…"

As Honoka grew flustered, Shizuku looked at her from the screen with eyes that said, *What is this girl even saying?* But Shizuku was the one feeling uncomfortable because of her silence. She began to try to wrap up the conversation herself.

"The only time blood relation is an issue is when doing things like that. If she's satisfied with just being with him, then the fact that they're siblings isn't an obstacle. I actually asked Miyuki."

"…Asked her what?" replied Honoka, her expression making it clear she didn't want to listen, but she had to hear.

"About what she thinks about Tatsuya."

"…And what did she say?"

"That she loves him."

"Oh… Then she does…" said Honoka quietly to herself rather than crying it out despite her crimson cheeks.

"In a nonromantic way."

"…That's what she said?"

"She told me she doesn't love Tatsuya the way a girl would fall in love with a boy. It didn't seem like it was simply because she's his sister, though."

"?" But Honoka looked like she was having trouble deciding how to interpret the extra bit of information Shizuku had tacked on.

"But…" Shizuku hesitated.

"But?" repeated Honoka, the same word but in a different tone, urging her to continue.

"*But I think that's just what she tells people, since she doesn't realize it herself. I think she does love Tatsuya as a woman.*"

The continuation was a categorical conjecture without a hint of hesitation.

"So you think so, too…"

Honoka didn't object to her friend's conclusion, even though it was somewhat (?) outside the realm of common sense.

"*Yep. So I think the battle will end when she realizes it.*"

"What do you mean?" Honoka asked back honestly.

"*You have to take the top spot with Tatsuya before Miyuki recognizes how she feels.*"

But as she heard that it was highly probable that Miyuki would eventually sort out her feelings, the future began to weigh on her.

"But I can't do it…" muttered Honoka, her shoulders falling.

"*Only give up when it's over. What happened to you might have been a disaster, but I think you can use it to appeal yourself.*" Shizuku encouraged her with a slight degree of forcefulness—that was really all the force she could manage.

"Appeal to Tatsuya?"

"*Mmhmm. You might as well just tell him everything now.*"

"But he might think I'm being annoying…"

"*It's all right. I'm sure Tatsuya wouldn't feel burdened.*"

The statement wasn't empty consolation. It was an odd kind of trust, and Shizuku truly believed it was true.

Right about when Shizuku was lighting a fire under Honoka…

Tatsuya was face-to-face with Lina, who had transformed into Angie Sirius.

Scarlet hair, golden eyes. It was all an optical illusion, but her features and height had changed, too—he couldn't see any of the actual Lina in there. With this, even if she didn't hide her face with a mask, anyone who didn't already know her true identity would probably never link Angie Sirius with Angelina Shields. In fact, it seemed to Tatsuya that *not* hiding her face was more effective.

Tatsuya carefully watched his opponent. He hadn't been goofing off for the last half month, either. With Yakumo's Cocoon as his practice opponent, he'd accumulated a wealth of countermeasures for her information-falsifying spell Parade.

As a result of his training, he could tell that Lina had used Parade for the exterior alterations but wasn't currently overwriting any coordinate information. With the feedback he was getting now, even if she did tamper her coordinates henceforth, Tatsuya figured he could still keep track of her.

Of course, this situation wasn't one he could think optimistically about, either. The fact that Lina hadn't messed with anything besides her appearance wasn't because she was overconfident or letting her guard down. It was doubtless because she wasn't sure she had enough magical power for it all.

Which means her spell requires that much capacity.

The code name Sirius was given to the leader of the Stars, the USNA military's most elite magician force. In other words, the magician with the most powerful magic abilities in the entire USNA. And she had to focus all her resources on this one spell.

The shining ray of light that had shot through the dark night to attack Tatsuya and Naotsugu Chiba. That attack's identity was probably a high-energy plasma beam. Which meant the name of the spell that had created it was…

I don't think there's much doubt. That was Heavy Metal Burst.

The strategic-class spell Heavy Metal Burst, belonging to one of the Thirteen Apostles, Angie Sirius. It converted heavy metal into high-energy plasma, then further amplified both the pressure increase caused by the ionization process that turns gas into plasma as well as the natural electromagnetic repulsion between positively charged ions, scattering the plasma over a large area.

Incidentally, very few people aside from Angie Sirius could use spells that converted matter to plasma. However, when simply ionizing atoms, the generated plasma as a whole has a neutral charge, which didn't cause repulsion. The scope and speed were obvious reasons nobody but Angie Sirius could use Heavy Metal Burst, but there was another factor as well: Only she could realize the process of discharging electrons outside the plasma cloud *while* maintaining the process of ionization.

Heavy Metal Burst supposedly emitted the high-energy plasma in all directions, radiating out from the blast center. The plasma that had attacked Naotsugu Chiba had been a directional beam.

She didn't just converge it. She controlled its effective firing range... and its area of diffusion.

The reason the plasma ray hadn't damaged any of the buildings along the road after missing Naotsugu was because the attack never reached them. Maybe the spell was constructed in a way that the energy dissipated after passing by the target, or maybe she set up a force field that would act like a stopper at the beam's end point.

What could have allowed her to do something like that? At a mere glance, he couldn't tell for sure, but it was probably...

...that staff.

This was the first time he'd ever seen the staff Lina was holding. It was likely what made it possible. It was probably—no, definitely a spell assister developed by the USNA. If their positions had been different, he wouldn't have been able to keep himself from praising the technology.

But right now, it's an incredible threat.

He didn't understand the details of how the plasma flow control system worked, but that didn't mean he understood nothing. If he "saw" it again, he'd be able to come up with a countermeasure. Maybe that was wishful thinking? No—Tatsuya denied that immediately. Nothing good would come of being weak at a time like this.

No, right now the problem was...

...whether I can take a direct hit and still have energy left for a counterattack.

Tatsuya had virtually unlimited restoration ability against physical attacks, but he could only Regenerate—he couldn't defend.

Furthermore, "unlimited" referred to a wound's severity, not the number of times he could pull it off.

The beam earlier had been significantly slower than the speed of light. At most, it was one-third of that. It was less than a lightning bolt, which traveled around six hundred times the speed of sound before hitting the ground. The plasma beam had been maybe a hundred times the speed of sound.

And yet, it wouldn't take two milliseconds for it to cross the sixty meters between them. It would literally be the blink of an eye. It would be impossible to dodge it after seeing it.

However...

If a physical object moves at a speed that fast, even if it's a rarefied gas, it would create a powerful shock wave. If that didn't happen, that can only mean that it creates its travel path beforehand.

If he could sense the creation of that "path," then he could get out of the line of fire.

Tatsuya mobilized all his senses and focused on Lina.

Under the streetlight, separated by darkness, Lina abruptly averted her eyes from his. She spun around on her heel, then cast a quick glance over her shoulder—he could see a thin smile.

It was clear she was calling him out.

Tatsuya wavered.

It was obviously luring him out, but he was already well within the trap's jaws anyway.

He didn't think she'd let him go if he didn't take her up on her invitation, either.

Having a shoot-out in a place like this was out of the question, even if it was to throw off her aim.

As Tatsuya tried to decide what he should do, he saw Lina's feet kick off the road.

He threw away his hesitation.

Lina's scarlet hair quickly grew distant as she ran—or, more accurately, jumped away.

Leaving Naotsugu behind, who was completely frozen and at a loss, Tatsuya used the same kind of gravity-control spell as Lina to chase after her.

"It's Major Sirius—she's made contact with the target!"

"Any response?"

"No, ma'am!"

The secret command center set up inside the Japanese branch office of the USNA military's dummy corporation had descended into a nearly panicked state.

Ever since step one, they'd needed to change their capture plans, but that wasn't enough to make Virginia Balance's arms and legs shake.

In fact, she'd even predicted the intervention of armed personnel thought to be an agent in the Japanese military.

The reason was something else.

Lina leaving her position on her own judgment had started the chaos.

The Stars commander, Sirius, was granted the right to act independently, so Virginia couldn't quite call it a breach of military discipline. But there was currently a team-based operation in progress. Just because it was technically allowed didn't mean the major could do whatever she wanted.

And it was Balance who told Lina to use her own judgment when using the Brionac, but to do something with it in the middle of traffic had been completely unexpected.

"The target has begun following Major Sirius."

The new report caused some calm to return to the air in the command center.

Thinking about recovering the Stardust along with the rest of the cleanup was quickly becoming a headache. But for now, the plan was back on its original track—thought, at least, everyone except for Colonel Balance.

I should have been more thorough with the operation's exit conditions...

"Summon the relay vehicle."

Her voice was level as she gave the order to the operator, concealing any irritation she felt inside.

It seemed as though light invaded every last corner of the city, but there were spots where it would abruptly cut off.

Dark, blank areas created by the city of Tokyo that never slept.

The park he'd been lured into was one of those gaps between streetlights.

Actually, the place was more like a vacant lot than a park. The hedges surrounding it had been maintained, but there were no benches, much less playground equipment. And only a token number of streetlights had been placed there. It was probably public property claimed during wartime as an empty spot for dealing with disasters, but it had likely been neglected during the redevelopment process.

Lina's golden hair shone under some of that sparse streetlight.

The darkness hung over her like a lid. It was cloudy tonight, with both the moon and the stars hidden, but Tatsuya could tell at a glance that was not all it was.

There was an optical spell in play here that obstructed cameras aboard surveillance satellites and stratospheric platforms.

He was inside the enemy's encirclement. He knew it was a trap when he jumped in, so he wasn't surprised or panicked at this point. Instead, what he found unexpected was that there was no trace of any active magic other than the concealment.

Avoiding interference between spells, then...

That meant the magic Lina was trying to use was incredibly

advanced even for her—powerful enough to make her allies decide that leaving her to attack independently would be more effective than acting as a group.

• Canceling her camouflage was probably to focus her mind on this attack spell as well.

So it's Heavy Metal Burst again.

"Tatsuya."

As his conviction about what cards she held in her hand strengthened, Lina spoke.

"I didn't think you'd be concerned enough to come."

"Having you flit around all the time would be annoying."

When she heard his contemptuously nonchalant answer, Lina gave a cold-blooded smile. "You're quite confident. But this time, your head was a little too big for your own good."

Lina brought the staff she was holding beside her up, grasping it under her arm, and pointed it at Tatsuya. "You'd better surrender. I don't know how you disable magic, but you won't be able to mess with the Brionac."

For Lina, that line was nothing more than a simple recommendation to surrender.

"Bree-oh-nake"... That's how she'd said it. *So not "Bu-ryu-nak"?*

But in Tatsuya's mind, the clue in her words assembled the puzzle pieces nearly to completion.

Names always meant something, and the name of a weapon usually gave an indication as to some of its attributes.

Preoccupied with observation and his thoughts, Tatsuya had forgotten to give Lina a response.

She took that as a refusal.

He couldn't criticize it as a hasty move. It may have been an accident on his part to forget to answer, but staying silent when asked to surrender customarily meant refusal.

Lina grabbed one side of a crosspiece sticking out horizontally from the staff.

It had to be what served as a grip, because—

A two-layered spiral of psionic light ran through the Brionac's bottom two-thirds; through the thin, eighty-centimeter-long pole; and then, in the staff's thicker upper third, a magic program was instantly constructed inside a forty-centimeter tube on the end of the grip. Upon detecting it, Tatsuya tried to activate Program Disper—

Only to realize he didn't have time.

The staff's tip glimmered.

A tightly bundled ray of light shot by Tatsuya's right arm.

It had only grazed him—but his arm carbonized from the elbow down and blew off.

His body twisted on impact.

He gave into the momentum and used it to jump over the hedge behind him.

Lina let go of the grip, then positioned the Brionac like a long sword and charged.

She closed the distance, then aimed at the hedge Tatsuya had hidden behind and swung horizontally.

The raw wood immediately burned and scattered—but only the shrubbery in the hedge had been hit.

The plasma hadn't reached the man behind it.

Holding his right shoulder and hiding his right half behind him, the now-kneeling Tatsuya watched as the light-giving plasma blade disappeared like an illusion.

"Brionac… 'That which pierces.' One of the weapons the Celtic god of light Lugh possessed. Does that naming mean you've reproduced the mythical weapon?" wondered Tatsuya, still kneeling, as Lina walked over to him.

There was no sense of pain in his voice. Lina assumed it was because he had a high resistance to it; not unusual among unique soldiers who had been trained in anti-interrogation methods.

"Is that what you're worried about? You know you're on the brink of life or death right now."

Inside the staff, another magic program instantly activated.

The spell that broke a tightly bound clump of metallic particles apart into high-energy plasma.

The event—the high-energy plasma created by the spell—changed its form according to Lina's will while inside its container.

With the electricity and the scorching blade right in front of his nose, the last piece clicked into place in Tatsuya's mind.

"Yeah, names can be important. People like names that mean something. The various legends say that the Brionac was a spear that could create a bolt of lightning to pierce its targets, or that it was a spear that could fly around on its own, or that it was a bullet made of light. I bet the key lies in the 'on its own' part."

"The Brionac, a legendary item modeled after a mythological weapon."

"To think you've put FAE theory into practical use... I shouldn't have expected anything less of the USNA's technological power."

Lina had been listening to Tatsuya talk without much interest until then, but when he said the term *FAE*, her eyes widened and her expression stiffened.

"...How do you know about FAE theory?"

When he saw her expression, he gave her surprise of his own. "Is it that strange? FAE theory was originally a hypothesis advanced by Japan-America joint research."

"That research is top secret! And it was all supposedly canceled!"

"But it wasn't really. That sacred imitation in your hand is pretty damning proof of that, isn't it?"

Tatsuya gazed at the Brionac. "FAE—Free After Execution," he said, deeply moved. "In Japanese, it was called variable post-discharge event theory, but the term *free after execution* is a better description of what it is. Events created as a result of magical alteration are events that should never have been part of the world in the first place. Therefore, restrictions posed by the laws of nature are looser directly after the alteration occurs. You could alternatively say that there's an extremely short time lag before the laws of nature kick in when a magic-caused event occurs."

Tatsuya gave the explanation in an unwarranted lecturing tone of voice, creating an odd lull in the middle of their death match.

"FAE theory posits a few things about magically created plasma. Even though it's supposed to scatter in complete randomness, it's easy to give it a direction for movement. And despite its original cooling rate, returning it from its heated state to normal temperatures can be done within any arbitrary amount of time. If its scattering characteristics are suppressed, then it's even possible to keep it in a certain shape. Like that."

Lina, missing a chance to interrupt Tatsuya's long-winded speech, just kept her grip on the weapon's handle.

"But the time lag of when physical laws are predicted by FAE theory to kick in is less than an instant. It was thought impossible for the magician to be able to add more definitions for the event they created within such a short time after triggering the spell."

Then Tatsuya made a face like he was in the middle of shrugging his shoulders. "And with good reason. It's not possible for a human to define an event in less than a millisecond."

And then pure, honest admiration crossed his face. "And to imagine...you lengthened the time lag for the laws of nature to apply by executing the spell within a bounded barrier container that blocked the very world's physical laws from having an effect on it."

It was a manifestation of natural emotion for Tatsuya, as a boy who wanted to walk the path of science.

"You have my honest praise. I raise my hat to you. Whoever created that Brionac is a true genius."

"Tatsuya!" yelled Lina suddenly, cutting him off. She gripped the Brionac, whose plasma blade had disappeared, then positioned it again to shoot.

Her voice made it sound like she was forcing herself to rouse her spirits and will herself to fight.

"I'll say it again. Surrender! With only one arm, you can't use your martial arts. You don't have any chance of winning!"

Upon hearing Lina's shout, Tatsuya gave a cold-blooded smile. It was even more inhuman than the one Lina had given him earlier—enough to chill her to the bone.

"What would you do with me as your prisoner?"

But contrary to his expression, his voice had no coldness in it.

"Human experimentation?"

In fact, it was more like he was gently coiling around her, softly exposing her evil deeds.

"Like you did with *them*?"

It sounded like the whispers of a demon.

Despite her misfortune, Lina was smart enough to understand that "them" referred to the Stardust. The nervousness and shock caused the blood to drain from Lina's face.

"It doesn't really need to be said, but...I refuse to be your guinea pig."

"Then I'll just cut off all your limbs and drag you away with me!"

The Brionac's tip aimed at the foot of Tatsuya's kneeling leg at extremely close range.

Then Tatsuya shoved his handgun CAD, the Silver Horn custom Trident, into the end of its nozzle.

With his right arm—which had been burned away.

"Your arm?!" cried Lina.

Her cry made her late to trigger the spell.

But Tatsuya had already formed his.

He guided the aim of the gun barrel—the targeting assistance mechanism—of the CAD he'd shoved into the bounded container.

Then, inside the re-created mythological weapon filled with the power of the USNA's strongest magician, his dismantling spell Mist Dispersion activated.

Metal grains, now changed into a gas of normal temperature, spurted from the Brionac's nozzle.

The gas pressure caused the Trident to fly out of Tatsuya's right hand.

But Lina was the one affected more.

Her tight grip had worked against her.

The unexpected recoil sent both Lina and the Brionac flying backward.

The impact of her slamming into the ground shook the Information Boost armor covering her.

Too impatient to recover the Trident, Tatsuya activated Regenerate.

The CAD's structural information and its coordinate information relative to his body reverted, and the Trident returned to his hand in a repaired state.

He fired off six instances of Dismantle, nullifying Lina's magical defenses and piercing each of her limbs.

The shots bored small holes the size of a needle into her arms and her thighs.

Without time to express her agony with a scream, the pain tripped her mental breaker.

A blanket of white swallowed Lina's mind.

"...Lina."

After finishing a certain thing up, Tatsuya returned to Lina, then looked down at her limp, unconscious body lying on the ground and spoke, knowing she wouldn't hear him.

"You'd be better off quitting the army as soon as you can."

Her naïveté had saved him in their earlier battle.

Judging only by their combat strength, Tatsuya should have had a rougher time.

After his arm had been blown to ash, he'd canceled his Program Dispersion. The reason was because he wanted to avoid taking even greater damage when the plasma dispersed once the structural information holding the beam together broke down. If she had lowered that first shot's degree of convergence and fired the plasma so that it dispersed more from the very beginning, it would have roasted more than just his arm. Half of Tatsuya's body would be gone, and he'd have lost his freedom of movement. Of course, he still could have reverted his physical body to its previous state in an instant, but he wouldn't have been able to use his winning move—a sleight of hand using his right arm to stage a surprise attack.

In terms of things Lina could've done from the start—she shouldn't have added the needless process of creating a "path" to limit collateral damage when she'd fired her original shot, either. The shock wave created along the firing path would have definitely done enough damage to block Tatsuya's counterattack.

And when she mowed down the hedge before, she shouldn't have tried to avoid hurting him. It was a basic rule of combat—to take away an enemy's ability to resist, you had to keep dealing damage.

She also didn't need to go along with his long talk about FAE theory. There was literally zero reason she needed to be shocked just because he'd exposed a secret weapon's operational principles.

For the last attack, she should have adjusted the power to stop after burning the surface of his skin instead of aiming for his foot. She lost a decisive amount of time when she changed the Brionac's aim. It wasn't the hesitation from being surprised that his right arm had regenerated that was truly fatal—it had been the lag from having to move the Brionac.

"Sirius, commander of the Stars…I really don't think you're fit for this job," he said to himself again, picking her up in his arms.

[14]

The first thing that leaped into view upon opening her eyes was the ceiling of a familiar large utility van—her team's mobile relay station.

The air clung to her skin like stagnant, tepid water.

But she would obviously have caught a cold left out in that chilly air, so complaining about the lack of ventilation would be asking too much, thought Lina.

Still only sort of awakened, she looked left and right.

Not out of any particular goal, but…a sense of something being wrong quickly swelled within her.

Something was going on.

And when she arrived at what it was, it instantly wiped all her remaining drowsiness away.

"Nobody's here…?"

With her mind clear, it didn't even warrant thought—it wasn't possible. The vehicle itself was a large van sold as something that could be used as a camper as well, but her people hadn't come out here to play.

If they'd encountered an accident, they might have gone outside to look.

Lina being defeated was itself a major accident. It was fully believable that they'd split up for multiple objectives, such as recon, support, and rescue.

But for everyone to be gone at the same time—*that* was impossible. *Why?!*

Her teammates never would have voluntarily abandoned their mobile relay station all at once.

Then had someone…?

Suddenly realizing something, Lina went to the onboard information system's console. She'd remembered that it always recorded everything going on in the vehicle at all times. The arrangement made her feel ill at ease, but right now, those recordings would be a boon. She decided to replay the last ten minutes of footage for now.

——Nothing appeared on the display.

Huh?

Lina's eyes and mouth froze into a shocked expression at the unexpected result. A moment later, she wore a fake smile, even though nobody was watching. She thought she'd used the console wrong.

Once again, this time more carefully, she set the playback starting time to ten minutes earlier.

——It still showed nothing.

She changed the command to play in 4× reverse speed from the current moment. She changed the rewind speed. She changed the playback starting time to an hour before. Two hours before. Three.

The result never changed. The recording data had been deleted.

Frantically, Lina checked to see if other data, apart from the onboard monitoring, was there. But all the storage was empty. The data had been completely deleted, including what the vehicle needed to operate.

As Lina hit the keys with a look of desperation, she suddenly struck the console with her hand. Her palm and fingers stung with pain, but she was so riled up she didn't even care.

Right. I need to report this to the command center.

But once again, this led to Lina losing her temper.

All the communication instruments had been cleverly destroyed so people wouldn't be able to tell by only looking.

After slamming her hand on the console a few more times, she ran out of energy and plunked herself down into a seat.

Her hands were throbbing and hot.

Slowly, she raised her hands, looking to see if they were injured.

Fortunately, she wasn't bleeding anywhere.

Becoming hysterical and hurting herself was too much to be called childish. Knowing the unsightly display wouldn't be revealed to anyone else, Lina breathed a slight sigh of relief.

And after calming down a little, she realized something even more wrong about all this.

"No injuries...no pain?"

First, she looked at her thighs, then rubbed her left and right shoulders in turn.

But the wounds that had delivered such intense pain that she'd passed out were nowhere to be found.

They weren't just gone—there weren't holes in her clothes anymore, either. Nor any bloodstains.

"What's going on...?"

Lina suddenly felt reality slipping away from her.

——How much of it had been real?

——Had she really been injured?

——Had she only been made to think that way?

——Could they, too, have been...?

No... Exotype magic... A mental attack?

A chill ran through Lina's body and caused it to shiver.

Have we...have we been misunderstanding something really important?

What if Tatsuya isn't the one who cast the matter-energy conversion spell, and he actually has a high affinity for mental interference magic...? An illusion master?

...If he is, that would explain a lot.

The reason his right arm went back to normal after being burned off—if he used an illusion to make it seem like that had happened, things would make sense.

And if he was better than me at illusion magic, it wouldn't be impossible for him to see through Parade, either.

When he nullified Muspelheim, too—considering the existence of mental interference spells that apply directly to someone's magical abilities, it all makes sense.

Those spells need delicate control, so he could have disrupted my mind only a little, just enough to keep me from realizing it, to stop me from maintaining the spell. I think that would be a lot easier than destroying the spell itself.

I mean, Tatsuya is a disciple of a ninjutsu *user famous for his illusion magic. It's perfectly sensible to assume Tatsuya himself is an illusion master, too.*

Her mind in chaos, Lina continued to think.

Tatsuya had no way of confirming whether his misdirection (not that it was anything crazy—he'd just repaired the wounds in her limbs and her clothes) had caused Lina to start getting the kind of wrong ideas that would work in his favor.

Besides, there was a more important matter he needed to deal with right now.

There were only twenty minutes left until he had to pick up his sister.

He wanted to finish making the necessary arrangements before then.

Inside a fully automatic car, Tatsuya opened a strictly encoded voice communication line.

"Oh, hello, Mr. Tatsuya. What's the matter?"

"I'm sorry for calling so late, Mr. Hayama."

The butler of the Yotsuba house, or more aptly Maya Yotsuba, was the one to answer.

Tatsuya had called a hotline that went straight to Maya.

"I daresay it isn't that late, but unfortunately, the mistress is currently attending to matters and can't answer the phone."

"Ah—well, I apologize." Considering the time, she was probably in the bath. He certainly should have expected that.

"You needn't apologize. To my memory, this is the first time you've ever given her a call. It must be something quite important."

The old butler was right—this was the first time Tatsuya had ever been the one to open this direct line.

Truthfully, it got on Tatsuya's nerves to have to rely on the Yotsuba, something he avoided whenever possible. But he couldn't be stubborn about it this time. Unlike the No-Head Dragon incident and the GAA invasion, this wasn't something he could use brute force to get through.

Hayama, part of the Yotsuba family core, would understand the current situation even better than Tatsuya. But the proper method for asking them for help was for Tatsuya to explain it in his own words.

"Well, I just came under attack by a small USNA military force. I fought off their first wave thanks to the intervention of Naotsugu Chiba, the Chiba family's second son, but he was hit by an attack from the Stars commander, Angie Sirius, and incapacitated. After that, I engaged Sirius…"

Once he defeated Lina, Tatsuya hadn't wasted the time to tie her up, instead heading for the parking lot adjacent to the park.

He didn't need to capture her. Even if she recovered her senses, Lina wouldn't be able to move. Even if she blocked her sense of pain, as long as her motor nerves were severed, she wouldn't be able to stand up or even crawl. He shot her limbs in a way that ensured that.

And if she'd had significant pain-tolerance training, she wouldn't have lost consciousness in the first place. Tatsuya had decided that for the time being, Lina wouldn't recover her senses.

What he needed to prioritize was her backup team.

The optical (light wave–oscillation-type) spell blocking "vision" from the skies above was still in effect. This was an obvious measure, since Lina wouldn't want her true face being photographed. But at the same time, it also meant she couldn't leave this place.

The USNA military would never abandon their Sirius.

In order to retreat, they'd have to split their people and recover Lina.

The time they took to do that was an opening Tatsuya needed to take advantage of.

They'd probably predict a surprise attack, so they'd be exercising caution now. After all, they'd just seen their star beaten down before their eyes. Even despite that, though, Tatsuya didn't have the option of leaving the backup team alone.

He couldn't kill Lina.

Not only couldn't he kill her, he couldn't capture her, either.

She was far too important a figure to either kill or capture.

Tatsuya had already sent one of the nationally recognized strategic-class magicians, aka the Thirteen Apostles, to his grave. It wasn't on purpose, but its effects on the global balance of power were not insignificant. There would be far too many variables to consider in terms of affecting the global situation should he erase another one of the strategic magicians factoring so heavily into the world's military balance.

But her support personnel were a different matter.

They were a group possessing clear harmful intent—and who had probably attacked him with the malicious goal of making him a human test subject. That was equivalent to someone trying to kill him.

There was no room for a lenient response. He needed to make them fully aware of the cost of pulling Tatsuya Shiba into a secret struggle.

He hadn't had the luxury of splitting his attention between Lina and her support unit when he was fighting her, but when he'd stretched out his sensory tendrils again, they hadn't moved from the positions he'd originally sensed them at. The unexpected defeat of their ace probably had them awaiting orders from the main force. Nothing else could explain this slow response.

They might not have been able to help it, but Tatsuya still felt it was naive of them.

Every mission needed a built-in procedure for retreat in case of defeat.

He might have even called this carelessness.

Although…

I'm more grateful that they were so careless.

From the start, it was clear as day that if he faced them all head-on, they'd drive him back through sheer numbers. Considering that they'd set up the one-on-one situation with Lina, they'd been nothing if not careless.

Of course, there were surely other reasons that they couldn't make a big spectacle of things in another nation's capital.

For Tatsuya, though, those reasons just needed to be overturned and taken advantage of.

Not wasting time with a targeting action, he used only his own abilities to take aim, then pulled the trigger of the CAD still in his hand.

His target was the electronic equipment in a utility van.

With his first shot, he disconnected the communicator wiring; with his second, the outside camera's power cable; and with his third, the inside camera's power cable. Magic was never meant to be used for this sort of delicate mechanical operation; this was all thanks to Fujibayashi and Sanada ganging up on him and putting him through the wringer.

The portable terminals would have still had their communication functions, but Tatsuya ignored that and put his hand on the utility van's door.

It wasn't locked.

No anti-theft systems using biological verification, either.

Instead, he was welcomed by a volley of bullets.

The gunshots made almost no noise because they were either using fairly advanced suppressors or the explosives themselves were special. As Tatsuya hid behind the door, the mechanical noise of the submachine guns' bolts opening and closing actually sounded louder.

And those soft gunshots quickly ended, too.

One of the things Tatsuya had a lot of practice with when it came to dismantling magic was disassembling firearms.

Men burst out of the thrown-open door at him, wielding large knives.

An activation sequence expanded inside the vehicle.

Draw the attention of close combat personnel, then use projectile weapons from behind—or in this case, attack magic. A classic tactic, but he had to admit it was an effective one.

If only their opponent hadn't been Tatsuya, someone capable of recognizing activation sequences on sight.

If the sequence was still expanding, he didn't need Dismantle to deal with them—he could just hit them with a psionic bullet.

Tatsuya thrust his empty left hand in front of him.

Creating a compressed psionic bullet—the fundamental form of the farstrike he'd been practicing so much lately—in his left hand, he fired it into not only the activation sequence around him but all the enemies as well.

He *saw* the sequence shatter in its entirety.

The enemy magicians did a good job of blocking the reverse psionic flow, but the time they took to do that meant they couldn't parry the psionic bullet that flew at them; they didn't seem to be preparing their next spell, either.

Three close combat troops had jumped out of the vehicle, and two of them had an unsteady posture.

Farstrike didn't affect the physical body, instead striking at the astral form—a person's soul, particularly the part in charge of the flesh, rather than the one in charge of the mind. The better a person was at controlling their body with their mind, the more easily psions hurt them. But gaining proficiency in controlling one's mental soul offered the chance to learn to parry the psionic bullet itself or ward it away.

In other words, those with only half-baked training on how to mentally control their bodies were the easiest fodder for farstrike.

The two people trying their best not to fall over in front of Tatsuya were those sort of people. The other one must have been a stout believer in maintaining good physical condition, one who wouldn't even consider doing any such eastern-style training in the first place.

And it was the simpler sort of opponent who was more dangerous.

Tatsuya took the initiative.

He closed in, stopping right before he was in range of a kick, and stuck out his right foot.

He'd switched his right-hand CAD with the knifelike armament device he'd stolen from Lina.

He swung that right hand up in front of his left shoulder, in a reverse shuriken-throwing form, and hurled it at the center of the enemy's chest who hadn't been affected by the farstrike.

A surprise attack with a projectile from point-blank range.

The knife had enough momentum behind it that the man wouldn't emerge unscathed just by knocking it away. In fact, his judgment to dodge it meant he was definitely a professional.

But his evasion was just what Tatsuya had ordered. It was a logical movement—and therefore easy to read.

The man pivoted his left side back, moved from outside Tatsuya's knife hand to inside, then knocked the knife's trajectory away from his body.

The move put the soldier's right side forward and the knife

knocked to his left. But the next attack didn't come from Tatsuya's exposed right back but from below.

Tatsuya's right foot bounced up.

Kicking with his right foot was an irregular motion, as that was where his weight had been for the knife throw, and it caught the man off guard. The man had been bringing his posture back, cautious of a left hook or a left spin kick, and Tatsuya's foot hit the back of his right hand.

The man didn't let go of his knife.

Enduring the shooting pain in his wrist, he tried to bring Tatsuya down with an opposite kick.

The only way to use your pivot foot for a kick was to jump off the pivot foot. Both Tatsuya's feet were now off the ground. If the man could stop the momentum of Tatsuya's kick, he'd have the better position and be poised to ruin Tatsuya's balance—if, anyway, this had been a pure contest of martial arts.

Tatsuya activated the gravity-control spell he'd been preparing in his virtual magic region. The spell was for flying, had a duration of three minutes, and restricted the number of trajectory changes to ten. He bent his blocked right foot underneath him, rising in the air without first touching the ground again, then whipped out a spinning left kick.

This time, the man's response didn't make it.

Tatsuya's right shin dug into the man's neck.

He felt it hit with a dull sound.

It was a feeling familiar to Tatsuya—the sensation of kicking someone's bone and breaking it.

The man's body flew sideways.

Tatsuya's body, ignoring inertia, slid to the left.

A knife pierced through his afterimage—one of the man's comrades had struggled through the farstrike damage to throw it.

Flight spell still effective, Tatsuya planted both feet back on the ground.

Then used the magic to propel himself off it.

With a speed impossible for a human—or at least, impossible with Tatsuya's muscle mass—he rushed into range of the second man.

Tatsuya placed his right-hand CAD into its holster and switched to a knife.

Rather than stopping himself with magic, Tatsuya planted his feet to take in his body's kinetic energy. With a ground-shaking footstep, he absorbed it, and his right hand flew into the man's chest.

It was a strong palm strike, not a fist, to right above the man's heart.

The man fell over backward, unable to take the fall gracefully. From his crouched posture, Tatsuya kicked off the ground with both feet at once.

His flight magic had one round of maneuvering left.

A bullet from behind rushed below his feet, which had risen two meters in the air.

A gun attack from inside the vehicle. They must have taken out a pistol instead of using their submachine gun, which was now in pieces. But actually, he'd expected the strategy sooner than this.

Tatsuya pulled a gun from his waistband.

It wasn't a gun-shaped CAD but a live firearm. This, too, was something he'd stolen from Lina.

He twisted in the air, then sent a return bullet at the shooter leaning out the window. His bullet caught the man in the chest. His body slid out the window—and down onto the floor inside the vehicle.

Tatsuya went over to the original third man.

With his right foot, he stomped down on the man's shoulder, and with his left foot, he folded his target's neck in from the side.

Without the effects of his spell, he then landed neatly behind the fallen enemy.

Panicked gunshots rang out one after another. Using the third man as a shield, Tatsuya responded with fire of his own.

It was hard to aim without damaging the inside of the vehicle, but fortunately for him, there was only one shooter there.

Suppressing the gunfire, Tatsuya charged into the van—only to suddenly deflate.

Aside from the two he'd shot to death, two other men had fainted.

The CADs wrapped around their arms told Tatsuya they were backup magicians.

His farstrike had worked better than expected. His special training with Yakumo had benefited him more than he thought.

Just to be sure, he stepped on the pit of their stomachs, once each, to check for a reaction. Then he threw the unconscious bodies outside the vehicle along with the corpses.

It was a good thing Lina's gun had a small caliber, since the bullets hadn't gone all the way through them. No flesh had been shot off, and there wasn't that much blood splatter, either.

After pilfering a data cube and making a backup, Tatsuya erased everything left on the onboard computer.

Whoever came next would probably clean things up nicely, but he gave the gore a simple wipe up and then left the utility van behind.

All the while keeping up the act that he hadn't noticed a hidden observer's eyes on him...

"...By the time I brought Angie Sirius to the mobile relay van, the backup team I'd taken down was nowhere in sight."

"Whoever was observing you took them away, then?"

"They probably decided it was more important than continuing to watch me. Naotsugu Chiba, who had been put out of combat, was nowhere to be found when I returned to him, either."

Once Tatsuya finished his report, Hayama hummed briefly. The complete lack of emotion may, perhaps, be called the wisdom of age.

"The observer was likely someone under the Saegusa family's yoke."

"The Saegusa? Not the Chiba?"

"Tokyo is currently part of the Saegusa family's sphere of influence. I have gotten word that Mr. Kouichi is ordering his men to act. He seems to be plotting something."

Tatsuya knew that "Mr. Kouichi" referred to Kouichi Saegusa, current leader of the Saegusa family. The names of Ten Master Clans family leaders were common knowledge to Japanese magicians.

"They may have responded with close combat skills, using as little magic as possible because they were aware of that observer's eyes, but we cannot call it desirable that the observer is watching you now."

Of the incidents Tatsuya had repeatedly encountered since April, he hadn't taken the initiative on a single one of them. It was always him getting wrapped up in everything. Still, he was aware it was a poor act that would make a bodyguard stand out too much, so he couldn't object.

"However, I'm fully aware that you have committed no grave mistake, Mr. Tatsuya. And while it is your responsibility to protect Lady Miyuki, a candidate for the next head of the family, that responsibility does not belong to you alone. Lady Maya, too, believes that other families learning of her position now would be too early. Of course, this is Mr. Kouichi. They may have a faint guess, but..."

When Hayama said "guess," he probably meant that Kouichi Saegusa had surmised that Tatsuya was related to the Yotsuba. Tatsuya was privately impressed—they only had a *faint* guess of it?

"Still, we wouldn't want more evidence than expected to fall into their hands. Please send the backed-up data here. We will do something about the USNA military for the time being," Hayama continued smoothly. It didn't seem to Tatsuya that he was trying to boast.

The Yotsuba family was conspicuously fewer in number than the Saegusa or the Ichijou. But that didn't mean they had less combat power. In fact, it was safe to assume each individual was of superior quality. And even though they had fewer people, they still had enough to accept extralegal business from governmental agencies, serving as for-hire counterterrorism trump cards. The Yotsuba family was highest ranked among the Numbers in jobs that involved eliminating sabotage groups and assassination teams, all while keeping it hidden from the public eye.

"Without an excuse to make the JDF act, Mr. Kouichi should back out for the time being as well."

Tatsuya didn't know about their other henchmen, but if Hayama said it, then even Tatsuya could believe it. He sent the data over their line and then bowed his head toward the camera.

As soon as Miyuki saw Tatsuya when he came to pick her up, she gave him a dubious expression. "Has something happened?"

"No, nothing," he said—but it was clear it wasn't the truth, and he spoke it only because others could be listening in.

As Tatsuya escorted her to the car, she exchanged goodbyes with a ladylike smile. After getting into the self-driving car and setting off...

"Brother, you aren't hurt, are you—?"

...she was suddenly all over him, to the point that even Tatsuya was surprised. "No... Miyuki, calm down a little—"

"I shall not calm down! This blood... You fought with Lina, didn't you?! And it wasn't one-on-one, either, was it?! I smell a fight against at least ten people on you!"

Just as Tatsuya perceived "information" using his vision, Miyuki did through touch. And in Miyuki's case, that wasn't all—she could interpret instinctual recognition through smell, too. Tatsuya was sure there were no physical traces left on him at all, but she seemed to have sniffed out the lingering scent of battle.

"Please just stay calm."

He was honestly happy she was worried about him. But he was also honestly concerned that if she didn't calm down, they couldn't have this conversation.

"You know that nobody can *leave injuries* on me if I don't let them, right?"

The words, sounding slightly perplexed, caused his sister to startle.

Quickly, her excitement began to fade. After five seconds or so, she finally regained her calm.

"...I'm terribly sorry, Brother. That was shameful of me."

His sister tried to make herself small, both her words and body language speaking to her embarrassment.

Tatsuya gave a modest smile—partly forced—and shook his head. "Not at all. I'm sorry for worrying you."

"No, that's not... It is natural for a sister to worry about her brother!"

The thought *Is it?* reflexively came to the back of his mind, but he didn't commit the foolish act of saying it.

But he did think this to himself:

Sure, it may be ordinary to worry about a family member, but maybe acting this passionate about it is another matter...

"I am aware that no matter how many times Lina challenges you, she cannot defeat you. Nobody can defeat you, though you may search the entire world," she declared with her usual fervor, causing Tatsuya to realize he was giving her a detached sort of look.

Her trust didn't weigh heavily on him. Tatsuya knew that if Miyuki believed in him, he'd respond to that belief as much as he was able. That was his determination, his pride, his resolve.

But apart from that resolve, he'd also objectively analyzed tonight's incident as dangerous.

If his opponent hadn't been a mentally inexperienced sixteen-year-old girl, if it had been someone with the force of will to put all their combat abilities on full display, he knew he could have been the one who was defeated.

But cluing in the one he protected to such diffidence would be bad, even aside from his job and his responsibilities.

So for now, he purposely gave her a strong-willed reply. "I wouldn't lose to anyone—not with you waiting for me."

That, however, had been an overstatement.

At the very least, it could be seen as "going too far."

A haze hung over Miyuki's eyes.

As she looked upon her brother with a floating, passionate gaze, he realized his own mistake.

But now that he'd said it, he couldn't take it back.

Actually, even if he'd succeeded in retracting the sentiment, he couldn't have changed the situation.

…Well, I guess it's better than her asking about every little thing, he decided to himself, somewhat out of avoidance.

Without any other means to go home, Lina arrived back at her apartment complex after the date had already changed. It had taken her quite a long time as well. Her only consolation was that the sun hadn't come up yet.

Every last one of her armaments had been stripped from her, but for some reason, the Brionac remained in her hand, so she didn't feel hopelessly in danger.

But her information terminal, even her spare one, had been taken away, so she couldn't call for a car to come pick her up.

Since she only ever used digital currency, she never carried a wallet with her. Besides, she didn't have any personal possessions on her anyway to avoid the risk a mid-mission search would present. Thanks to that, she couldn't use any twenty-four-hour public transportation, and she'd had to go back to where she lived *unaided*.

Not only had her specialized CAD been taken but her multi-purpose CAD had been, too, meaning she couldn't use flight magic or speed-running magic as she wished. When she finally spotted her apartment building after a sporadic series of jumping spell assemblies, she almost broke out in tears. If any of her acquaintances had seen her like that, she might have turned the Brionac on them out of pure reflexive shame.

Thanks to the biometric identification security system, she didn't have trouble getting into her apartment.

But as she breathed a sigh of relief, she felt an irresistible anger well up within her.

What the hell do you have against me, Tatsuya?!

Objectively speaking, there were piles and piles of reasons Tatsuya might resent her. However, this was her emotions at work.

Still, her training as a soldier had endowed her with the ability to remember what she needed to do right now despite all that. So she opened a transmission line to the command center.

But no matter how many times she called, she got no response.

A cold sweat formed on her spine. She shook her head vehemently, trying to drive off the ominous premonition.

Using a spare portable terminal, she called the command center again. Her last ray of hope was that their transmission functions were down—but even that was finally dashed by the unending stream of call tones.

She had to come to terms with the fact that something had happened to the colonel and the others.

Lina quickly equipped her CAD and other armaments, then dragged her worn body out onto the veranda and fluttered into the night sky.

Her destination was the building that housed the secret command center inside.

It would only be after an hour, after she'd finished a thorough search, that she'd learn nobody was there waiting for her.

The next morning.

Print and video media both frothed at the news that a small USNA Navy–affiliated vessel cruising in Japan's offshore territory had begun drifting because of engine trouble and was secured by the JMDF.

For some reason, a high-ranking military attaché at the USNA's Tokyo embassy had been aboard the ship, but that wouldn't be reported.

On the same day, a beautiful transfer student at First High was absent from school for a second day due to health problems.

[15]

Tatsuya, who was watching the morning news broadcasts while eating breakfast, realized he was nodding off unconsciously and hastily stopped his neck from moving. Fortunately, Miyuki's eyes had been on the television screen, too, so it didn't seem like she'd noticed.

"Could it have been a device malfunction? It doesn't seem as though it ran afoul of any poor weather, like storms or thick fog."

Miyuki was currently preoccupied with confusion about the news that a small American navy vessel had been drifting in Japan's offshore territory around Chiba Prefecture's bay.

"I can't imagine their instruments all failed at the same time. Maybe the issue was with their power source," he suggested. "After all, with how far automation has come in this day and age, a simple human error wouldn't have caused them to lose their steering."

His sister nodded, not doubting his words for a moment. When he looked over her innocent (?) figure, he felt like it was cleansing him, right down to his corrupt core—but of course, he knew that was no more than an illusion.

Even still…

This response was too fast, even assuming our aunt issued a direct order.

Considering the time at which the drifting vessel had been secured, it would mean that after Tatsuya contacted Hayama, she'd finished sorting out the aftermath of the attack Tatsuya had faced within not a half day but half even of that.

The Yotsuba's operative team might have been talented, but it was impossibly fast if they'd had to go from step one.

Which meant...

Their forces were already in position by the time I contacted her.

He didn't know what her intention behind that was. The timing might simply have been coincidental, or she may have been trying to interfere as little as possible.

It was also possible she had waited until Tatsuya came to them, head bowed.

Even if they did, I still don't feel I owe them anything.

It didn't matter what was going on behind the scenes—if things turned out better as a result, that was enough for Tatsuya.

Miyuki nodded when her brother mentioned a power source–related issue, then quietly considered him.

He didn't seem to have any suspicions.

It pained her to deceive him like this, but even she occasionally had things she didn't want him to know.

She wanted him to believe that she was ignorant of the situation.

Miyuki brought their dishes into the kitchen, then left the rest of the work to their HAR (home automation robots) and went upstairs to the second floor to change into her uniform.

With her mirror in front of her, she breathed a little sigh.

She'd known about that news without needing to see it on TV. It had been after Tatsuya had left for his usual morning training.

She'd received a phone call from Maya.

Maya's news was that they'd eliminated all the USNA military forces that had threatened Tatsuya.

Miyuki didn't know exactly who in the Yotsuba family had done it, so Maya had been the only one Miyuki could show her gratitude to. She knew it was a method of controlling her, but this time, she actually felt thankful. Including for how Maya had kept it a secret from Tatsuya that Miyuki had asked for Maya's help, even when both she and her brother were planning to betray the woman.

It was a dirty move... If Brother knew the truth, I'm sure he would stop liking me...

Miyuki didn't want Tatsuya to think she was a stupid girl.

But at the same time, she didn't want him to think she was too clever, either.

From her heart, Miyuki never wanted to be a burden for him.

And at the same time, she absolutely wanted to avoid making him think he didn't need a little sister anymore.

Once her brother decided she could do her job independently as leader of the Yotsuba...he might leave her.

And even if he didn't, he might put distance between them.

That possibility was a nightmare that tortured her.

Miyuki and Tatsuya were siblings related by blood. Once they grew up, it was natural she'd leave him—and natural he'd leave her.

And she knew she'd eventually have to get married, too.

She knew she'd have to take a husband who wasn't her brother.

Miyuki didn't wish for it, but society, this nation called Japan, wouldn't allow it. Not as long as she was a talented magician with highly desirable magic genes to pass on.

And that wasn't too far in the future, either—it was close at hand.

Currently, magicians were expected to marry early. Female ones in particular were expected to marry quickly and bear children even faster. This was because for each new generation of magicians, their innate abilities tended to improve. Scientists called it "magic adapting to genes." There wasn't much of a difference in generations for top-class levels, but when comparing average abilities, it was true that the current generation's was higher compared to their fathers' generation, which was in turn higher compared to their grandfathers'. Eventually they would probably reach equilibrium, but at the moment, the birth of a new generation was very much anticipated.

To the point where female students attending the National Magic University commonly took time off from school to raise children.

The same expectations didn't apply to engineered magicians whose life spans were unstable, but even they were in their second generation. When it came to the third generation, everyone was looking at them as though they had a duty to give birth as soon as possible. The Shiba siblings' mother, who had married late, and their aunt, who insisted on remaining single, were rare exceptions. And even those exceptions wouldn't have been allowed if not for physical reasons exacerbating the issue.

As it was, Miyuki was a perfectly healthy specimen and so didn't meet those criteria.

In fact, she possessed particularly excellent factors that made her a hopeful for the next leader of the Yotsuba.

In truth, she didn't want any other man besides her brother to embrace her. That was how she truly felt. In fact, to be completely honest, she didn't want any man besides her brother even touching her at all.

It wasn't a morbid distaste for it, like a physiological rejection, so she was fine with things like dancing. But to bluntly spell out her feelings, she was only okay with Tatsuya touching her. It was only okay for Tatsuya to do with her as he pleased.

She looked at herself in her underwear in the mirror. As she did, she thought to herself. These fingers, this hair, these lips, this chest, the secret places she wouldn't show to anyone—if it was Tatsuya, he could touch her. If it was Tatsuya, she wouldn't care what he did to her.

——*Both my body and mind, everything about me, belongs to Brother*——

These were her true sentiments, a prayerlike wish from the bottom of her heart.

But she knew those feelings would never be fulfilled.

So this is what she thought instead:

I'm all right being a bad sister... No, I'd much rather he think I was a bad sister. If that's what it will take for him to stay at my side...

Meanwhile, she decided that she would do her best to secure Tatsuya's affections, whether that would be to keep herself from being seen as evil or boring.

That was Miyuki's current dilemma.

Entering classroom 1-E, Tatsuya sensed a strange mood in the air. He scanned the room with his eyes and quickly found the reason.

The twenty-five seats in their class were arranged in alternating male-female columns in alphabetical order. In front of Tatsuya was Leo, to his left side was Mizuki—and the source of the dark clouds was in a window seat another row over.

Erika was staring out the window glumly. She almost looked like an aura of distaste was exuding from her body.

Well...I can't blame her. Tatsuya had a good idea why she was unhappy. Considering the commitment he'd seen from her in the summer, he was confident the particulars of last night were probably hard to accept.

As Tatsuya simply gave Erika a glance and then took his seat, a voice next to him asked, "Oh, Tatsuya... What do you think happened to her?"

Mizuki may have been addressing him, but half her mind seemed occupied with Erika. But that wasn't the whole of it—she'd obviously guessed, quite sharply, that Tatsuya knew what was going on.

The next thing he realized, Mikihiko and even Leo were giving him the same look.

But there were things he couldn't give them even if they asked. At least, there was no way he could tell them that Lina had defeated Erika's brother last night.

"I wonder what it could be?"

In the end, all Tatsuya could do was feign ignorance.

They didn't press the issue, a good virtue as friends. Even if it was for different reasons—Mizuki because that simply wasn't her personality and Mikihiko and Leo because they personally knew everyone had things they didn't want to talk about.

But even that couldn't defeat the uncomfortable mood swirling in their midst.

The awkward atmosphere persisted, too. For lunch, the five classmates were all apart for the first time in a while—"classmates" specifically, rather than "friends," because Miyuki and Honoka were acting the same as always.

The change came only after school let out.

Like he'd told his sister last night, Tatsuya immediately went to negotiate with the robot club (there was some monkey business involved) and personally rented Pixie from them, since they were her temporary owners.

The point was to question her, not to play with her, but the robot club's garage wasn't fit for such a thing. Nevertheless, leading her around the school in her outfit would have stood out too much. He wasn't in the mood for others casting doubts on him (namely *on his hobbies*), and considering his objective, her standing out at all would have been an issue.

Due to the circumstances, he first had Pixie change into a girl's school uniform. He borrowed the uniform from the art club through Mizuki; it was a model they used for portraits. Pixie's frame was different from a human skeleton, so he was worried whether she'd be able to change into it. But the 3H's body was more flexible than he'd thought, and she had no problem removing her maid dress and putting on the uniform. There were some unnatural lines around her lower body, but he'd known that would happen, and so he'd borrowed a uniform one size too big, making it less conspicuous. She'd look like a regular student to a mere passerby in the hallway—and just for the record, Tatsuya felt nothing watching a robot change clothes.

With all that done, Tatsuya brought Pixie into an empty classroom in the lab building and began his questioning.

He quickly got used to how odd it felt to hear her active telepathy echoing in his brain. But he really couldn't get used to Pixie's inorganic optical sensors (her eyes) and the passion there. Feeling uncomfortable in a way he never had before, Tatsuya continued his inquiry.

He asked about the vampire incidents. Especially the strangeness of the victims having a large amount of blood loss while not having any notable wounds on their bodies. He asked about the mechanism therein and about their motives. It had been weighing on Tatsuya's mind ever since he'd first learned of the incidents.

"Were the parasites responsible for the victims' blood loss?"

"Yes."

"Why did you need blood from a living person?"

"Blood loss was not our intent. It was a side effect of mistaken propagation."

"Explain in more detail, please."

"Our propagation process starts by cutting off part of ourselves and sending it into a recipient—a human body we perceive as capable of hosting us. The separate body spreads through blood vessels while absorbing psions and psycheons in the bloodstream. It permeates the recipient's physical body by exchanging itself for their blood."

"Wait… Exchange itself for their blood? You're bodies of information—you don't have mass. Where does the exchanged blood matter go?"

"It is used to modify their body during assimilation. Should assimilation fail, the separate body is expelled from the recipient's body as vitality."

"I see, so that's how it works… Continue."

"Should permeation of the body succeed, we can control its information body—its ethereal body."

"An interplay between physical bodies and information bodies? The same basic tenet as magic."

"The ethereal body is also a route to the mental body. If we can access the recipient's mental body through their ethereal body and merge with it, our propagation succeeds. Unfortunately, however, we have had no successes."

"Why not?"

"Unknown. I wanted to know this as well. For some reason, the idea alone remains within me."

"...How many of your group are in this country?"

"Immediately prior to inhabiting this body, there were seven—eight, including myself."

"Can parasites communicate with one another?"

"Yes."

"How close do they need to be?"

"They can communicate from anywhere within this nation's borders."

"Where are the other parasites right now?"

"Current locations unknown. My contact with them was severed upon inhabiting this body."

Pixie continued to smoothly answer Tatsuya's questions. Her face itself was impassive, but her thought waves sounded happy—and that probably wasn't his imagination. He didn't know how much in the way of emotion telepathy could express or how much of it one could disguise, but as far as he could feel, she was legitimately happy to be helping him.

To him, a monster was showing him kindness. It may have been a coldhearted way to put it, but he still couldn't help feeling unpleasant about the whole situation. Still, since its host wasn't a person but an object, it made it a little easier. He didn't have to feel guilty about treating it like a possession and using it however he needed to.

It was after his questioning had just reached a breaking point that Erika came into the classroom—and saw just the two of them in it, one person and one robot.

"Tatsuya, do you have a second?"

Had she been listening in for the right moment, or was it a pure coincidence? He didn't know. Eavesdropping he could forgive, since it was Erika and he'd been getting all his answers through active telepathy anyway. She would've heard only Tatsuya's questions, no matter how hard she tried.

He didn't have any complaints as to her suddenly coming in. It wasn't as though he'd been in the middle of changing, and this wasn't even his room, so he didn't feel like demanding that she knock first. It was just that...

"I don't mind hearing you out, but you seem like you're out for blood. It isn't as though I don't feel anything, you know."

...he wished she'd calm down a little.

"Oh, uh, sorry!"

Erika didn't seem aware of it herself. When Tatsuya pointed it out to her, her face turned red with embarrassment.

"No, it's okay, as long as you understand."

She truly didn't seem to realize it, and the coiled springlike mood clinging to her quickly dissolved into the air.

That meant that whatever she wanted to talk to him about was taking up all her mental processes. For whatever reason, he felt his sister did similar things, too, and he had to consciously suppress a dry grin from coming out.

"Pixie, please lock the door."

"At once, sir."

As the robot went, Erika came before Tatsuya, as if to take the robot's place. He gestured for her to sit down, but she didn't want to. She stayed standing, looking down at Tatsuya, who was sitting in a chair.

It wasn't like he didn't understand how she felt, so he didn't force the issue. "What did you want to talk about?"

"You know what."

"Well, I have a guess."

"Yeah... It's about my brother making a sorry display of himself last night."

Erika's answer was what he'd expected, but that hadn't been the *only* thing he'd expected. "Is that all?"

"That first for now."

I see. She has an order, Tatsuya thought.

Erika continued, "Who was he up against?"

The question was extremely forward, without any preface at all. But she hadn't waited for him to say something before asking it—maybe it had her quite flurried.

"Commander of the Stars, of the USNA armed forces—Angie Sirius."

Tatsuya's answer in response was also forward and blunt.

Erika seemed at a loss, as though she hadn't expected him to give an answer so quickly.

"What did you need to know that for?" asked Tatsuya this time, plunging into the hole her bafflement left.

"I mean…isn't it obvious?" Erika seemed taken aback by the frank cross-questioning, but she gave an immediate, strong-willed expression as she answered him.

"I can make a good guess, but…you shouldn't, Erika."

"You trying to say I can't do it?"

This wasn't the unconscious anger from a few moments ago. Erika was quite aware of the anger she was displaying.

Tatsuya accepted it without batting an eye. "Yes. Not because of your actual abilities—but because of how it would end up."

"…What do you mean?" Her anger swelled at the first half of his sentence, but changed to dubiousness in the second half.

"Did you see the news this morning?" he asked. "Videos or printed, either one."

"Yeah, but which news do you mean?"

"The news of the small, drifting USNA vessel."

"Right, that… Wait?!"

"You're quick on the uptake." Erika's face had changed completely, and Tatsuya's praise was not flattery. "Sirius probably won't be showing up again. I don't think anything good will come of this for either of you if you dig it back up."

Erika didn't give an acknowledgment or a denial to Tatsuya's advice. "Tatsuya…" she said instead, looking at Tatsuya as though he were a strange, unknown monster. "Who…who *are* you…?"

No, it wasn't "as though he were"—that was *exactly* how she was treating him.

"We, at least—the Chiba—we couldn't do something like that."

"Is that so?" Tatsuya wasn't trying to feign innocence, but he had no other answer to give her.

"Not just us. The Isori, the Chiyoda, the Tomitsuka—I bet none of them could do it, either. I don't know what you did or how you did it, but the only ones who could get results like that would be the Ten Master Clans, and only then the—"

"Could you give it a rest?" answered Tatsuya shortly, implying this wasn't something he could answer.

But Erika didn't seem to understand.

"—only a family with a lot of power. Either one with their footing in the capital or one that could operate regardless of area."

She didn't stop talking.

"Erika, stop."

"Excluding the Ichijou, since they're based in the Hokuriku district…then the Saegusa or the Juumonji. Or…the Yotsuba. Tatsuya, could…could you be—?"

"I said stop."

"!"

Tatsuya hadn't raised his voice with her. It wasn't his voice's volume that silenced her but the willpower contained within.

"Any more than this would make us both unhappy," he told her quietly.

Erika had her fair share of experience living through savage battles.

She hadn't gone silent because he'd overawed her.

It was precisely her densely packed experience that informed her.

She was very foolishly about to step over a boundary.

"…Sorry."

"It's fine as long as you understand."

The same words as before. The same light tone as before.

But this time, a cold sweat broke out on Erika's back.

"Erika, nobody will have anything to gain from you trying to figure out who Sirius is. So please, let's put an end to that matter."

"…Right."

And she knew Tatsuya had changed the subject partly for her sake, so she nodded without resisting the proposition.

"Anyway, what's the other thing? I think it's probably about the parasite remnants."

"Well, it wasn't that hard to figure out. If you didn't know that much, I'd assume I was talking to an impostor."

Erika had finally gotten back into the swing of things—at least it appeared that way, which was probably intentional.

"Was that a compliment?"

"Well, I know I wasn't trying to run you down."

Erika seemed to be rapidly getting her feet back under her as she put on the act. Tatsuya was slightly envious of how quick the turnaround was.

"I don't plan on leaving them alone, either. Don't worry—once I learn anything, I'll tell you," said Tatsuya, casting a meaningful glance toward Pixie.

Erika glanced at her as well, and the corners of her lips turned up in satisfaction. "Promise, got it? In exchange, I won't keep anything from you about this incident, either."

And it was very much like Erika to include the "about this incident" condition.

"Yeah, I promise."

But this level of distance between them was about right for how long they'd known each other.

"Bye then, Tatsuya. Sorry I interrupted."

"No problem. Give my regards to your brother, too."

With her hand on the door, Erika's spine shivered, but she didn't say anything more before leaving the classroom behind her.

Tatsuya didn't say anything else to her, either.

After leaving the classroom and her secret talk (?) with Tatsuya, Erika walked quickly down the hallway. Once she'd left the unpopulated lab building and returned to the main Course 2 building area, she rested her back against a hallway wall.

Erika heaved a sigh.

A drop of cold sweat streaked down her temple.

Belatedly, the thought that she wasn't herself today rose in her mind. Normally, she wouldn't have ever done something like that, like stomping on a tiger's tail.

——No, that was no mere tiger's tail—it was a dragon, and she'd rubbed its scales the wrong way.

——Thanks to that, she knew.

——She now knew that she didn't need to know.

...*I'm the worst.*

Erika's lips twisted into a self-deprecating smile.

Now that she knew what lurked in the background, several things made sense to her. But she couldn't tell it to others.

He'd warned her not to speak of it, not to let anyone know. She understood that.

And the warning hadn't been directed only at her, either.

What am I going to tell Brother...?

That was probably what Tatsuya had meant at the end.

At first, Erika hadn't liked that someone had been so set on investigating Tatsuya that they would use her brother for it, and she'd wanted to take Tatsuya's side and get in their way.

She'd wanted to protect his secrets.

And now, somehow, she'd been driven into a different position: no longer wanting to but needing to.

She knew Tatsuya probably wouldn't try to get revenge even if she did spill his secret.

I feel like he'd just smile and ignore it even if I slipped up and said something.

But now she'd changed her mind. There was the worst case to think about.

And she didn't feel like testing it.

Not only were Tatsuya's own abilities so incredibly troubling, there was *that family* to think about on top of that.

Ahh... I really screwed up this time. "Involve yourself not with gods and ye be not cursed," huh?

And then she thought to herself, *How did we even end up on that conversation?*

Now that she thought about it, there was almost a sense that he'd guided her into figuring it out.

That can't be right... Tatsuya may have an awful personality, but I have to be thinking too hard about this.

Erika forced her doubts away with a laugh—while straining to avert her eyes from the thought that *yes, he'd probably do something like that.*

Did I step on a hornet's nest? thought Tatsuya, still watching the door Erika had left through.

He'd believed the intervention yesterday by Naotsugu Chiba was the Chiba family putting out feelers, whether at the behest of the Saegusa family or that of a Saegusa-incited Japan Ground Defense Force intelligence division, but it seemed that Erika, at least, hadn't been involved.

She may have simply not been informed, though.

Well, whatever. She would have figured it out sooner or later anyway.

He'd already shown various things to Erika. Not just his strength but even Miyuki's Cocytus. With her sharp wit, even if she hadn't gone overboard today, it would have only been a matter of time.

Consequently, I should be able to get her involved.

Tatsuya hadn't plotted this development all the way through, but to him, things seemed to have turned out all right in the end.

The presence of collaborators was indispensable in keeping secrets from others.

There were always things the secret holders alone would be short-handed for. This was because those who would try and ferret out your secrets did so without letting the person know. At times like that, having a third-party collaborator was convenient for appearances in several ways.

After coming to that rather egoistic conclusion, he brought an end to his silent monologue.

"Pixie."

"Yes, master?"

Tatsuya understood intuitively that during his conversations with Pixie, telepathy wasn't being used to convey words but rather concepts. That the images trying to be conveyed were being translated into vocabulary that would let him understand.

Servant clothes would have been one thing, but someone in the same school uniform as him calling him "master" made him feel restless. But that's what Pixie felt, so as long as they communicated via telepathy, it was something he'd have to get used to.

In fact, he was relieved it wasn't being translated to something like "my lord" or "milord"—though that was mostly his own linguistic sensibilities.

What she (?) was using was active telepathy, so she couldn't tell what Tatsuya was thinking. She moved directly in front of him, reading from the manual programmed into her electronic brain the proper movement patterns for when her name was called.

"Before you inhabited that body, you all appeared to move as an organized group with a common objective in mind. Does one of you correspond to a leadership position?"

"There exists no command structure among us."

"Then how did you keep on acting as a group?"

"Strictly speaking, each one of us is not a perfectly autonomous individual. We are both individuals and the whole. We possessed the ability to think individually, but we shared our consciousness."

"Do you mean that one mind was having multiple thoughts?"

"Yes, but not only thoughts. Perhaps it would be closest to express it as a merger of several lower minds with incomplete egos and isolated thought capabilities into a single higher mind."

"I understand. But in that case, if a lower mind had a different objective, wouldn't the higher mind have lost its unity for it?"

"When attaching to a living host body, we cannot avoid the effects of their most primordial desires. We were integrated within a mind possessing both survival and reproductive instincts, and thus did we decide our actions."

"To survive and to increase your numbers. A simple way of life indeed for *living creatures*."

"That is correct. We had been obeying our most prioritized desires as organisms, acting with the goal of survival and self-replication."

"If you share your mind with the rest of the group, couldn't you have created a different system of collaboration for purposes other than survival and self-replication?"

"Though we are unified in the broadest sense, we each have our own ego, so we respond individually to the specific desires of the host body. It simply happened that we had been prioritizing a common goal, which I should think is why you felt that way about it, master."

"I see…" Tatsuya stopped and thought. She didn't interrupt with anything unnecessary, either because she was a human or because she was inhabiting a machine. "Then since you've inhabited an inanimate object, you're now removed from that shared objective, making you an outcast. When something like that happens, don't you try to eliminate them?"

"We have no desires relating to the elimination of outcasts. However, it is possible that they will prioritize attacking me if they judge me an obstruction to their goal."

"I see... One more question. You said you were disconnected from the rest of your group at the moment. You can't sense their presence at all?"

"I would likely be able to sense them if they were in a state of heightened activity. Conversely, if I were to come within a certain distance of them, they could sense me."

"I see." Tatsuya pretended to think for a moment, then immediately gave her a new command. "Pixie, go back to the garage, change into your old outfit, and stand by in sleep mode. I'll have more for you later."

"Right away, sir. I eagerly await your command."

Pixie gave a proper—in other words, stiff—bow, then headed off for the garage.

Mentally listing the equipment he'd need, Tatsuya walked off toward the student council room to pick up Miyuki so that he could return home for the moment.

The world had become smaller in the 2090s. However, that meant it turned into a world that pitted magicians directly against non-magicians. Magicians who were acknowledged as effective military power in the last world war and the sporadic border conflicts after it were then severely restricted from leaving the country, except on official government duties. For magicians, the world had shrunk to the size of their borders.

Meanwhile, those who weren't magicians could fully enjoy the benefits of advancements in public transportation. Machines meant for transporting people over land, sea, and sky alike had gotten faster, allowing them to more easily visit foreign countries. It was now an age where you could board a direct flight and be on the other side of the planet in ten hours with no layovers. Compared to a hundred years ago, the world had definitely gotten smaller.

Because of the circumstances that led to the global war outbreak, every nation trod very carefully when it came to possible illegal immigrants staying for a long period of time within their borders. In exchange, foreigners who stayed for short periods of time were on the rise in many countries. Even here in Tokyo, seeing people of different ethnicities walking the streets had become the usual state of affairs.

So even when a white-Hispanic man, a young mestizo (half-Caucasian, half–Native American) man, and a young half-Caucasian, half-black woman were walking together at dusk on the east side of the Sumida River, no Japanese person thought it was odd. Nor did a single civilian watch them with suspicion as the group of three entered a certain hospital—a large place but one not often used.

There were beds in the hospital's basement.

Putting it that way may make it seem as though nothing was out of the ordinary, but these beds were not normally the sort a hospital had in it.

They were black leather and didn't have much cushioning; rectangular boxes that could be more suitably called bunks than beds. And the nine of them weren't positioned in two horizontal rows of four and five, but rather all were in a radial pattern. One young man lay on each bunk for a total of nine. All of them had Northeast Asian features, but their faces were pale. Also, they had lain down without any pillows, and their chests weren't moving—so they were either corpses or comatose. The only ones in the basement room were these nine young men, and the three Hispanics who came down the stairs.

The white man went into the empty space in the center of the beds, with nine heads facing inward. The dim lighting gave him a somewhat conjurer-like mood.

The young mestizo man checked his wristwatch. He held his arm up, waiting for something. After about ten minutes had passed, he looked at the half-Caucasian, half-black woman standing on the other side of the ring of beds. It must have been a signal. The woman nodded slightly, then raised both her hands in front of her face.

The young man assumed the same pose. Between the young man and woman, the man clapped his hands and tapped with his foot at the same time.

The applause went on.

The foot stamping continued.

The pair clapped their hands and stamped their feet along with the older man, moving around the outside of the circle of beds. When the young man and woman had changed places, the older man gave a much stronger clap.

As his clap echoed, the human bodies resting on the beds rose.

One, then another.

Eight apparently dead people on those black bunks had been revived.

A buzzing noise like the wings of bugs began to fly across the dim basement room, through not the physical dimension of Fact, nor the information dimension of Idea, but the mental dimension.

If their words were to be translated…

"I/We have finally awoken."

"I/We are still lacking."

"Is it one person/thing I/we lack?"

"Have I/we not enough vessels?"

"No. As you can see, the collaborators have arranged the vessels."

"Chinese necromancy is certainly something."

"Yes, I/we shall have to admit that it is beyond my/our level."

"The longing to live in the face of death. A suspended ego."

"I/we could not think of a way to assimilate with my/our hosts while in suspended animation."

"Therefore, I/we learned. Now I/we know how to move into a host."

"Next time, even if my/our flesh is destroyed, I/we can quickly resume activities."

"It is also easy to retake the one person/thing I/we lack."

"Let us retake what I/we lack."

"Let us go and search for what I/we lack."

That was the kind of conversation they were having—the three individuals who had come here across the ocean and the eight parasites.

After returning home, Tatsuya went to the phone before changing. He wouldn't be using the one hooked up to the big screen in the living room but the one with enhanced security features in his bedroom. Normally, the phone did real-time encoding, even with some of its functions dedicated to video processing, but Tatsuya made a voice-only call to the Yotsuba butler, Hayama. It was pretty much in sync with the time he'd been sent in the message.

"Mr. Tatsuya? Right on time."

"Thank you for last night, Hayama."

They both did away with the *normal* prefaces. Tatsuya had done it because Hayama had. It wasn't that the old butler was busy and wanted to get this over with, though. Tatsuya could sense there was something he wanted to tell him.

"As I said last night, there is no need for thanks. Protecting Lady Miyuki is the second-highest priority for the Yotsuba, after all."

"Hayama, with even you speaking so imprudently, I find myself at a loss."

"It doesn't pose an issue, so long as one considers the time and the person. Besides, unlike that one, I do not possess the nerve to be hostile to you, Mr. Tatsuya."

He did, at least, seem to have the time to go along with meaningless chatter.

But Tatsuya didn't have that much time himself. He decided to ask why Hayama had directed him to call specifically on a secret line—and he couldn't exactly respond to Hayama bringing up the trouble with Aoki from months ago anyway.

"What did you need to talk about? You couldn't send it through a text message, and you didn't have the kind of time for me to go there personally, so it must be something urgent."

"*Oh yes, that's right,*" responded Hayama in a voice like he'd just now remembered. But Tatsuya knew it was an act. Even if he couldn't make the judgment based on the elderly butler's voice, he knew it because of his nature.

"*Mr. Tatsuya, it appears Section Three is getting involved with our little demon episode. I wanted to make sure you were aware of that.*"

"Section Three... Section Three of the Japan Ground Defense Forces counterintelligence department, the funny team? They're part of the Saegusa faction, right?" asked Tatsuya.

He heard a laugh come through the receiver. "*I'm sure they'd hate to hear someone belonging to a certain Independent Magic Battalion calling them funny, but yes, you are correct.*"

"If they have an interest in this, I expect they're not trying to exterminate them. The Saegusa must be going through them to investigate... no, to try to capture the parasites, aren't they?"

"*I would like to commend you on your correct answers as always, but unfortunately, we still don't know their goals. It is likely, however, just as you've described, Mr. Tatsuya.*"

Sounds like a huge pain, thought Tatsuya from the bottom of his heart. There were already so many factions and influences intertwined with one another—and now another player had appeared on the stage. And to make things worse, they might have been on the Saegusa's side, but they seemed to have a different goal from Mayumi.

"Thank you very much for the vital information."

Still, he couldn't just flip over the game board and end it all. However much of a bother this got to be, you couldn't reset reality like a video game.

"I judged that this, too, was necessary to protect Lady Miyuki's well-being. Never forget that fact, Mr. Tatsuya."

"I understand perfectly."

Yes—he couldn't risk the world where Miyuki lived. Hayama's admonition hadn't been much more than a reminder, but Tatsuya accepted it without resistance.

Seven PM.

The students had already left school, and very few faculty remained, leaving the school building to wallow in silence. The gate was shut as well; until tomorrow, save for a few exceptions, nobody would be let in or out. Even the teaching materials and school store products, as well as the students' meals, had been transported out the rear gate via an underground tube.

The only ones allowed in or out were faculty members on night duty, security personnel from the contract company, system maintenance engineers who couldn't do their work except at night, and those with special dispensation from the school or student council.

It seemed like a slight overstepping of student autonomy, but this was something Mayumi had introduced when she was student council president. No shortage of ideas and authority from the Saegusa family seemed to be wrapped up behind everything, but if you were in the position to take advantage of it, those secret circumstances didn't matter. Tatsuya was truly grateful to not have needed to submit an application with logical reasons to be in school after dark to the faculty room.

Tatsuya had arranged several things on his way back to his home, and by the time he'd arrived at the school again, it was with a filled bag on his shoulder. He showed his nighttime entrance permit, which had a student council president–approved pass code embedded in it, to security, then received three visitor ID cards. Without these ID cards during the night, the security system would flag him as suspicious.

As to why he had received three—

One was, of course, his own. He handed the second to Miyuki, who was following behind him. She accepted it with a satisfied smile on her face.

Tatsuya hadn't actually planned on bringing her here. His *plan* was to have her watch over the house in his absence.

Unfortunately, when he'd been issued the nighttime entrance permit, Miyuki had placed a condition on it: He had to bring her along.

The authority to issue the permit lay with the student council president, Azusa. However, Tatsuya then had to sit through about three hours' worth of a heated debate that seemed to lend credence to the gossip that the vice president was actually the one with the power in the current student council.

After failing to convince his oddly stubborn sister, Tatsuya had no recourse but to allow her to come.

Miyuki—and one other person.

He handed the third permit to Honoka, whom they'd met at the station. Perhaps it didn't deserve mentioning, but Tatsuya never planned to bring Honoka from the start and had given the thought even less consideration than he had with his sister. Unfortunately, the permit-issuing conversation had occurred in the student council room, meaning Honoka was there, too. He could truly call it nothing if not careless of him.

But refuse her as he might, he couldn't state his *true goal* out loud with Azusa and Isori listening as well. If it had only been Honoka pleading with him, he could have dealt with it, but when even Miyuki took her side, it was impossible to keep denying her. And unlike Miyuki, Honoka took the ID card from Tatsuya's hand with an obliged look on her face.

The reason he'd given when applying for the permit was to check on the 3H type P-94, which was still behaving oddly. But his real reason was to take Pixie and use her to lure out the parasites.

There was one thing he'd learned from questioning Pixie—that the parasites wouldn't leave Pixie alone. It was still no more than conjecture, but Tatsuya had confidence in this particular deduction. If the link with one of their mind-melded "parts" had been suddenly severed, they should want to recover it. They would doubtless come to contact her in some form or another. That's what Tatsuya's idea was.

He had no way of searching out the parasites, and he didn't need to do a thorough search anyway—until the day before yesterday, at least. But now that he *owned* the parasite possessing Pixie, he couldn't stick to his detachment. He could see some major problems coming if he were to neglect Pixie in her current state. More importantly, he wanted to finish this business with the parasites. He'd been expecting a rematch against them from the start. That was why he'd asked Yakumo to teach him—why he'd been training with him. He'd done nothing more than create a chance to change his stance regarding Pixie from passive to active.

Even he didn't expect to reel in all the parasites tonight in a single net. But if he could lure out even one or two, he was sure he'd be able to get a clue as to where the rest of them resided.

Considering the danger of what he was about to try, perhaps Tatsuya should have been firmer and denied Miyuki and Honoka's request to join him. Several *things* about him were probably just a little bit numb when it came to danger.

Tonight's plan hadn't been more than an independent action from the beginning. Considering the events leading up to this point, as well as the necessities, he'd asked for support from Erika and Mikihiko. He'd accidentally decided, with a slight lack of thought, that if those two were going to be helping him, then it would be fine for Miyuki, who knew the circumstances about as well as he did, and Honoka, who was in a way related to the whole thing, to come as well.

First High rules said you had to be in uniform when you came to school even if it wasn't a school day, but that rule didn't apply to nighttime entrance. You needed to have a communicator-embedded ID card on you, but that meant you didn't necessarily have to wear your uniform. At least, that was the official reason. Behind it was a desire to prevent students from loitering about in the city in their uniform at night.

For the school, it was a kind of risk prevention—also known as "playing it safe"—and Tatsuya understood that. He was dressed for fighting in his usual blouson. Miyuki, taking a page out of his book, wore an activewear-style outfit, with half coat, stretch pants, and tall boots.

However, Honoka was wearing her uniform under her coat. It made Tatsuya doubt whether she understood what they were about to do, but he wasn't one to let that show in his voice or expression.

"Honoka, did you not go home today?"

It was instead Miyuki who spoke for her brother's doubts using an inoffensive expression.

"Huh? No, I did."

Honoka lived by herself; the room she was renting was closer to the school than the siblings' house. She would have had plenty of time to change.

"Umm, should I...should I not have come in my uniform...?"

"It's not a totally bad thing..." said Tatsuya. "It just might be a little inconvenient."

He didn't want to say anything to criticize her, but he could predict a variety of accidents happening tonight. And Honoka didn't seem to have thought about that. With a bit of regret, he reflected that he should have explained this to her more properly.

As though sharply picking up on Tatsuya's thoughts, Honoka began to look down as they walked through the hallway.

"Brother, would it be possible for us to stop by Honoka's apartment?" Miyuki was the one who set to work dissolving the awkward mood. "You can wait here while Honoka gets changed."

She probably wasn't consciously assisting her rival. She'd only suggested a solution because Tatsuya was worried.

"Yeah. It's a little late to visit, so… If that's all right with you, Honoka, that's what I'll do."

"No, not at all! Um, I don't really mind it at all if you come with us. If you have the time to spare, then please come and visit."

Unrelated to Miyuki's intentions, this was the best outcome Honoka could ask for.

While they were having a conversation that had begun with them at odds before coming full circle to the point where they meshed like well-fitted cogwheels, the three arrived at the robot club garage. It was locked, of course, but the thing about locks was that you didn't usually need to do much to open them from the inside. Tatsuya booted up his portable terminal's close-range communication mode, then sent the encoded message plus encryption key he'd created just that day.

The response came back immediately.

"Did you call for me, master?"

A single door, even an armored one with strength unbefiting of its thinness, was no obstacle to telepathy.

"Open the entrance for us, please."

"At once, sir."

There was an answer, and immediately the garage door was opened.

Just inside was the figure of a doll in maid clothes, bowing deeply from the waist. Though an evil spirit resided within, its preprogrammed basic movement patterns seemed to be strictly observed.

Tatsuya waited for Pixie to raise her head, then took out the first item from his bag.

"Pixie, please change into this."

Even so late at night—actually, precisely *because* it was night, in a sense—he couldn't bring her along for a walk in this outfit (namely, the maid clothes). Nevertheless, a student uniform would be no good, for the previously stated reason. For their mission tonight, the first thing Tatsuya had procured was clothing for Pixie to wear.

Pixie must have decided a response was unnecessary for this level of thing. She abruptly began to take off the balloon-sleeved dress she had on.

Tatsuya watched, eyes implying it was natural. This was the second time he'd watched her change clothes, the first being after classes had ended, and he wasn't possessed of the sort of propensity to confuse dolls with people. For him, Pixie getting changed was almost like taking the seat cover on or off his motorcycle.

"Brother?! How can you watch that so calmly?!"

But for Miyuki, it seemed to be something impermissible.

When he looked, Honoka, too, was directing a criticizing gaze at him.

"Why? Miyuki, Pixie is a robot, you know."

"She may be a robot, but she's still a girl!"

"Well, she may be shaped like a person, but she isn't modeled *that* precisely to resemble the human body..."

As Tatsuya said, a 3H was a humanoid robot built to be mistaken for a human *with* clothes on, and the details hidden under the clothing were entirely different from a woman's naked body. The cheap dolls people used for pseudo-sexual acts had a much higher degree of reproduction for *those* kinds of parts.

For instance, Pixie's upper body was close to that of a woman wearing a skin-colored leotard but only down to her waist. The exterior of her torso from the waist down was clearly something one would recognize as robotic, and if one made her wear tight bottoms, one could tell even just from the back that she wasn't human. The default of a skirt with a wide hemline was for that very reason.

But for the two girls, her subjective appearance was a higher priority than that objective truth.

In the end, Tatsuya was forced by his sister to stand facing away from Pixie, while Honoka stood between them in order to conceal the robot's modesty.

It wasn't to say he didn't feel like it was unfair, but at the same time, it also wasn't as though he needed to see her changing. Tatsuya obediently kept his back turned until the two gave their permission.

"It's okay now, Tatsuya."

Addressed by Honoka's voice, Tatsuya first confirmed his sister's expression just in case, then turned around.

The outfit Tatsuya had brought here was a highly elastic sweater under an open jacket with a standing collar and a knee-length skirt with three layers of frills to hide her waistline.

Alongside a longish scarf wrapped twice around her neck.

He had purposely omitted any type of hat that would hide her face. He also had her wear thick tights and boots, which emphasized her legs' silhouette while concealing the finer details… It was an effect for which he'd made full use of the advice from the female petty officer who'd lent the clothes to him and was in charge of the Independent Magic Battalion's supplies.

Honoka was messing with Pixie's hair using a brush she'd taken out of somewhere, but Pixie didn't mind it, not budging an inch while standing perfectly upright. Regardless of how much they faked the outside, it served to indicate she was a doll, not a human, but Tatsuya had no intention of making such advanced demands of her.

He didn't mind as long as she didn't elicit questioning walking down the street.

With regards to that point, Pixie's current form earned passing marks.

"Pixie, come with us."

Instead of declaring that their mission had started, he gave her an order.

Arrogantly, as if commanding a slave.

Indifferently.

◇ ◇ ◇

Erika stood riveted to the floor in front of her older brother's room.

From her perspective, this hesitance was completely unexpected. She couldn't believe such a timid part of her still remained.

She had no diffidence entering the main building, though she had wanted to avoid meeting her father and older sister. She didn't feel like seeing her eldest brother, either, though she didn't have as much resistance to seeing him as she did toward the first two. Fortunately, at this hour, the eldest son wouldn't have been back home yet.

In any case, getting this over with quickly and going back to her own room would be best, and standing around doing nothing in the hallway was the worst. After all, she had plans after this today.

Erika energized herself, then said, "Brother Tsugu, it's Erika."

"Come in," came the answer after a slight pause.

His voice didn't sound displeased, but it wasn't very welcoming, either. Actually, he was probably forcing himself to suppress his less-than-stellar mood.

Fighting the impulse to turn and leave that very moment, Erika opened the door.

"What could be the matter at this hour?" he asked.

Naotsugu was sitting in front of his writing desk. He had his chair turned and was facing Erika with his whole body. But Erika glimpsed signs that someone had just been sleeping in the bed across from the desk.

The two siblings were in opposite positions from the day before yesterday, but Erika didn't bother pointing that out to him.

"I just had something I wanted you to know."

Erika's tone of voice was an inarticulate one. The smile Naotsugu was forcing himself to make caused it.

"I'm all ears."

Her brother's response was not a very enthusiastic one. In less subtle terms, it felt like he was only listening out of obligation. But that didn't mean he was making light of Erika; it seemed like he was preoccupied with other things.

"I have a name I wanted to see if you knew: the 101st Brigade's Independent Magic Battalion."

"How do you know a name like that, Erika?"

Erika had managed to rally her spirits at the door, but then she nearly crumpled under the weight of her brother's unenergetic responses. But now, Naotsugu showed intense interest in the name she had mentioned.

"Actually…"

Even after coming this far, hesitation coiled insistently around Erika's legs. But she couldn't think of a cleverer way of doing this.

"My classmate Tatsuya Shiba—the one you're protecting—is a special-duty soldier in the Independent Magic Battalion."

"What…?"

Naotsugu couldn't conceal his surprise at the truth Erika had revealed after willing away her hesitation—or rather, her fear.

"I apologize. I should have told you this earlier when I heard of it, but someone calling himself Major Kazama strictly forbade me from talking about it, saying it was a matter of national security."

"Major Kazama…? The 'Great Tengu,' Harunobu Kazama?!"

"The…Great Tengu?"

This time, it was Erika who tilted her head in surprise.

Exaggerated nicknames were often given to magicians, mostly as a bluff to make opponents cringe in fear, but "Great Tengu" was conspicuous even among them. It was so overblown, it made her think there was an actual story behind it.

"You're familiar with Major Kazama, then, Brother Tsugu?"

"Yeah… He's an old magician known as a world-class expert on mountain and forest warfare. He's currently known as *the* best commander Japan has when it comes to leading paratroopers."

Naotsugu's face and voice contained a mixture of excitement and reverence.

"You know about the Dai Viet conflict, right? At the time, he aided the Vietnamese military in guerrilla warfare against the Great Asian Alliance, who planned to advance south to the Indochinese Peninsula. Apparently, the GAA forces—mainly the Goryeo advance party—feared him as a demon or a god of death."

Naotsugu exhaled slightly. His excitement turned to yearning, and his reverence became a sigh.

"That was in his midtwenties… He wasn't much older than I am now, so in a way, he's a legend. Of course, the nerve center of our military at the time had wanted to avoid a direct clash with the GAA. They were angry with him, and apparently his path for advancement went off course because of it."

Forgetting even the problem in front of her in her brother's story, Erika felt like heaving a fed up sigh.

They had their own example of a meritorious man who would become a sacrifice for the peace-at-any-price principle. Maybe it would destroy the nation in the future. Erika knew that was not something a teenager like herself needed to think about, but she couldn't help it.

"So the rumored Independent Magic Battalion was the force Major Kazama was leading… Well, several urban legend–type stories about him make sense now. And if you're saying Tatsuya Shiba is one of them, I understand a little more how he has such skill despite his age."

As Erika monologued to herself, Naotsugu sounded like he was speaking to himself as well.

Thanks to that, Erika was able to pull her mind back to her original goal.

"Brother, I met Major Kazama during the Yokohama Incident. If it hadn't been the emergency it was, Shiba would have never revealed his secret. That was how important and confidential it was. I could feel it."

"Hmm… Well, the battalion itself acts like a secret unit. If a high school student is an unofficial member, then yes, there must be quite a good reason for it."

"The reason I broke my oath and told you about Shiba was because I wanted you to understand exactly that."

"Then you want to tell me not to tread any deeper in his personal affairs than this, right?"

"Yes. If we poke the bush and the snake comes out, I'm sure it won't do you or the Chiba family any good. Especially if the snake might turn out to be a venomous cobra."

"Hmm... Yes, you have a point. Still, I may be a student, but I'm already in the military. I can't disobey an official order."

"Then couldn't you only obey your orders as they were given? Keep acting the bodyguard, and if an attack on him happens, you could deal with it and stop there."

"I see... I get it. I'll try considering it from that angle."

...It seemed she had managed to successfully convince her brother without letting the name Yotsuba slip. Erika bowed to hide her relief, then left the room without meeting her brother's gaze.

After returning to her own room—which was in a separate building—Erika read the message on her information terminal, which was on her desk with a blinking message notification light.

"Aoyama Cemetery, huh?"

Without the time to settle into her chair, Erika took off the clothes she was wearing and threw them aside. The act was ill-mannered, unbecoming of a "young woman of a good family," but her mind was so exhausted from persuading Naotsugu that just energizing herself was all she could do.

She put on her under-armor—underwear made of multifunctional synthetic rubber that was bulletproof and bladeproof—then put a fake leather rider's jacket and shorts on over them. Knee protectors that wouldn't hinder movement, and synthetic fiber gloves with an ultrathin layer inside the palm and finger areas. After checking that she had everything in her jacket pocket, she got her weapon and headed for the separate building's front door. Her outfit, with the shorts and boots ending below the knee, was stylish and meshed well with her coquettish good looks, but she wasn't off to the shopping district tonight.

The members of Erika's "royal guard" were waiting outside her building. They were the core of the Chiba unit for the vampire incidents—in other words, they acted as Erika's arms and legs.

"Let's get going," she announced casually.

The men followed behind her, not a hint of unhappiness to be seen.

The apartment Honoka was renting was a really snug lease. In terms of the floor plan, it had a living room, a dining room, and a kitchen, but it wasn't actually as big as that would sound—there was only a small, obligatory dining room next to the kitchen.

Still, having her own room separate from the living room was probably something nonnegotiable as a girl. Opening the front door and immediately being able to see the bed you slept in wouldn't feel very good even for Tatsuya, a man.

In that living room, Tatsuya and Miyuki were having tea together. Honoka had hastily thrown it together after stopping Pixie from trying to help in accordance with her original production goals. They'd gotten coarse tea, which was probably Honoka's preference.

Speaking of Honoka, she was currently changing in another room. The soundproofing was perfect, but a vague air of commotion still got to them. Of course, both the siblings had enough good manners to pretend they didn't notice.

When Honoka appeared next, the siblings had just finished drinking their coarse tea.

"Sorry for the wait!"

She burst out of her room, her outfit the same general style as Miyuki's.

A half coat on her upper body. A turtleneck sweater visible underneath it. But instead of long stretch pants for her legs, she'd combined a mini culotte skirt with thick leggings. They were also called stirrup pants, the sort where the hems flared out, leaving only the toes and heel visible.

Her half coat's hem came exactly down to hide her culotte skirt, and at a glance, it might have looked like she wasn't wearing anything on top of her leggings.

Her outfit coordination was quite eye-catching—particularly to the male eye.

Still, it wasn't completely impractical. Her leggings were heat retaining, woven with fibers that made the material especially tough. Tatsuya knew that the same type of fibers were used in field battle–use coats. After a quick top-to-bottom glance of what she was wearing, he nodded slightly.

"All right, let's head out."

He didn't know how she'd interpreted the action, but she followed him, her expression one step away from breaking out into a grin.

In her hair, to the left and right, were the two crystals she'd received from Tatsuya. For a slight moment, Pixie acted as though she were drawn to their glow, but neither Tatsuya nor Miyuki, nor Honoka herself, noticed.

"Brother, where are we headed to now?" Miyuki asked at the top of the escalator that led to the train platform, judging that there was nobody around at the moment. Miyuki would follow Tatsuya wherever their goal happened to be, but that didn't mean she wasn't curious about where they were going.

"Aoyama Cemetery."

Honoka was curious in her own right, but when she heard the answer, her face became taut. Considering the time of day, and setting aside affection and trust, maybe she couldn't help it. Miyuki, who didn't so much as bat an eye, was surely in the minority of teenage girls.

"I'm sure we're not going there for an off-season test of courage. Is it just that *ghosts tend to crop up in places like that?*"

"You're quick on the uptake."

There was a slight tinge of happiness, though suppressed, on Tatsuya's face as he indirectly affirmed his sister's guess.

"Well, it was something you thought of, Brother."

Miyuki returned the not-altogether-not-a-smile with one of her own.

"Umm, Tatsuya," Honoka mumbled, feeling a little thorn in her chest at that. "It's late, so won't the park be closed...?"

Until the day before yesterday, Honoka would have flinched at the pain from the thorn and backed off. But the prodding from a good friend last night was still there—not in her mind but in her heart. So she squeezed herself into the conversation, from one stair up on the escalator.

Miyuki looked surprised, but Tatsuya didn't appear bothered. "We probably can't get inside. But even so, it wouldn't matter. If we get close, they'll come out for us. That's why we brought Pixie along."

As a result of questioning Pixie, his idea was that the other parasites wouldn't tolerate *her* current way of being.

For the other individuals, who moved in concert as living beings, Pixie, who had lost her desire to self-replicate, was something removed from that. If there were extremely few individuals, they would try to recapture her from her prison inside the machine Pixie. If they were controlled by the basic impulses of self-defense and species preservation, their movement patterns to do so should be the same as humans'.

"And if anyone stops and questions us, you'll be here to do something about it, right?"

Tatsuya knew more than just hearsay about her skill at optical camouflage—he'd seen it for himself. The Blackout Curtain, used by the USNA's backup personnel, was far less advanced a technique and required far less skill in comparison. Honoka was the perfect magician to conceal them.

Although, this was simply lip service on Tatsuya's part. He couldn't imagine a situation in which they'd actually need to hide themselves.

However.

There was something Tatsuya still didn't fully understand.

Honoka didn't get that sort of joke.

"Please leave it to me!" she said confidently, almost peacefully, pounding her chest.

What an overreaction, thought Tatsuya, in an awful misunderstanding.

Underground, in a medium-rise building on a street corner in Ichigaya: Here was where the JGDF counterintelligence department's Section Three had its *headquarters*.

If their HQ in the Ministry of Defense was the front-facing core of the JGDF's intelligence activities, this underground room was the one behind the curtains, one of the *true* cores. It may sound strange to have more than one core of something, but this was a product of risk analysis, set up so that if their HQ went down, their functions could keep running.

Of course, using an abnormal organizational structure brought with it some major side effects.

Intelligence groups always came with the concept of the left hand not knowing what the right was doing, but that concept was strikingly conspicuous here. People refraining from doing whatever they wanted on their own would have been a saving grace, but the reality of it was that each section had its own backers and operated in many arenas at once according to those backers' wants. The JGDF's intelligence department in particular contained an ugly disunity in its organization.

"Observation target currently moving toward the city. Sister and two others with him."

The patron of this underground room was a major conglomerate of electronics manufacturers, which was also the second-biggest munitions industry group in the nation. And the Saegusa family was deeply embedded in their federation. It would be apt to say the Saegusa were the true patrons of counterintelligence Section Three. And right now, apart from Mayumi and the others in the Saegusa-Juumonji alliance, they were also acting on the will of *the Saegusa's current leader*.

"Running video verification… One of them is Honoka Mitsui, first-year student at NMU's Affiliated First High School."

"A classmate. Odd tastes, bringing his sister along on a date like that."

The person in charge gave a response that seemed scornful, but depending on how one interpreted the words, it could have also sounded envious.

"The other one… No, she's not a human. It seems to be a type P-94 Humanoid Home Helper."

"A humanoid HAR terminal? Where could he be bringing it?" The man tilted his head in confusion and said to another staff member, "Have we gotten into the cabinet service systems yet?"

"No, sir, it has tough protection… My apologies, sir!"

The man in charge didn't scold his subordinate for the almost whining remark. He understood that if the public transportation system's control brain allowed hacking that easily, terrorists would be the bigger worry.

"Chief, the train with the target on it has changed course."

"Akasaka…? No, Aoyama?" muttered the chief, predicting the cabinet's course from the monitor display. After a pause, he gave the order.

"Position operatives disguised as police officers along Aoyama Road. If the target group uses magic, pretend to arrest and capture them."

As affirmatives to his commands and communicator-aimed instructions were flying about, the chief continued to stare at the monitor.

Colonel Balance sat, exhausted, in an embassy-prepared, rent-by-the-week, fully furnished apartment.

She had allowed a break-in to their operational headquarters, if only a temporary one, and on top of that, she'd been kidnapped without the chance to put up any real fight, and then she'd been humiliated when a foreign vessel had rescued her as she was drifting out at sea. The huge failure was a deep blow to both her career and her pride.

Surprisingly, neither her home nation nor the military officials staying at the embassy had any particular criticisms. This mistake had humiliated not only her but also the special team dispatched as temporary HQ security, as well as the navy, for allowing the seajacking of a small vessel in the first place. (The USNA Navy's pride, however, was in much worse shape than hers.) So she understood the situation didn't allow them to blame her alone.

But she had enough energy left to guess that wasn't the only reason. Still, she couldn't deny that she was in a malfunctioning state.

When the doorbell rang suddenly and she looked up, only then did she realize that night had long since fallen.

She heard the female sergeant assigned to be her bodyguard answer the doorbell. Then she heard a sharp intake of breath from the woman.

"Excuse me, ma'am."

Both the footsteps approaching the living room Balance occupied and the voice asking her for permission to enter sounded rattled.

"Enter."

Balance straightened her posture on the sofa, making sure to give her reply in a firm tone. She couldn't show weakness to someone of lower rank—the officer training within her, more than her own intent or emotions, made her act that way.

The living room door opened and closed carefully. In front of her, a tall woman in a pantsuit saluted. A noncommissioned officer chosen for her personal combat abilities over her appearance or education, her skills and courage were both some of the best. Balance rated this sergeant so highly she believed things might have turned out differently last night had she been present.

And yet—her face was pale, drawn back.

Sensing this was no trifle, Balance rose from the sofa. "What's going on?"

"There is someone who wishes to meet with you, ma'am."

"What...?"

It was a secret that Balance was staying here. But if it had just been someone from the military (the USNA military, that is) coming to see her, her sergeant bodyguard wouldn't have any reason to be this nervous. Not even for the embassy staff. In other words, the visitor was an outsider, despite the USNA military's information control—and what's more, an outsider who knew that she was *here*.

Too impatient to give a command to the sergeant, Balance used a remote control to transfer the video monitor on the doorbell to the large screen in the living room.

A young girl stood there on the display—pretty, wearing a classical dress and a mysterious look on her face.

Balance's surprise exceeded its limits. She froze for five solid seconds.

"...Who is that?" she asked, finally managing to reboot her mind, then becoming aware of two well-built men waiting behind the girl. One courteously held a coat, probably the girl's. They were probably her attendants—bodyguards.

A girl, probably in her midteens, with two bodyguards, all clearly out of the ordinary.

Balance knew she had to be careful here—but she couldn't stop the situation from feeling surreal.

"Her name is Ayako Kuroba, ma'am," declared the sergeant. She made a gesture, as though gulping, but after hearing her next words, Balance couldn't blame her.

"She says she's an agent of the Yotsuba family."

"It is an honor to make your acquaintance, Miss Balance. My name is Kuroba Ayako. I'm sorry to intrude. I've come today as an agent of the Yotsuba family."

The girl introduced herself in clean, crisp English.

Without, however, using any honorific tones normally expected when addressing a soldier—a high-ranking officer.

If she'd learned such perfect pronunciation, it was hard to imagine she didn't have the vocabulary necessary for it.

In other words, the slight was on purpose.

Ayako having given her own last name first was probably just as deliberate.

"Colonel Virginia Balance, USNA military JCS. I apologize for my rudeness, but I'd like to ask a question of you before hearing what you've come here for."

"Oh, what might that be? I do hope I am able to answer."

She seemed even younger in age than Major Sirius, but she appeared to be a better negotiator.

Even better than the one with all kinds of experience as commander of the USNA military's top-class force of magicians, despite what had happened.

This girl before her was no ordinary one. Balance made sure, once again, to keep that in mind.

"The Yotsuba family... Are you referring to *the* Yotsuba?"

She purposely made her question ambiguous, on the slim chance that she'd misunderstood.

But despite her fluid way of asking, the girl smiled pleasantly. "Yes, you are correct. I've come here today to make a request as an agent of Maya Yotsuba, leader of the Yotsuba family, one of the Ten Master Clans."

Even though Balance was prepared—already knowing that the chances of being mistaken were roughly zero—the way the girl had said it so easily made it quite difficult to accept.

The Yotsuba—of Japan.

For anyone related to magic, they were, in a sense, Untouchables. Especially to those concerned with magic usage in the military.

It wasn't as though each individual had destructive power rivaling an entire army, like Major Sirius did.

The Yotsuba's way was the opposite.

Right now (and for now), they acted in accordance with the Japanese government, but some even said that if they were to go underground and become terrorists, it would be the trigger for a fourth world war.

The group treated the concept of magic so radically seriously that they went beyond respected and were instead simply feared.

"A request?"

"Yes. I would very much like it if you were to hear it out."

"Please go on."

Belatedly, Balance realized that a guest had visited and they hadn't served her tea.

But far more belatedly would be diverting the conversation now to prepare drinks.

Balance focused on the words about to come out of the girl's mouth.

"Very well, then. Miss Balance, we would like you to cease the interference with our country's magicians being carried out at your command."

"..."

It was more than plain interference she was commanding—it was an intelligence war, a mission to investigate Japan's unofficial strategic-class magician, then secure (read: kidnap) or disable (read: assassinate) them. Balance had, of course, thought of the possibility that her "request"—the Yotsuba's demands—would involve it. Actually, she'd predicted it as a high chance.

But the "cease" demand was more unreserved than she'd expected, and she couldn't immediately react to it.

"I believe you are aware of what Japan's Ten Master Clans system is and how it works, Miss Balance."

The girl's tone suggested she'd be glad to tell her if she didn't know. Feeling a sense of antipathy, Balance nodded. Feigning innocence would be meaningless.

"Our leader, Maya Yotsuba, has concerns over your excessive interference. She has said that since our nations are allied with each other, she did not want to make this affair into a trigger for any sort of conflict."

"...Is that a warning? Will you light the trigger if we don't withdraw?"

Instead of answering Balance's question, Ayako gave another pleasant smile.

"Miss, did you sleep well last night?"

"That was you?!"

Before she knew it, Balance had risen from the sofa and leaned forward. Were the table slightly narrower, she might have grabbed the girl's collar.

"Umm, what do you mean? Respectfully, your face doesn't look well, so I simply offered my concern."

Ayako said that, but there wasn't a hint of worry on her face.

She was smiling. Without trying to hide her *I-know-how-it-is* look, informed about everything.

"Miss Balance, please allow your nerves to settle. If at all possible, we would very much like to build a friendly relationship with you."

"A friendly relationship...?"

Balance realized, though not because the girl had told her, that throttling her now would be not only pointless but actively harmful. She returned to the sofa. The words the girl had then said only served to rub Balance the wrong way even further.

"You are aware of the Yotsuba's power. And we are well aware of yours, Miss."

Balance's emotions were hitting rock bottom, but her logic told her to listen to what the girl had to say.

This girl, who named herself an agent of the Yotsuba family, hadn't said she knew the USNA military's power or the Stars' power. She said they knew Balance's power.

Which meant...

"The leader has said that if you would arrange things to withdraw from this incident, Miss, we will not forget our gratitude to you personally. And that, should there be an opportunity in the future, we would be able to assist you."

It was an attractive proposition.

If she created a personal connection with *the* Yotsuba, it would be a weapon that would make up for all the position she'd lost last night and then some. She'd just learned of their true strength firsthand.

The girl smiled gracefully.

The discordant scales tipped toward logic—the logic of avarice.

The devil, in the form of a beautiful young girl, had handed her a contract. And Major Balance intended to sign it.

As soon as Tatsuya alighted on the walkway outside the Aoyama bridge station, he sensed eyes observing him, clinging to him like wet paint. Not just one or two pairs, either. During his conversation with Hayama

on the phone right before leaving, he'd predicted surveillance. Still, such a passionate investment of manpower exceeded his expectations.

He was pretty sure they hadn't learned of his and Miyuki's relationship to the Yotsuba—or even predicted it. Thus, there wouldn't be a large force to stage an intervention following him around.

Besides, he didn't think Japan's intelligence agencies, despite their support from the Saegusa, would run the risk of clashing with the Yotsuba.

What would happen if they stirred up trouble? The COIA, Public Safety, and the intelligence bureau would have already learned the answer from the incident the siblings' mother and aunt were embroiled in when they were still young girls. They were only incidental to their revenge, not the targets themselves, but nevertheless, the memories of such thorough destruction weren't the kind to be forgotten in a mere two or three decades. To say nothing of the fact that the Yotsuba's power—their power to enact violence rather than their influence—had strengthened even more since then.

Tatsuya stopped thinking about it there. A new set of eyes had joined the group, watching them.

A new—and abnormal—gaze.

A different quality from a human's. The gaze of a demon.

Giving a mission to observe three high school students and one household robot to professional secret agents meant there was no helping the fact that they relaxed their efforts somewhat.

Part of building a career was learning where you could let up a bit. That wasn't to say there were no incredibly serious people who would throw themselves completely into everything and never cut any corners, but here, because relaxing one's efforts and slacking off seemed similar, the situation was different.

"Letting up" always tended to give a bad impression, but at its core, it referred to how someone paced themselves. It meant not pouring ten units of energy into something that only needed five.

. Instead of always putting in ten units of energy, regardless of the job's difficulty, only using five for jobs that needed five would, despite being slower to finish each individual piece of work, end up completing more work in the end. Growing accustomed to something was just one more skill to learn.

But it was true that letting up wasn't solely advantageous. There were downsides.

These middling spies disguised as police officers had completed many tailing and spying missions. Their bountiful experience was unconsciously directing them to withhold some of their focus, and this time it worked against them.

The mission they'd been given was to immediately capture and kidnap the targets under the guise of an arrest should they use any form of magic.

Their magic-usage detector went off.

They didn't react to the change on the meter—they reacted to the alarm itself.

——A moment later, a brilliant light washed over their vision like a flood.

An unexpected preemptive strike.

An unlikely hostile act.

And just like that, their counterattack sunk to the bottom of a sea of illumination.

"Tatsuya, I put everyone who was watching us to sleep."

"Nice work."

Despite thanking the prideful Honoka, it was a fair struggle for Tatsuya to keep his face from drawing back.

The strange presences drew steadily closer. Nonhuman...parasites, almost without a doubt. The humans watching them would cause issues for their dialogue.

Using magic arbitrarily on the streets was an illegal act. There was no way the gazes sticking to them like cling tape belonged to well-meaning citizens or proper public servants, but because they were improper, being seen having a magical shoot-out would be even more inconvenient. Tatsuya had told his companions about the observers so they would take care not to carelessly use magic until the eyes were off them.

In fact, had Tatsuya been allowed to finish, he would have said that part.

But Honoka made the move before he could.

And if anyone stops and questions us, you'll be here to do something about it, right?

Honoka had made a wonderfully broad interpretation of that sentence. In reality, she was on cloud nine, excited that Tatsuya had asked her for something for the first time ever.

Normally, she was relatively opinionated and prone to assumptions, so not even Miyuki, much less Tatsuya, had paid it any attention. But today was somewhat different from usual.

Honoka's specialty magic was light wave–oscillation magic. Her best techniques were light-controlling ones.

After learning about the observers' locations from Tatsuya, then warping and amplifying light around herself and spotting them, she'd promptly created a big ball of awful, strobing light literally before their eyes.

The light of a brainwashing spell—Evil Eye.

When Tatsuya realized that, even he started to panic.

The subliminal effect had just been to put them to sleep, so he didn't interfere with its activation, but he wasn't confident that judgment had been the correct one. In magic, spells with subliminal effects were treated as bad as illegal-level spells that directly harmed a person's physical body. If any actual police officers had caught her, she'd have gotten more than a warning. They'd have slapped her with a jail sentence, despite being a minor—an imprisonment under the pretext of "volunteer labor using magic."

Astonished at the speed and precision, which were incomparable to the terrorist organization Blanche's leader, and her skill at triggering Evil Eye against four opponents at once, Tatsuya felt an immediate need to change locations.

"Let's get away from here before their friends come running," he suggested to his friends, belatedly thinking, *Maybe bringing Honoka along was a mistake after all...*

"What a troubling young lady..."

Fujibayashi sighed unconsciously. She was sitting in front of the monitor of a psion-wave radar that could detect unlawful magic usage. It was combined with an urban-area surveillance system—it used mainly the roadside cameras, in conjunction with a poison gas detector and an illegally high-output electromagnetic wave detector.

"But she's incredible. Her name was Honoka Mitsui, right?"

From behind her, she heard a voice plainly praising her skills as a magician.

The easygoing, grandfatherly remark, without any ulterior motives, caused Fujibayashi to want to sigh again. "That's right, Grandfather. She's Honoka Mitsui, a freshman at First High."

Retsu Kudou nodded to himself in thought. "Considering her name and her specialty type of magic, I wonder if she's part of the Elements bloodline of light."

"I don't know that much. Shall I investigate?"

"No, there's no need to go that far." The elderly Kudou shook his head at his granddaughter's question, maintaining his likable smile.

"Anyway... The strong attract the strong, and unusual powers attract unusual powers, I suppose. There are many interesting people around that boy."

"True—and not only in the ability aspect but the personality one."

As she made that casually biting comment, Fujibayashi's fingers, covered in thin gloves meant for operating devices, quickly danced over the touch panel console.

From a systems' point of view, the urban-area surveillance system was stubborn and hard to use, both on the hardware and the software side. Instead, it provided flexibility on the management end. Even a few government officials had been indiscriminately caught on camera at bad moments. Without manually restricting its records, they couldn't have put together such a comprehensive surveillance system.

Even for these vampire incidents, in order to secure exemption for unlawful magic usage, it had been arranged by the Saegusa and Chiba so that data would not remain in the system.

Mayumi had been in charge of that, as an information control measure, but with her exams just around the corner, Fujibayashi was replacing her.

Of course, in her case, she was managing the console on her own, without anyone making her do it. Unlike Mayumi, Fujibayashi didn't have the mind to leave this to others. She knew that while the Saegusa leader was helping his daughter with information concealment, when it came to Mayumi's soldiers, he was also having Fujibayashi keep an eye on Mayumi in secret—and that her grandfather was in turn keeping an eye on *that*.

She was operating the system as a proper user, rather than hacking into it, so technically the work was easier than usual. At the same time, the control scheme was inflexible and incommodious.

But there was no helping that.

She'd been the one to accept Mayumi's request, but her real role had been to manipulate things into having that happen so she could get in. She couldn't do whatever she wanted this time.

Especially not with her grandfather watching her from behind.

For both her and those who had dispatched her (meaning the person who had plotted to have her as the replacement), this situation where the elderly Kudou was present was an unforeseen one.

Fujibayashi didn't ask him why he was here.

He may have been her grandfather, but that didn't mean they were particularly close. She knew that as a member of the Fujibayashi family, she couldn't act too familiar toward the previous leader of the Kudou family.

And if sparks did ignite between the Saegusa and the Yotsuba, it wouldn't be strange to see Retsu Kudou acting to extinguish the flames.

Kyouko Fujibayashi's grandfather was one of the very few people who knew Tatsuya Shiba's true identity.

"Birds of a feather flock together...or perhaps he was the one they flocked to, rather than the other way around. Either way, the stars he was born under must not have been very peaceful."

"Yes. Perhaps it only looks like he has them wrapped around his finger, when he's actually wrapped around theirs," agreed Fujibayashi idly, still watching the monitor.

If she had turned around to look at her grandfather's face, she might have realized there was something underlying his remark.

But it didn't happen.

When he'd said "birds of a feather," he'd meant Kazama and the other members of the Independent Magic Battalion, including her. Unfortunately—or perhaps fortunately—his granddaughter didn't catch on.

As predicted, they didn't enter Aoyama Cemetery.

They hadn't needed to.

As the three people and one machine enjoyed a leisurely (?)

nighttime walk along its high walls (built after the war to prevent misguided individuals from taking photos and doing other things irreverent toward the dead), they sensed a clear presence closing in from the front.

"Master, three parasites are approaching," came Pixie's telepathy.

Tatsuya stopped. He'd allowed her to use telepathy, rather than making her use her onboard speakers, in order to draw out the parasites.

He'd also ordered her to convey her thoughts to Miyuki and Honoka as well.

As Tatsuya came to a halt, so too did the girls, bringing themselves up to his sides.

Neither of them appeared scared, but they couldn't hide how tense they were.

Tatsuya wasn't exactly immune to the tension, either, so he wasn't unhappy with their attitudes.

As they previously discussed, he pushed the SEND button on his portable terminal. It would send his current location, acquired from his navigation system, to Erika and Mikihiko. They would probably head here right away with a party of soldiers from the Chiba family. The plan was to wait until they were in position, then shift to capturing the parasites.

Of course, he had no intention of waiting for his friends to arrive should the parasites do something different.

Tatsuya removed his silver partner from his left inside pocket. He let his right hand, holding the handgun-shaped, specialized CAD—the Trident—dangle naturally at his side, then waited for the demon-possessed humans to arrive.

Miyuki stood back-to-back with him, covering his six, with her information terminal–shaped CAD. Honoka, her right hand hovering over the bracelet CAD on her left wrist, stood beside him, looking in front and behind them in alternation.

The stance was fairly sure-footed, and he found a smile rising to his face in spite of everything.

The unexpected act had loosened his tension.

The wellspring had been concern over the two girls' safety. But now that he was assured of their prowess, it had gone away.

He focused again on what lay beyond the streetlights' luminescence.

Three figures, approaching them from the front. No hesitation in their gaits. As Pixie herself said, the parasites could obviously detect her location.

The distance closed farther, without either party making a move.

When they were close enough to tell their clothing apart, *two* parasites who had drawn near them stopped.

The remaining one continued toward Tatsuya.

As its form grew clearer, he felt a strengthening sense that something was wrong.

He quickly figured out what it was.

A conflict between the information coming to his eyes and what he could personally sense.

The man wore an extremely average peacoat and chinos. The coat wasn't to hide his body type—and *this time*, he wasn't wearing a mask. His eyes, mouth, hands, and feet were nothing out of the scope of the ordinary. Nevertheless, despite the man's human form, Tatsuya could feel something decidedly not human. Perhaps it was the demon's energy...?

As Tatsuya watched the man closely, the closing of the distance between him and the parasite stopped when they were close enough to hear each other's voice and make out the other person's expressions.

"Tatsuya Shiba, we want to talk."

Tatsuya had no intention of speaking up first, so the parasite kicking things off was as he'd planned. And the fact that it was via the form of mostly peaceful conversation was also technically within his expectations.

But he was a little surprised the parasite had called him by name. "What should I call you?" asked Tatsuya in exchange.

The man possessed by the parasite almost opened his mouth but was unable to resume the conversation. Tatsuya thought to himself that losing one's words over something so trivial was quite human of it. It looked like the person's emotional base didn't change despite his personality being hijacked.

Or perhaps the term *hijack* indicated a mistaken understanding. Guessing by what he'd heard from Pixie, the parasites' main body only had primitive awareness. It seemed to him their emotions hadn't progressed past an equal point, either. Maybe he should assume they hadn't enough individuality to hijack a person and that they used the assimilated person as a base to construct a new individual. Tatsuya decided to assume that moving forward.

"Marte."

As Tatsuya thought about it, the parasite gave a short answer. A name to reply to the question of what to call it. Bits and pieces of information told Tatsuya it meant "Mars" in Spanish or Italian.

It made sense. The man's Japanese pronunciation was fluent, but his features were clearly Caucasian. Tatsuya only had informational knowledge, since he'd never been outside the country, but the man in front of him was possessed of Hispanic characteristics. Whether Marte was his real name or a code name—well, it was exceedingly likely to be a code name—it wasn't strange for him to introduce himself as such.

Tatsuya, of course, didn't know that there were rank groups in the Stars like planet-rank and satellite-rank. He knew only about the literal "stars," as the name of the group would imply. Therefore, he didn't understand that the name Marte was a reference to the Stars' planet-rank code of Mars or that it originated in the host's envy and regret of having once had the training to be a planet-rank candidate but ultimately failing to join the Stars.

"Then, Mr. Marte—or should I say Señor Marte?—what on earth do you want?"

Thus, this question had no deeper meaning. The man's "Mars" code name was no more than a label to Tatsuya, and he diverted the conversation offhandedly.

"'Mister' is fine, *boy*."

In turn, the parasite calling itself Marte mocked him irritably. But all Tatsuya thought was that he had quite a short temper.

"Sure. Anyway, what is it?"

Tatsuya wouldn't have minded a contest of traded provocations to stall for time, but he saw his companions steadily losing their cool, so he decided to move forward with the conversation.

"…Tatsuya Shiba. We have no further intent to remain hostile toward you."

It appeared that this "Mr. Marte" found his full name a more courteous approach than "boy."

Not that it mattered much to Tatsuya (in the sense that he hadn't expected any courtesy from the start).

"I don't understand—you're being too vague about this. Who is 'we'? And who is the 'you' you're being hostile toward?"

More importantly, it was far more crucial that he resolve what the man was talking about.

"…We demons have no further intent to engage in any hostile actions toward you, the magicians of Japan."

He outright called himself a demon…

Not a devil, not a ghost, not a specter—a demon. That appeared to be how they perceived themselves. He hadn't heard this term from Pixie, so they must have discussed it ahead of time.

Tatsuya almost let out a pained grin. He was aware people called his dismantling magic the Demon Right. They'd dubbed it that because when he activated it, he pointed his right-hand CAD at the target. But that didn't mean he felt any affinity for the term.

"And? Wasn't there something else you wanted?" Tatsuya pressed. There were things he wanted to ask about the parasite's short statement, but for now, he decided to let him say what he would.

"In exchange for promising to end hostilities against you, we want you to hand that robot over to us."

Pixie gave a shiver. Or at least, it looked like it—Tatsuya was probably seeing things. No matter what was inside, robots had no connection to such biological reactions.

"...Now look, Mr. Marte. Would you mind talking a little more politely? I don't have any way to answer unless you explain why you want us to hand it over."

"I hadn't thought explanation necessary. In fact, you should have no reason to take that robot's part."

"We're the ones who decide if we have a reason or not."

Marte frowned at Tatsuya's answer. But even his displeased expression, considering the man appeared a generation older than him, didn't look strange.

"...We wish to release our comrade who is imprisoned inside that robot."

After hearing the answer, Tatsuya faked a confused head tilt. "Is your comrade not allowed to have a robot for a host?"

Marte's expression grew even more severe. "We don't know what you think, but we are living creatures. And our mutual connections are much stronger than you humans'. Is the fact that we want to get our comrade, a living creature, out of a lifeless vessel so difficult for you to understand?"

But his tone of voice was still controlled.

"No, I understand it," replied Tatsuya in a simple way, just like the man. But he did it because Marte's answer aligned with the information he'd already gotten from Pixie and didn't serve to draw his interest. On the other hand, it meant he'd gotten evidence to back up Pixie's claims. Wondering whether his reply was enough, he continued to speak, trying to plan the timing for their strike. "But how?"

"We will destroy the machine. Should the current host be lost, we can move to a new one."

"I see... That's his offer, Pixie. Do you wish to be released from there?"

"No, I don't, master!"

Tatsuya hadn't been serious with the question. As long as she had the desire for self-preservation despite residing in an inanimate object, he couldn't call it *right* to let it be destroyed. Also, the 3H's basic programming included the three laws of robotics: never to hurt humans, to obey humans, and to defend oneself as long as it doesn't interfere with the first two laws—insofar as they could be applied.

However, the intent of refusal indicated by the telepathy was much stronger than he'd predicted.

"I am me. My wish is to belong to you, master. That is who I am."

It didn't stop at primitive self-defense instincts. It contained an emphasis on the self.

"I do not care anymore what sort of being I originally was, nor where I received the wish constituting my core. I do not want to stop being me."

Tatsuya wasn't the only one who heard Pixie's telepathy. The three other parasites heard it—as did Honoka and Miyuki.

Honoka pursed her lips tightly.

A smile broke out onto Miyuki's lips.

"That's what she says, Brother."

"Yeah."

A faint grin was on Tatsuya's lips as well. Strangely, the unexpected, impassioned speech wasn't causing a pained grin.

For whatever reason, he felt no aversion to the feelings this demon living inside a robot had.

"Anyway, I expect you can guess our answer already, but..." said Tatsuya. "Before I spell it out for you, there are two or three things I want to ask."

"It seems you were more foolish than we thought, Tatsuya Shiba. We are disappointed... Fine, then. Say what questions you have."

"Before, you said you didn't have any intention of engaging in hostilities *against magicians*, right? Why wasn't it *against people* instead of *against magicians*?"

There was no answer.

No—curled in scorn, the lips were the answer.

"If we had accepted your request, you demons wouldn't act hostile toward magicians. Then how would you act toward non-magician people?"

"..."

"After you destroyed Pixie's body, what would you have her inhabit next? No, you don't need to answer that. I know without having to ask."

"...You possess only superficial cunning that requires no real wit." Seeing Tatsuya's steely gaze and the girl behind him preparing herself, Marte shrugged as if on purpose. "We don't get it. We're telling you we won't be your enemies anymore. Why are you not satisfied with that? We demons are not compatible with humans in the same way that you magicians are different from other people, am I wrong?"

"Really, now?" Tatsuya shamelessly interjected into the speech the parasite had suddenly broken into. It was more like a propaganda pitch than anything. There was no way he had the commendable mind-set of worrying about how shameless his tone was.

"My host was a magician as well," said Marte, making an exaggerated gesture to bring his palm to his chest.

Perhaps this man, before he'd been possessed by the parasite, had been an expert at inciting crowds. If he was, the code name Marte (Mars) was a mismatch. The name Mercurio (Mercury) seemed more suitable.

In blatant disregard for Tatsuya's chilling glare, the parasite's speech grew more fervent. "That is why I understand the way humans treat magicians."

"And what way might that be?"

"To humans, magicians are tools and lab rats. A magician's wishes are too trivial for humans to take notice of. They treat you as tools to use a power called magic and only see you as experiments to draw out even more of that power."

None of this was different from any old speech, but Tatsuya decided to let this parasite finish and see what happened.

"Why do you do right by people who think of nothing more than using you? You should have no such obligation. You have your own wishes, your own hopes. Don't you?"

Tatsuya watched Marte's face closely as he finished his speech. Marte returned the stare with a true look of sincerity.

Tatsuya sighed. "I don't think magicians are the only ones who get taken advantage of anyway," he responded carefully to the bristling parasite host. "How should I put this... This all sounds like by-the-book stuff." And then he twisted his lips into a scornful smile. "For someone who just treated me like a fool...you sure are stupid."

Rage wavered in the man's eyes.

Was it the parasite's emotion or the host's?

Marte tried to say something, but Tatsuya interrupted, continuing. "You won't harm magicians. That's fine—it really is. But you've already hurt my friends. My *magician* friends. Do I have any reason to believe that you won't hurt them in the future when you haven't given even a word of apology? It's no different from the catchphrases that proclaim to 'protect a magician's human rights.' You're feeding me lies and trying to get something out of me. The sheer audacity of the idea."

Tatsuya paused his long remarks, then smirked once again, as though he found this all a bore. "Come to think of it, I never gave you my answer. Well, it's *no.*"

"You impudent little—"

"Yeah, yeah, 'you're going to regret this.' There, I said it for you. It's embarrassing even talking to you."

Death shone in Marte's eyes.

He waved his right hand and a knife appeared from his cuff. Judging by the cord connecting to the handle, it wasn't just a dagger—it had some kind of gimmick built in.

The other parasites took out their own knives as well.

When Tatsuya saw them, he narrowed his eyes coldly. "So easy to understand. I'll make this easy for you to understand, too." With as much affectation as he could manage, he grinned. "Put down your weapons and surrender peacefully. If you do, we won't have to hurt you. I promise you treatment—you'll be happy lab rats."

"You…human…*dog!*"

The parasite that controlled the human was now being dominated by the overwhelming emotions of its host.

A Möbius loop of control and submission.

The "magician" Marte probably had a lot of hatred and bitterness toward the humans who'd controlled him before he'd been possessed.

There was enough anger in his scream to betray that.

Without an activation sequence expanding, the signs of magic activation appeared. As Tatsuya thought, the parasites didn't seem to need activation sequences nor incantations to use magic.

Of course, Tatsuya was much the same. Before the parasites' magic triggered, Tatsuya's dismantling destroyed the information bodies about to alter events.

An unusual ability, the natural predator of all magicians—the direct dismantling of information bodies.

That spell, Program Dispersion, was effective even on nonhumans.

A silent battle with no sound or light.

But Marte, who had taken an offensive position predicated on being able to activate magic, stood petrified at the unexpected situation of his magic being canceled.

Tatsuya wasn't about to let the opening go unpunished.

His four limbs shot through where they connected to his body, Marte fell over onto the road.

Even with the parasite inside, he couldn't go against his fundamental anatomical structure. He might be able to ignore the pain, but he couldn't move his limbs now that the tendons were severed.

Tatsuya pointed his empty left hand at the parasite on the road.

If he destroyed his physical body, the parasite would scatter in search of a different host.

If he had Miyuki freeze him with magic, he would self-destruct and escape.

The parasite didn't require activation sequences, so even if he couldn't move his body, he could probably still use magic.

In order to disable the parasite, he'd have to deal damage directly to the mental information body.

He clenched a ball of psions in his palm.

There was no guarantee doing this would have any effect.

But Tatsuya didn't hesitate. If this didn't work, then he'd just have to bring along a caster skilled in ancient sealing spells.

Hesitation now would do more harm than good.

He simply willed "rejection" and thrust his left hand toward the parasite.

The tough, compressed psionic bullet struck the parasite in the chest.

Not its brain but its heart.

This was something he'd decided after discussing Pixie's information with Yakumo. The parasites didn't possess physical organs but a person's mind. Therefore, there was no essential reason to strike one part of the body over another. In that case, they'd concluded, it was best to strike at the place most deeply connected to the rest of the body—the heart, which distributed fuel for the body's cells.

The effect was more dramatic than expected.

Like a lobster fished out of the ocean, the parasite's body bent and stretched madly.

He writhed.

The body infested with the parasite was rejecting it.

Tatsuya's thoughts, fired into the parasite, were rejecting the parasite, while also being rejected by it in turn.

"Brother!"

But unfortunately, he didn't have the time to carefully observe.

Miyuki's cry sounded desperate.

But Tatsuya hadn't taken his "eyes" off her.

If any danger was threatening her, he would have sensed it without her saying anything.

Sure enough, when he turned around—

On the other side of Miyuki, who had frozen her opponent's clothing rather than the actual limbs and was now suppressing their magic with her Area Interference—

—was Honoka, having a hard time with the enemy's armament device, which he controlled via wires, and Pixie, who had shielded her from an attack.

"Honoka!"

"I'm all right!" she answered firmly.

A strong light shone in Honoka's eyes.

It was the light of her will, her desire to never become a burden for them.

The light in Honoka's eyes…

…and in her hair ornaments.

Tatsuya felt a rapid heightening of psi-wave activity.

It was a sign that her thought energies were amplifying.

It wasn't magic.

It was more direct—thought interference.

A moment later, a powerful psychic blast fired out of Pixie.

The event-altering force, unrefined in its precise control but ferocious, shook the interference field Miyuki had constructed.

An interference field made by *Miyuki*, whose strength was preeminent among all currently living magicians.

Tatsuya fired a newly constructed psionic bullet into the parasite his sister had been fighting.

A dance of rejection reproduced.

But right now, that wasn't what Tatsuya or Miyuki were concerned with.

There, a simple kinetic state alteration event influence—in other words, a psychokinetic blast—had been fired.

Honoka's eyes were spinning at the sudden powerful psionic wave, and Pixie stood in front of her to protect her.

The parasite they'd been fighting blew far away into distant vision.

◇ ◇ ◇

Fujibayashi, dumbfounded at the sight unfolding on her monitor, pulled back to her senses at an amused laugh audible from behind her.

"…Well, what a surprising, interesting thing he's shown us."

When his granddaughter swiveled around in her chair and gave him a stare incriminating him for his imprudence, the Kudou elder cleared his throat. Then, his tone suggesting he was trying to excuse himself, he said, "That last psychokinetic blast came from the 3H, didn't it? I've never heard of anyone developing robots that could use psychic powers."

Fujibayashi was sitting at the monitor console of a psi-wave sensor. There was no mistaking the measurement results displayed in front of her.

"…Neither have I. I don't believe it's possible for current technology."

"I shouldn't think so. With present technology, it's impossible to reproduce preternatural powers, whether magic or psychic. Which would mean a nonmachine element resides in that 3H."

"…" A slight breath, which could have been interpreted as a sigh or a groan, escaped Fujibayashi's lips.

"So the demon has inhabited the robot, has it?"

"…"

"I've received reports about the parasites, but I didn't hear any-thing about this."

"We haven't received reports of it, either," answered his grand-daughter with a hard expression. "I've only heard about it through personal conversations."

"No, no," replied the Kudou elder, waving his hand to soothe her. "I wasn't criticizing you, Kyouko. I don't exactly have the right to anymore. I was just thinking about how fascinating it was."

The poker face Fujibayashi was wearing broke down.

She looked up at him, unrest in her eyes—and saw glimmers of ambition on her grandfather's face, the likes of which she hadn't seen on him in a very long time.

"To think—that you could use a humanoid robot this way…"

◇ ◇ ◇

The usual Fujibayashi might have noticed something.

But right now, she was upholding the usage procedure set out by the system—as an operator, not as a hacker. Under the circumstances, even the Electron Sorceress couldn't notice an onlooker using methods the system hadn't been designed for.

The onlooker watching at that very moment, Maya Yotsuba, took the shade-shaped monitor device off her eyes, leaned back in her seat, and closed her eyes.

In terms of the time, it was about ten seconds.

Then, after storing the monitor inside her desk, she took the handbell on the desk's side and shook it. A clear sound rang through the quiet room where she sat alone.

"You called, Mistress?" asked the elderly Hayama, her butler and confidant, as he opened the door and walked over in front of her.

"Would you please call Mr. Aoki?"

"Of course, Mistress."

With a polite bow, the butler Hayama left the room again.

This time, there was a slight wait.

She heard no footsteps, but a hastened presence drew near and knocked on the door.

"Come in."

"Excuse me, Mistress," came Hayama's relaxed voice.

The sense of restlessness was emanating from beside him. Along with Hayama had entered another butler, this one significantly younger (though still older than Maya).

"I'm sorry for calling you so late, Mr. Aoki."

"Please, don't be. I would instantly go to the ends of the earth should you call me there, Mistress."

Aoki hadn't mastered the art of teleportation—the concept hadn't been realized anyway—so physically he couldn't be there *instantly*, but he always spoke theatrically, so neither Maya nor Hayama minded.

"Forgive me for the suddenness, but there is something I'd like you to obtain for me."

"Yes, Mistress."

Aoki was the treasurer entrusted with the Yotsuba's asset management. If she'd called him, it was for more than mere shopping. Either it was something expensive even for the Yotsuba (and exorbitantly expensive for the rest of the world), or it was a rare or unsold product that was difficult to purchase in the first place.

But even so, no tension colored Aoki's face. He knew answering these types of requests was his entire reason for being here, and despite having problems on the personality front, his actual abilities were certainly no less than first-class, both when acting legally and illegally.

"I'd like you to buy the 3H P-94 on loan to the Magic University's Affiliated First High School as soon as possible. You may spend as much as you need and use whatever methods you need."

It wasn't unusual for Maya to suggest money was no issue, but she rarely outright told him to do it by any means necessary.

"If you can't obtain it, then manage things so that its proprietary rights are not transferred from its current owner. Especially so that it doesn't pass into the other Ten Master Clans' hands. You don't need to worry about money in that regard, either."

And her laying out precise methods and conditions in case he failed was a first, at least for Aoki.

"At once, Mistress."

Aoki looked rattled for a moment, but he bowed to her respectfully, without letting his nerves show in his voice.

After Aoki withdrew with hurried steps, Maya gave a searching glance to Hayama, who was still waiting beside her.

"...Wasn't there something else you wanted to say?"

But in the end, he hadn't been able to maintain his poker face, and Maya decided to urge him on herself.

"I understand it may be rude, Mistress, but…"

His interest drawn out, he bowed as he gave a few prefacing words. It was a practically clichéd phrase, but the odd tone of voice signaled to Maya that the topic wasn't a very pleasant one.

"Would it not be wise to refrain a little more from making use of Hlidskjalf?"

Nevertheless, she couldn't stop him from remarking—admonishing her—at this point. The advice was painfully true, as expected. Maya frowned, but she couldn't display any anger, either.

After all, Maya, its operator, knew more than anyone else—with the exception of the six remaining operators with the same access rights as her—that using it had more than just benefits.

"…It is a pure and complete product of scientific technology. There should be far less risk of side effects than with magic, which still has no shortage of black boxes."

"Lady Maya, forgive me, but that wasn't what I meant by my remark."

Maya herself knew her argument was just splitting hairs, and once Hayama cut that away, she gave an awkward sort of look.

"And in terms of black boxes, Mistress, we don't even know where the Hlidskjalf mainframe is set up. There have been no lies yet, but there is no guarantee it will remain that way."

Hayama's claim certainly had logic behind it.

And Maya understood the dangers he hadn't described.

"Yes… I believe you're right, Mr. Hayama. I seem to have been relying on its information-gathering abilities too much lately."

"Its capabilities are certainly a lot to give up. In my humble opinion, perhaps Mr. Tatsuya would be able to learn where the Hlidskjalf mainframe is located. Or perhaps that if we can directly access it, we can gain exclusive control over it."

For Maya, those remarks were completely unexpected. Taken by surprise, she thought for more than a few moments, then finally shook her head.

"It's still too soon."

Her answer left room for interpreting *what* was "too soon."

Hayama bowed, then left his mistress alone in the room.

"This isn't good, though..."

Miyuki had been taking care of Honoka, whose eyes were spinning—or, more specifically, who had gotten dizzy and fallen. But when she heard Tatsuya's monologue unintentionally escape his lips, she turned around.

"Yes... You're right. Brother, shall we leave this place for now?"

The answer he got was an exceedingly natural one, and he almost simply agreed.

Well, we could, but...

He got the feeling that if he started taking her quick-witted nature for granted, it would come back to bite him one day. Still, something else warranted more concern at the moment.

The reaction earlier, that large-scale psychic display, must have been seen by the Aoyama/Akasaka area. Undesired guests would be upon them presently for all sorts of reasons.

The parasite who had been writhing around until just now had settled down, as though his power had run dry. Tatsuya had already tied his hands behind him just in case, but even he didn't know how much of a point there was to the maneuver. For the moment, as long as the vessel—the host's physical body—was still intact, it couldn't escape from there. But if it came to it, there was one final method: having the opponent self-destruct.

Yeah... Wonder if there's some ancient spell for the job.

"Tatsuya!"

"Sorry we're so late!"

Speak of the devil—well, think of them—and hear their voices. It looked like they'd finally made their entrance.

But he didn't intend to blame them for being "late." They'd been searching around for the parasites on their own, not slacking off. He couldn't complain.

Yes, he told himself—complaining about them waltzing in nonchalantly *after* the entire quibble had ended would be unreasonable.

"Umm…Tatsuya? Your face looks kinda scary."

"My face looks tough to begin with."

"Well, that's not really what I meant, but… If you're doing it on purpose, it's a lot scarier."

Tatsuya glanced at Mikihiko, who was hesitating a little for some (?) reason, then addressed the extra person—the one he hadn't expected. "Leo, you came, too?"

"Yeah. I got them to let me tag along. Partly for rehab."

"Well, don't overdo it. Anyway, Erika?"

"Hmm? What?"

When he addressed Erika, who was looking at the captive with a harsh look, a surprisingly calm voice came back.

"We need to leave this place as quickly as possible," he said, going straight for the matter at hand. "Did you prepare a way to carry the three of us?"

Relieved that she hadn't done something excessive like suddenly driving a stake into their captive's heart, Tatsuya gave a quick glance around, but he could only see the *two* motorbikes that the *three* of them had used, no other vehicles. But even beyond that…

Tatsuya hadn't seen which two had ridden tandem.

"Huh? Why?"

Erika, who had turned around at Tatsuya's words, was making an honestly mystified face.

"What do you mean *why*, Erika?"

This remark was not Tatsuya's. Mikihiko had interrupted with a face that couldn't hide his impatience.

"Didn't you sense the thought waves before? That was a lot of magic power that just scattered all over. I don't think the regular police will be the only ones coming this way."

"But we were prepared for that from the start—is what I'd like to say...but I guess we shouldn't make trouble for the three of you."

Aside from her slightly watchful look, it was the same Erika as always. At least, to the extent Leo and Mikihiko wouldn't notice.

"Umm, we can take him to the storehouse at Miki's place. Is that okay?"

Erika had said "storehouse," but of course it wasn't a literal storehouse. The act of purposely bringing them into Yoshida family jurisdiction rather than a Chiba family facility meant they had an appropriate spell or technique to seal the parasite's magic and bind it.

"Is that okay, Mikihiko?"

"Huh? Of course it is. I mean, that was our job to begin with."

By "our," he must have meant "ancient mages." Maybe he wanted to say sealing demons was an onmyouji's job (although Yoshida's family were Shinto, not Onmyou practitioners).

"All right, then me, Miki, and I guess Leo will take over here. You three should go home."

"Wait, why?" asked Tatsuya dubiously, ignoring Leo's anger at the *I guess* part. "We'll wait for you to load up."

The answer was a rather inarticulate one.

"Tatsuya, well, that is..." stammered Mikihiko.

Tatsuya followed his gaze. Pixie's skirt was torn here and there, and Honoka's half coat now had several additional unintended slits in it.

"...We'll call a car."

"I think that would be best."

Tatsuya decided to leave this place to Erika's group.

The siblings' house was inside the self-driving vehicle control area, but Honoka's apartment was outside the control area for automatic cars. Honoka wouldn't be able to go home with the self-driving commuter he'd summoned with his information terminal. The four ended up transferring to cabinets at the station.

Not having much attention on them despite their considerably unconventional fashion was a welcome aspect of cities.

Without drawing more stares than he thought they would (though with Miyuki with him, it was impossible to draw no attention whatsoever), Tatsuya and the others climbed into a four-seater cabinet.

"Oh, umm, Tatsuya…?"

Because the act of getting inside was so natural, Honoka only had doubts after the cabinet had already pulled away. They were going in the same direction, but they couldn't get out of the cabinet halfway there…

"I'll take you back," Tatsuya stated.

Hearing that, Honoka—who couldn't exactly admit that that was exactly what she wanted—fervently but modestly turned him down… even if she couldn't hide an expression of happiness.

Four-person cabinets featured the ability to change the seating layout to facing.

Next to Tatsuya was Miyuki, and across from them was Honoka.

Diagonally across from Tatsuya was Pixie (who was being treated as a passenger, not luggage). He glanced at the robot, then turned his gaze to Honoka—then repeated the process in silence.

"…Brother, if you don't give Honoka a word or two soon, she won't last," whispered Miyuki from beside him, unable to remain indifferent as their classmate became visibly tenser each time Tatsuya's eyes set on her.

"Right. Sorry," said Tatsuya, coming around at his sister's reprimand. It seemed like he was unaware he'd been doing it. "All three of you did a good job tonight."

His congratulatory words were probably a mere preface. Him counting Pixie as one of their number was proof. He did perhaps approve of Pixie doing a stand-up job in her own right, but it was clear from the way he didn't distinguish between humans and robots that he hadn't thought about it very much.

"And hmm. Honoka, how should I put it…? Do you feel any kind of exhaustion?"

His next words weren't an explanation but a question. Honoka shook her head, even while flustered at the sudden query.

"I see… Pixie, what about you? Are you exhausted—? Well, that's not the right way to put it. Do you feel any consumption of the psions and psycheons that comprise your main body?"

"The consumption is within the range of natural recovery, master."

"I see…"

"Brother, whatever might you be worried about?"

"It's not that I'm worried, really, it's just…" said Tatsuya, shaking his head at his sister. Then he turned his gaze to Honoka again. "When Pixie released that powerful psychokinetic blast earlier… Honoka, did you get a sense of what happened?"

"…No, why? What do you mean?" asked Honoka in response, unease wavering in her eyes.

The question had been significant enough that he couldn't blame her for feeling uneasy.

Although, of course, it hadn't been spoken with the intent to deliberately fan that unease.

"I'd like you to listen calmly."

Tatsuya himself was baffled enough to want to preface it with that.

"Just before Pixie fired the psychic blast, she'd been supplied with psions from you, Honoka."

"Huh?" Honoka's eyes went wide, dumbfounded.

"…Do you mean to say that Honoka provided Pixie with strength?"

"No, didn't exactly seem like that," Tatsuya replied, his voice showing an unusual lack of confidence. "It was similar to the process of injecting psions into a CAD when you want to expand an activation sequence. Something like…priming. Or maybe resonance."

Honoka turned a fearful stare on Pixie.

The robot girl—or rather, the parasite possessing the 3H type P-94—didn't seem to mind. Of course, her expressions didn't change, so they couldn't know for sure.

A magician and a machine had exchanged psions.

The phenomenon itself was a familiar one for Tatsuya and all other modern magicians as well. But the phenomenon occurred with a machine fitted with a system specifically designed to do that from a magical engineering perspective. A 3H didn't have any functions like that.

Machines didn't have any abilities beyond what humans gave them. They would never learn new functions on their own.

Therefore, this phenomenon hadn't occurred between her and Pixie's machine body but between her and Pixie's *actual* body. It was the only explanation.

He couldn't blame Honoka for feeling uneasy or being captivated by fear.

"Mizuki said something like that… There really does seem to be some sort of path between Honoka and Pixie. And it seems like—"

Suddenly, Tatsuya stopped talking. He seemed uncomfortable for some reason, like he was having a hard time getting the words out. Miyuki directed a dubious look at him.

He felt her unspoken question through his skin, and with a resigned expression, he continued, "…It seems like the medium for it is your hair ornaments, Honoka."

"Huh?"

Honoka's emotions had been busy with surprise and fear until now, but this time her surprise stood out most strongly.

She wasn't the only one who was surprised.

Miyuki stared closely at the elastic tying Honoka's hair.

"Specifically, those crystals. I don't have any idea what sort of logic is at work here, but…"

Honoka put her hands to her crystal hair ornaments. It was an unconscious act, not something she'd expected a particular result from.

But a moment later, something happened—something that seemed to prove Tatsuya's speculation.

An incorporeal light released from the center of Pixie's chest.

It wasn't a strong light. Visually speaking, it was about as bright as a lantern.

But the synchronization was too strong to doubt the connection.

Tatsuya's and Miyuki's eyes both focused on the hair ornaments.

Honoka closed both hands around the decorative jewels, almost as though afraid of them being taken away.

"Setting aside the operative principles for now... We'll have to find a way to control it," Tatsuya whispered, his tone soft, like he was trying to soothe a small and cautious animal.

Indeed, Honoka's caution changed to surprise as she returned his stare.

Tatsuya moved his gaze from her to Pixie. "It seems like buying Pixie was the right move, at least."

Tatsuya's high school group wasn't the only team active that night. He hadn't gotten in touch with Mayumi or Katsuto, so the Saegusa-Juumonji forces weren't doing anything, but the Chiba family had dispatched quite a few people to carry out Erika's intent. Erika having come running with only her small unit meant nothing other than they were the strongest out of all the members mobilized tonight.

Erika, Leo, and Mikihiko. For all but one of them, their grades left something to be desired. Their abilities in actual combat, on the other hand, went above and beyond. Even with adults added to the equation instead of just high school students, if you excluded skill at handling weapons, their capabilities would still place them in the upper ranks.

Of course, because they'd been the only ones acting, they were left in a situation where they had to wait for an escort car while keeping watch over the bound parasite…but someone more troubling found them before their escort.

"You there, what are you doing?!" came the loud interrogation as a car (with a motor) stopped on the other side of a streetlight. A pair of young men in police uniforms ran over to them.

When they saw the men, consternation entered Mikihiko's face, a brassy smile appeared on Leo's lips, and Erika silently directed them a challenging stare.

"What is this?! You're all in high school, aren't you? What are you doing here?!"

When they saw the two men lying on the road, hands tied behind them, the taller one sharpened his voice. That was, perhaps, the natural reaction for a police officer to have upon seeing civilians tied up and lying in the road at night.

"No, well, you see…" Mikihiko, thinking they were being questioned, racked his brains trying to find an excuse.

But Erika pushed him aside and gave an overbearing counterquestion: "I should be asking *you*. Who are you?"

"What was that?!"

"Hey, Erika!" Mikihiko hissed, staring at her in utter disbelief as the men bristled.

"Mikihiko." A hand grabbed his shoulder and pulled him closer. He turned around to see Leo with an amused grin.

"Didn't you hear me? I asked your names and rank," repeated Erika, sniffing away the threatening gazes the police officers were giving her. "What, you don't know? There aren't any policemen in this area right now. They were ordered to leave. Even that stupid brother of mine wouldn't cut corners at a time like this."

Erika's words came with no proof.

If they were actual police officers, they should have mockingly laughed her remark off.

But the young men in front of her appeared, unfortunately, rattled.

"What? That's not possible."

Their confusion went away in an instant. But Erika didn't let it slip, and she wouldn't have cared if she'd gotten no reaction at all anyway.

Because she hadn't been bluffing.

"If you were going to disguise yourselves, you should have pretended to be detectives in personal clothing. Then I would have at least heard you out. Well, that's *all* I would have done anyway," added Erika, nose in the air.

As the taller man moved to reprimand her, his colleague stopped him. That one stepped forward instead. Comparing the two, he wasn't as tall, but he had a more toned physique. He was notably more intimidating.

"You can try to get out of this with whatever nonsense you want, but we've caught you committing a violent crime. You're coming with us."

"Really? You're still gonna play the fool, huh?"

It wasn't enough to intimidate Erika, of course. Like before, she returned their provoking gazes with a cold stare.

"That's too bad for you," she went on. "We stopped these two men during an attempted rape. It was, what do they call it, a *citizen's arrest.* And we were just waiting for actual police officers to get here. This is no place for imitations. Am I making myself clear here?"

Mikihiko watched his childhood friend as she smoothly concocted a reasonable-sounding story. He knew it was a lie, but it was very convincing—and because of it, he was a moment late noticing a presence creeping up on them.

"Miki!" "Mikihiko!"

Without a sound—not metaphorically but literally silently—a dark shadow came upon him from overhead. By the time he was aware someone had jumped over the wall surrounding the cemetery, it was too late for him to intercept them.

He felt an impact on his shoulder.

He only realized someone else had knocked him away after he'd unconsciously fallen in a forward roll.

Leo had raised his arm overhead, blocking a swung club. Mikihiko could guess how powerful the blow was just from the sound it made, and it was enough to easily break any normal person's bones. But Leo had caught the blow with ease. And while he did so, he shot out a fist that cut through the wind toward the person who had just now landed.

"Ugh!"

But he pulled his fist back after making only a shallow blow on the assailant's body.

Then, under the feeble streetlight, Mikihiko saw the glimmer of electricity.

The man was wearing a suit that could pour a high-voltage current into anyone who came into contact with it.

Leo backed off a step, clutching his wrist. The man wielding a club assumed a stance for a follow-up attack.

"Leo, get back!"

Mikihiko whipped his left arm around. A folding fan–shaped CAD flew out of his sleeve, and he caught it with a practiced motion.

He tried to fire a support spell at the man who had attacked Leo, but then some kind of ring struck his CAD from the side. He didn't drop it, but he had to cancel the spell.

The object that had canceled Mikihiko's spell curved around and flew back to where it came.

After it had returned to the hand of the enemy who threw it, he finally realized it was a sort of boomerang. Of course, a normal boomerang would lose all its kinetic energy upon collision with a target, not return to the user. It must have been some kind of magical weapon.

Leo, having been hit by an unforeseen electric attack, had rolled onto the road to avoid the club being swung down at him to create some distance, and he was still recovering his posture.

Mikihiko didn't have the time to be concerned with him.

There was more than one enemy.

No sooner than he heard the *shh* of compressed air releasing did a bullet the size of two old-fashioned juice cans strapped together come flying at him from the other side of the street.

Mikihiko launched a mass of wind to intercept the shell.

The moment after he saw it stop in midair, a net shot out of it and spread out, flying toward him. On each of the octagonal net's corners, there was a super-small rocket motor, flaring with fire to make up for the canceled kinetic energy.

They make *those?!* Mikihiko squawked in his own mind.

It wasn't all that fast, but he had no idea what kinds of gimmicks this net had in it. He used a jumping spell to dodge it.

A figure waiting for him in midair. A torus-shaped throwing weapon closing in on him.

Meticulous positioning, like a chess problem.

And an average caster would have been out-positioned by it.

But Mikihiko wasn't average. He'd gotten back all his former strength from when they'd called him the wonder child, and he'd gone even further.

By jumping once again in midair, using the air as a foothold, he evaded the three rings as well as their owner's attack.

From the air, he looked down at the man who had missed his swing with a slender weapon—probably something like a horsewhip.

There was shock in the man's face as he looked back up.

It was finally Mikihiko's turn.

He reached out with a bent leg.

His foot touched the man's forehead.

That very movement was a "seal" that triggered magic.

An electric net spread out from the point of contact between his foot and the man's forehead, quickly rushing over the man's body.

Mikihiko kicked off the wind again and landed on top of the wall.

From there, he searched for signs of Leo and Erika.

Leo had recovered from the initial attack. He was having a bare-handed battle with the man holding a club. He wasn't taking damage from the electricity, probably because he'd wrapped himself in a suitable spell. The man he was up against was quite skilled in his own right, but Leo had the edge in both speed and power.

The issue was Erika.

One of the men who had spoken to them first had been a lousy performer, but he was a very skilled fighter.

After all, he was bearing out Erika's driving strikes. Either he was wearing special armor underneath his uniform or the uniform itself was specially made.

But tough was all he was—he couldn't do anything against Erika's sword attacks. Every time her sword hit him, fine particles erupted from the surface of his clothing and scattered. Erika, cautious, hadn't taken the final step to finish him.

If her weapon had been a little longer, he wouldn't have given her so much trouble. But her weapon today was a short club that could transform into a *kodachi*. Avoiding the particulate sprays, which were likely to be drugs, she was forced into a dip-in, dip-out style of fighting.

Now that he had a bird's-eye view of the situation, Mikihiko realized something. The three of them were being pulled away, little by little, from the parasites they'd tied up.

The men hadn't stepped closer to the parasites than the three were yet. But if they kept dragging them away at this rate, their captives could be gone before support arrived.

They had to finish this quickly, even if it meant being somewhat forceful.

It was a moment after he made the decision. The opponents had probably also decided they couldn't hold out any longer.

With regards to the opportunity, Mikihiko's decision and the enemy's decision matched...

...and the enemies were one step quicker to move.

He heard the sound of something falling toward him from overhead.

Both Leo and Erika separated themselves from their enemies, Leo kicking his away and Erika showering hers in a flurry of strikes.

"Get down!" he shouted, just as a cocoon of air covered Erika and Leo.

Mikihiko had created a defensive barrier.

The bomb falling from overhead burst before hitting the ground, swathing the streetlights in a curtain of smoke.

He heard several metal pieces dropping in succession.

The wind Mikihiko created blew away the smoke curtain.

Then it became clear what had happened.

A metal arm, hanging out of the air by thick wires, had grabbed up the parasites' bodies and was now quickly retracting. The wires originated from a jet-black vessel that had at some point appeared in the night sky, blending in with the darkness.

It was surprisingly small and quiet, but there was no trace of it using magic. Without a sound, without any magical waves—and because of that, they hadn't noticed the unknown flying ship that had risen above them.

The captives themselves had disappeared into the gondola.

Erika let out a shock wave, then took a stance as if to slash upward. Her slashing attacks didn't have strategic-class magical power, but she might be able to cut the gas tank of a flying ship and shoot it down.

"Don't, Erika!"

But Mikihiko stopped her, and she grudgingly disengaged. She knew as well as he did that shooting an airship out of the sky in a place like this would cause a massive tragedy.

The assailants had vanished from sight as well while Erika's group was preoccupied with the airship. It was clear the fake police officers and the airship belonged to the same force.

"Well, that throws a wrench into things…"

Mikihiko nodded deeply, feeling completely the same.

Erika turned around to him, an awfully insincere smile on her face. "What should we tell Tatsuya?"

"Well, we should call him, right?" asked Mikihiko, looking to Leo for help.

Leo shrugged at the stare. "Well, it's late, and we'd be bothering him."

"Ah-ha, that's right—it is quite late. Let's just do it tomorrow."

The three of them laughed empty laughs, which were caught by the night breeze in the capital and blown away.

"Sample secured."

At the JGDF counterintelligence department Section Three, with its base of operations in the basement of a certain building in Ichigaya.

When the report came in from the dispatched stealth airship, the assistant division chief (they only used company positions in this department rather than JDF ranks, for camouflage) nodded with relief.

"Despite the accident, we seem to have accomplished our objective."

When the agents disguised as police officers had been put to sleep by the group of high school students and the Home Helper Robot, the word *demotion* had flashed across the back of his mind. But now he sighed in relief. It looked like he would get through this without damaging his superior's mood.

He knew that the "samples" they'd captured were the "vampires" making the rounds in the news, but he didn't know that the vampires' identities were former magicians possessed by things called parasites. He also didn't know that one of the vampires they'd captured was an ex-soldier from the Old Mexico region in the USNA or that he'd retired because he'd lost his magical abilities after an accident during training. All the assistant division chief had gotten was an order to capture vampire samples.

He'd been keeping a watch on Tatsuya's group because he'd been told that there was a high chance they'd make contact with the vampiric samples. As for why a bunch of high school kids, despite being up-and-coming magicians, would be related to these vampires—well, that was unknown to him.

However, when his subordinates had been easily disabled, the notion that they were *mere* high school students had disappeared. But that only presented more questions, like why high school students were that strong. In the end, though, it looked like his subordinates wouldn't have to worry themselves over *abnormal* high school students any further. That was another reason the assistant division chief was relieved.

Now his job was only to "preserve" the sample for a time. His subordinate, the division chief, would take care of the rest of the paperwork. Part of staying alive in a group like this was not prodding into higher affairs. He knew vaguely that the *request* to obtain samples hadn't been from the government but the wishes of their sponsor, and also that the *true* requester seemed to be *a certain family* pulling the strings behind that sponsor. But he had absolutely no intent to elucidate the details.

"Bring them into the 'ice box' as planned. And go heavy on the drugs, just in case."

After ordering his subordinates to disable the magicians by putting them into a state of hibernation with low-temperature anesthesia and to store the vampires into their facility, the assistant division chief got out of his seat to tell his superior that the operation was complete.

"I see that Kouichi still loves his schemes. Part of his personality at this point, I'd expect."

The words alone made it sound like her grandfather was complaining, but his voice actually sounded faintly amused for some reason. Fujibayashi decided not to ask.

Counterintelligence Section Three's sudden intervention via spy ship had surprised Fujibayashi, too, but her response after that was swift and exact as always. She immediately pinpointed the group the airship belonged to from its radio communications.

And then, as always, she'd broken into the Ichigaya basement room's line with skills that brought no shame to her moniker, Electron Sorceress.

"Your Excellency, what might Mr. Saegusa be after?"

She'd called him "Your Excellency" and not "Grandfather" simply because she knew she was on the job right now. Retsu Kudou understood that as well, so the aloof, distant title didn't bother him.

"Not even I know what's in Kouichi's head. I can make a pretty awful guess, though."

Nevertheless, the Kudou elder didn't seem to want to match his granddaughter's way of speaking, and his own tone of voice was the comfortable sort one would have toward a family member.

"An awful one...?"

"Mm. Maybe Kouichi found out Maya's interested in the parasites and decided he wanted one for himself."

"Ms. Yotsuba is interested in them?"

"The Yotsuba entrust their intelligence to a branch family called the Kuroba. And the Kuroba seem to have tried to wipe out the parasites. They're apparently still investigating things now."

"A branch family tasked with intelligence... The Yotsuba really are unique."

"Well, the twenty-eight families themselves are like branch families of the magic technician development laboratories. You're right, though. Aside from the Yotsuba, nobody has a system based on branch families."

Kudou gave a self-deprecating grin, probably remembering where he himself came from. Fujibayashi didn't bother to awkwardly comfort her grandfather, and instead waited for his next words.

"That all aside... He must have found out that the Yotsuba had a strong interest in the parasites and decided he wanted to get involved, too. He wants to get stronger than the Yotsuba, no matter what he has to do. It's certainly sad that he still hasn't escaped the nightmare from thirty years ago, but still…"

As Kudou spoke, it looked to Fujibayashi like he was reminiscing about the distant past. It didn't seem like a good past, certainly, so she addressed him in a slightly firm voice to pull him out of it. "What should we do, then?"

"What do you mean?"

"I don't believe that leaving counterintelligence Section Three to do as they please is a good idea."

"Indeed… Though had they played their cards better, we might have been able to." As Fujibayashi hoped, Kudou returned from his world of memories and directed his mind to the present. "Kyouko, can we leak this information to the Yotsuba anonymously?"

"I believe we can, but why?"

"Then that's all we need to do. Maya will think of a way to deal with the rest."

To have Maya Yotsuba settle Kouichi Saegusa's scheme… It seemed like a cruel mistreatment to Fujibayashi, who knew the circumstances. But she wasn't about to object to her grandfather's plan, either, so she set right to work at the console.

When the Shiba siblings got home from dropping off Honoka at her apartment and leaving Pixie in the garage they got her from, the date hadn't quite yet changed, but the time was still such that one had to call it the middle of the night.

Still, considering their age, it wasn't particularly late, either. The skirmish had been far from their full combat powers, but their tense nerves were keeping them on edge, too.

"Brother, it's Miyuki. Might you have a moment…?"

After eating, bathing, and finishing several other things she could find to do, Miyuki visited her brother's room. Rather than being in his lab in the basement, he was, unusually, studying something other than magicology—probably because he couldn't get to sleep, either.

Tatsuya had a textbook open as a sort of substitute for a sleeping pill. Despite the fact that they were siblings, it wasn't proper for one to visit another's bedroom (also their private room), but he figured talking to his sister might give him a good distraction.

"It's okay, you can come in."

"Yes. Please excuse me."

Tatsuya lowered his display from its vertical position on the desk's back to a horizontal one on the desktop, then turned around at the sound of the door closing.

"……What did you need?"

Only he could have prevented himself from stammering or his voice from cracking.

Nevertheless, it still resulted in an unnatural pause.

Without immediately answering her brother's question, Miyuki took a seat on his bed, her expression proper.

Tatsuya couldn't stop himself from wondering, internally, what was happening.

——He was certain his sister wore pajamas to bed.

——Had Shizuku's recent outfit infected her?

In short, Miyuki was in a nightgown.

More concretely, in a negligee.

She did have a proper gown on, of course, and her belt was tied tight.

But her skin was barely visible through the thin fabric over her upper chest and below her knees, making it more alluring than seeing it directly would have been.

It's fine because I'm the only one here, but… Does she not fully realize how old she is?

As her brother, he secretly feared for her lack of caution—but whether that was appropriate for the situation or not, there was no judge here to give a decision.

Miyuki, in the meantime, gave a happy smile as though satisfied Tatsuya was staring a hole through her, then quickly went back to a serious expression.

"I'm sorry, was I interrupting your studies…?"

"No. You know I don't need anything like that."

Depending on how you took that—actually, most people who heard that would have taken it as sarcasm, but Miyuki wasn't envious, nor did she admire him for it or even praise him. She simply accepted the words as the regular way of things.

Tatsuya stood from in front of his desk and moved to the bed. He sat next to his sister. With enough space between them, of course.

Urged by his questioning sidelong gaze, Miyuki nervously broached the subject.

"Brother… Miyuki is confused."

"Confused?" Tatsuya parroted back.

It was a sudden remark, though a reserved one. He looked at her with seriousness.

But his sister wasn't looking at him. "I just don't think I understand anymore. What is magic? What are we, magicians…?"

Perplexity passed over Tatsuya's face.

It was a more advanced question, and one he certainly hadn't expected. He considered this topic one belonging in the realm of philosophy more so than magicology.

It didn't seem like the kind of thing he could handle, but nevertheless, he didn't have the option of brushing off what Miyuki had to say.

"Why the sudden question?" he said, urging her on for the time being.

"Magic and psychic powers are fundamentally the same. Brother, you know more than anyone that this is more than just theory—it's fact."

"'More than anyone' might be exaggerating things, but... Why?"

"On the other hand, parasites—demons use magic, too. There was no difference in the activation process between the magic they use and the magic we use."

"Indeed."

Miyuki, who was staring at her clenched fists in her lap, turned to face her brother. Her hand rested in the open space Tatsuya had left, and she leaned forward, looking up into his face.

Unease wavered in her eyes.

"I thought...I thought it was because the demon had possessed a magician. I thought the demon was using magic through the magician's mind."

Behind that unease lurked fear.

"But when I saw the psychic powers Pixie used and asked you about it afterward, I realized I was wrong."

"The psychokinetic blast earlier?"

"Yes..."

There was a short pause before her next words. Miyuki was scared of putting the rest out there. She feared explaining her reasoning, and the possibility that Tatsuya would confirm it. That was what Tatsuya sensed.

"Telepathy is an ability that works between two minds. I didn't think it was strange when a parasite, which is originally similar to a mental body, could use it. And when I heard she used psychokinesis to create facial expressions, I figured it wasn't too farfetched and didn't worry about it."

Miyuki's face drew slightly closer.

He could see the flicker of emotion in her eyes, more clearly than before.

"However, with the psychokinesis earlier... It had a rough structure, but it couldn't have been anything other than a movement-type spell. A spell that triggered via resonance with Honoka, right?"

"...Yeah," nodded Tatsuya with hesitation.

He'd been ambiguous about it earlier, but he was nearly certain the phenomenon that occurred between Honoka and Pixie was "resonance"—where the energization of one's magic-calculation region heightened the energy levels of the other's magic-calculation region—the sort observed, rarely, between those closely related by blood, such as identical twin magicians.

"Three-H doesn't... Machines don't have the ability to generate magic. That means the psychic power Pixie used wasn't its host's ability... It was the parasite's—the demon's—ability."

Miyuki lowered her gaze for a moment. When she looked back up a moment later, her stare seemed to cling to him.

"Magic and psychic powers are the same thing. That would mean the demons have the same power as we magicians."

Tatsuya finally realized what his sister was so anxious about.

"In Japanese, the word *magic* figuratively means 'demonic method'... Does our power originate from them?"

His sister's face drew even nearer.

Just before it got close enough that Tatsuya could feel her breath, he stood up from the bed.

It looked as though he'd smoothly evaded her, but that wasn't it.

He squatted in front of Miyuki and brought his eyes to her level.

"Miyuki... You're overthinking this."

Lithely putting her hands down to support her tilting body, Miyuki received Tatsuya's gaze—and accepted it.

Tatsuya put his palms around his sister's shoulders and slowly sat her back up straight.

"In Japanese, magic might come from the term *demonic method*, but in English, for example, it means 'the skill of a magus.'"

"Ah," gasped Miyuki softly.

"We still don't know much about the forces that magic comes

from. We understand the system of causing an alteration in events by overwriting eidos using a magic program. But why can we do that? Why does the human unconscious have what we call a magic-calculation region? You could say we have no idea."

Tatsuya made a troubled face, the kind a master might give to a favorite pupil more talented than he to admonish her for a misunderstanding, and smiled a little.

"We're not even certain the magician is really the one producing magic. Just because a demon used magic doesn't automatically mean there's a link between magicians and demons."

"Yes...yes, you're right..."

"And besides, we think the parasites are actually independent information bodies originating in the human psyche. If they come from a person's mind, then their power is something humans gave them. You could have the opinion that magicians' magic doesn't come from demons but that demons' magic comes from human magicians."

"Yes... You're right, Brother."

The unease had been wiped from Miyuki's eyes.

Tatsuya felt like it was too early for her to be convinced, but this was more constructive than her making mountains out of molehills. He wasn't about to put a damper on it.

"You were having trouble sleeping because you were worried you might be kin to something inhuman like demons, weren't you?"

Tatsuya hadn't asked that with the intent to tease his sister.

But it flipped a switch inside of Miyuki, and her face immediately flushed a wonderfully bright red. She froze, forgetting even to hide her face. When she managed to restart herself, she spun around and put her back to him.

She climbed farther onto the bed, sitting with her legs disorganized— unusual for her—and remained stock-still, facing the wall.

It wasn't that embarrassing... thought Tatsuya, at the same time feeling like her reaction was oddly cute.

"In that case..."

He brought his lips close to her ear and whispered.

"...until you go to sleep..."

At a level that spoke of a mischievous intent.

And sure enough, Miyuki's body gave an exaggerated shake. The shake was so hard she might have flown into the ceiling.

"...shall I stay by your side?"

Miyuki slowly turned her head around to look at him, and with her face red, eyes upturned, and voice feeble, she answered.

"...Will...will you hold my hand?"

Maybe I went too far, Tatsuya thought.

Without any right to refuse, Tatsuya now had to sit at his sister's bedside in her room until she went to sleep, holding her delicate white hand.

Fortunately, she sent off for dreamland quickly.

Seeing his sister's happy sleeping face was enough of a reward for Tatsuya, but he still couldn't avoid feeling mentally exhausted by it.

Without turning the lights on, his gait unsteady, Tatsuya left Miyuki's bedside behind him.

Without a sound, he closed the door, then went back to his room.

On the way, Tatsuya realized something.

Miyuki, who had advanced education as a magician, based on just one facet of magic, had linked magicians to the demons.

She had seen magicians as something separate from other people.

If even Miyuki, who knew magic very well, could be entrapped by such an impression, then it wasn't strange for non-magicians, who didn't know magic very well, to see magicians and demonic inhuman beings in the same light.

No, it wouldn't be strange at all if they thought magicians were something other than human. Something altogether inhuman...

◇ ◇ ◇

The next morning.

Right after Tatsuya got to school, Erika, Leo, and Mikihiko grabbed him and pulled him out of the classroom. Mizuki watched with a confused, flustered expression, but rescue was beyond her abilities.

Their destination was the roof.

It was already first thing in the morning before the temperature rose, and they were outdoors, on the roof, exposed to all the wind. Nobody else was there, and Tatsuya didn't want to stay very long, either.

"You had something to talk about?"

He couldn't have the three of them clamming up on the roof. But his friends had gone on and on about unimportant trifles on the long way here, so even if he prompted them to get on with it in a somewhat irritated tone of voice, nobody could turn around and say Tatsuya had a short temper.

The three exchanged glances, then all gave resigned looks at the same time. Their faces remained that way as they spoke, the result of compelling an unprepared spokesman.

"Tatsuya, well, actually..."

The one who nervously started to speak was, perhaps as expected, Mikihiko.

"What, did you let the parasites get away or something?"

Tatsuya had only given them a chance to get this whole thing over with, but when he saw Mikihiko audibly gulp and draw his head back, a sigh escaped him in spite of himself.

"I'm not going to get mad at something like that, so quit worrying. Thinking about capturing more is a pain, but... We can't do anything about them now that they got away."

He didn't hide his disappointment, but this wasn't something they could never take back. Expressing as much, Tatsuya turned to return to their warm classroom.

"No, that's not it, Tatsuya!" cried Mikihiko, desperately trying to keep him from leaving.

"That's right!" continued Erika. "They didn't escape! ...Well, I mean, I guess they did, but..."

As the two of them stumbled over their words, Tatsuya turned his gaze to Leo.

"Someone swooped in and grabbed 'em," he confessed.

"They were that strong?"

Tatsuya's reaction might have been slightly different from a normal person's.

But for Tatsuya, that was the most interesting part.

It had been nearly a year since entering the same class as them. At this point, Tatsuya rated their abilities as almost on par with first-rate combat magicians and, more concretely, members of the Independent Magic Battalion.

They weren't up to Kazama's or Yanagi's level yet, of course (without using the Trident, Tatsuya couldn't match them, either), but pitting them against any of the middle-ranking soldiers would probably make for a good match.

"It may sound like we're being sore losers, but I don't think they were really that strong in terms of their abilities," explained Mikihiko.

"But they came fully armed," put in Leo. "Never seen a suit that shocked you whenever you punched it before."

"The guy was wearing awfully tough armor, but every time I hit it, this powder sprayed everywhere," said Erika. "I should have brought a weapon with more reach."

"I see."

Those were quite unique armaments. Thanks to that, he ascertained their opponents' identities immediately.

"And then the parasites got taken away on a black airship. It makes me so mad!"

"Well, I'm glad nothing worse happened."

Erika looked at him, a little confused, not at his words so much as his tone. "Tatsuya, you know who they were?"

"Probably. I didn't fight them personally, though, so I can only guess."

"Who were they?"

Considering the characteristics of the answer, it wouldn't have been weird for him to evade the question or just remain silent.

"The Japan Ground Defense Force's counterintelligence Section Three. I think they're the only ones who would use such interesting gear and a stealth-equipped airship."

But Tatsuya gave it to them straight. It didn't seem that they were trying very hard to keep it a secret. Maybe they were trying to get not just Erika but Leo and Mikihiko wrapped up in his own affairs as well.

"Is that...something you know because you're part of the Independent Magic Battalion, Tatsuya?"

Nevertheless—

"I don't remember telling you what unit I belonged to..."

—he had to tilt his head in confusion when she pointed out something he didn't remember.

"...Oh, you asked Miyuki."

"Well, after what happened, of course I'd want to ask."

Erika was referring to the MOVAL suit. Even she, who had a clue as to his true identity, hadn't gone so far as to link Tatsuya and the Scorching Halloween.

"After fighting the invaders with my real abilities, I had to tell you about my chain of command in case something happened, so it's fine. But don't tell anyone else."

"I know. I don't want them to nab me as a spy suspect."

Those who broke the law for the protection of state secrets were synonymous with suspected spies. Unlike the latter half of the previous century, even Japan had become a *normal enough* country to have a majority of its populace feel like that was disgraceful.

"Hey, if we know who we're up against, don't we know where they brought the parasites to?" asked Erika hopefully, very quickly pulling out of her earlier mood.

However:

"We can't narrow it down if we don't know what they're after," Tatsuya responded flatly, shaking his head. This was how reality worked.

"Right, right… They're a government agency, so they can probably have as many bases as they need," agreed Mikihiko.

"Well, they've got a budget," countered Leo. "They can't just have a hundred. But they're probably hidden all over the place, so well even a thorough search wouldn't work."

As they said, they were up against a state agency this time. They had far more quantity and quality of operational resources than a foreign power staking an illegal invasion. The home field advantage they'd had until now was on the enemy's side this time.

"Well, we don't have to worry about it much. Those guys who showed up yesterday won't be the end of it, and we know the parasites are after Pixie. We'll just have to make sure nobody can barge in this time. We'll set a trap."

A terribly evil grin spread across Tatsuya's face as he comforted the three of them. —And despite comforting them, Erika, Leo, and Mikihiko all winced and leaned away. But Tatsuya didn't seem to care about that one bit.

"Anyway, let's get back to class already. I'm getting cold."

Nobody here was the sort to complain about this level of cold, but that didn't mean they didn't feel it.

With nobody else objecting, they followed after Tatsuya.

Colonel Balance got the phone call right at the same time Tatsuya was having his conversation with Erika and the others on the school rooftop.

"I apologize for calling so early, Miss Balance."

"Oh, it's you."

Displayed on the videophone screen was a face she'd just met yesterday, a girl in her middle teens calling herself an agent of the Yotsuba, one Ayako Kuroba. This morning she was, once again, buried in ribbons, lace, and frills.

"Are you not going to—? No, excuse me."

Excluding times when the completion of her duties depended on it, Balance was fundamentally a moralist. Hence, why she'd almost gone out of her way to lecture the girl, clearly of schooling age, after seeing her too busy with things other than classes on a weekday morning.

"Thank you very much for your consideration," noted Ayako with a friendly smile, sharply picking up on what Balance was about to say—and how she changed her mind about it. *"But you needn't worry, Miss. I've already acquired enough credits to graduate."*

Balance didn't have a good understanding of what Japan's secondary education system looked like, so she couldn't discern if what the girl said was true or a lie. But she did understand that their relationship was cordial enough not to make an issue of it.

"No, I said something pointless. Anyway, did you have something to tell me?"

Balance asked this question as a way of putting things diplomatically. She didn't seriously believe Ayako would provide her with beneficial information today, either.

"Yes. Yesterday, the JGDF counterintelligence department's Section Three captured parasites. We discovered that one of them is a magician formerly belonging to the USNA military. I am here at the behest of our leader, who felt we should inform you of this."

Her saying "I am here at the behest of..." over the phone wasn't a problem. Balance wasn't that particular. The information she'd given directly before that was of far more consequence.

"The parasites have begun moving again?"

"One of our family has suggested that after the parasites' vessels were destroyed, they found new hosts. Here are the ones that have been captured."

As she spoke, she sent an encrypted data file to Balance's terminal. The military officer looked at the decoded file's contents, then checked one of the personal profiles, which included facial photographs.

"Three parasites have now been taken prisoner. This is the only one we've identified thus far, but if you wish, we can tell you where they are being held."

Just looking at the contents didn't give a good sense of how crucial this ex-magician was. But Balance didn't have the choice of leaving it aside.

"Please do, Miss Kuroba."

"Very well."

The girl bowed to her on the screen, and with that, the data was sent. Balance gave a simple word of thanks so as not to be rude, then hung up and immediately looked over the data.

Her expression changed into one of dangerous severity.

She went over to a specially encoded transmitter and quickly punched in a message.

The message contained instructions to prepare for mobilization tonight.

The recipient was Major Angie Sirius.

The first engagement of the day was first period, rather than homeroom or an assembly. Before them was the kind of task where students read a text, then answered questions about it, with a voice-reading function usable should the student wish.

Tatsuya usually just let the text automatically scroll by, but today he had earphones in. As he dismissed the synthetic speech coming in over the wireless receiver, he thought about something unrelated to classes.

He had, in fact, learned of counterintelligence Section Three's name and traits through the Independent Magic Battalion.

But he hadn't learned of it as just one part of several in the information bureau.

Within the information bureau, this section particularly was under the Saegusa family's influence. Their team was actively at the family's beck and call. More accurately, perhaps, at the beck and call of their sponsor, of which the Saegusa family was pulling the strings behind the scenes. But their name had come up as a candidate on his list of virtual enemy factions.

That didn't make sense to Tatsuya—assuming this incident had been carried out at the Saegusa family's behest. The method of bringing a stealth airship right into the heart of the city and stealing the parasites with it seemed far too violent for them.

Tatsuya didn't know their leader Kouichi Saegusa's temperament, so he couldn't say for sure this wasn't how the Saegusa family did things. But this style had been forceful, almost like a gamble. If they'd been doing this sort of thing in the past, they and the Yotsuba would have collided headfirst a long time ago.

So what could have been the intent behind this havoc?

Maybe Section Three *hadn't* carried it out on the Saegusa family's orders—maybe they'd been reckless on their own.

If the military has taken action that deviates from their sponsor's will…then their motive must have to do with an objective that relates to why the military exists in the first place.

What was a military's objective? It was an agency of force to actualize national influence and the only way the nation had to properly and directly resist other nations' direct violence upon them. Their characteristics were complex, not something you could sum up in a couple of sentences.

But if you were to treat them as a phenomenon, their goal was surprisingly simple.

A military's objective was to win.

Any other objectives were merely incidental. Victory itself took many forms, and in situations where you simply had to *not lose*, not losing itself was a kind of triumph.

In any case, their objective was to win. Anything after they'd won was governmental territory. Militaries had to think only about winning.

Therefore, militaries sought power.

Even if its intelligence bureau's complacency caused it to act recklessly, it was no more than the result of having sought power.

After he'd thought that far, Tatsuya felt a slight chill along his spine.

Was Section Three considering trying to put the parasites—the demons—to military use?

That struck him as incredibly dangerous. The main tool used in the smear campaigns spreading across the USNA now was criticism that they'd invited the demons into this world. That they'd done so with military-like ambitions. They were false pretexts, no more than agitation, but wouldn't plotting to put the parasites to military use give the anti-magician demonstrators that exact excuse?

Actually, it would be the same even if the Ten Master Clans were pulling the strings.

He changed his mind: The risks were the same whether this was counterintelligence Section Three making a rash act or if they'd done it on the Saegusa family's orders.

Improper behavior though it may be for a youngster like himself, he had to give the Saegusa a warning. He felt bad for Mayumi, who was about to take her exams, but he had to get her to make time for him. With that thought in mind, he sent a summoning text message from his own portable terminal to Mayumi.

——And though he said he felt bad to himself, he didn't actually care about Mayumi's convenience right now.

* * *

He got a response to the message he'd sent Mayumi in the middle of class, just a minute after he'd sent it. He had attached the "urgent" code to it, but...

She was *taking the general exams, right?*

There wasn't much time left until the exams. Though there was virtually no worry of her failing, it made him think, *Is this okay, Miss Exam-Taker?*

Still...maybe it was none of his business. He'd gotten a reply to his urgent message right away, so he wasn't in a position to complain.

As he was thinking about it, he opened the message.

Tatsuya had said, *There's something I want to talk about, so could we meet within the next day or two?*

And yet Mayumi's response was, *Please come to the student council room immediately.*

It seemed she was at school despite it being a free attendance day for her.

Right now, she wasn't in a classroom or the library but the student council room.

...Seriously, is this okay, Miss Exam-Taker? Tatsuya wondered genuinely.

Tatsuya was the one to bring the matter to her, and it was preferable to do this sooner rather than later, so he got up and went to the student council room. It was a full-blown classroom escape, but while it was difficult to fool the systems keeping track of the lecture progress, it wasn't impossible.

Using his ID card, which had been reset with entrance privileges without him knowing it, he opened the door. Since class was still in session, Mayumi was the only one waiting there for him.

After exchanging pleasant greetings—with Mayumi fine with it but Tatsuya wondering what attitude he should have—Tatsuya sat directly in front of her and then immediately started to give her the rough outline.

"...That's about it. I believe that airship belonged to the information bureau's counterintelligence Section Three, rumored to have ties to the Saegusa family. I don't know why on earth you wanted to make off with the parasites. But if you're considering using them for military purposes, that would be dangerous. We don't know for sure how to destroy them, so I think we should be sealing them."

"Counterintelligence Section Three? I may be a minor, but even I didn't know that despite being a member of the Saegusa. I'm surprised you know about that."

"I would appreciate it if you didn't ask what my information source is."

"...Well, you probably have a lot of your own things going on, so I won't. More importantly, why didn't you tell me you were going out to capture the parasites?"

"Because I figured bringing more people along would make them cautious, and we wouldn't be able to lure them out."

"Is that really all?" Mayumi gave Tatsuya a frustrated look momentarily. "It does make sense, I guess..." she muttered with a half shrug, though, after seeing his face remain completely steady, she aborted the gesture in the middle. "Anyway, you want me to explain this to my father, right? And get the information bureau to give back the parasites they snatched to Erika and the others?"

It didn't matter, but Mayumi had at some point started referring to Erika by her first name. Erika made a peeved face whenever she heard it (even though Mizuki did it and she didn't care, so it probably depended on the person), but Erika had never stopped calling Mikihiko "Miki," so from, say, Tatsuya's perspective, she got what she deserved.

...Tatsuya shook his head to drive the drifting thoughts from his mind. "I won't tell you to get them to give them back," he prefaced, then added, "but once you've verified the reason they took the parasites away, if they're trying to deal with them in any way other than sealing them, I'd like you to warn them off. Tell them that if the fact that the information bureau is taking advantage of the parasites leaks to the public and magicians face disadvantages because of it, they'll be the ones paying for the damages."

"That's a scary thought."

Tatsuya's voice had mild annoyance mixed into it, but the light wavering in his eyes spoke volumes that this was not a mere whine or complaint.

"Considering what's happening in the USNA, I believe the threat is necessary."

Mayumi knew as well as he did that the bitterness toward magicians was getting more severe by the day. If the same thing happened in relatively small Japan, then Japan might end up seeing clashes that didn't just end at arguments well before the USNA did.

"...Will do. I'll talk to my father. But I can't promise any results, so don't expect too much. Unlike Juumonji, I don't have free reign over the Saegusa."

Tatsuya expressed a bit of surprise at what Mayumi added on.

"...What?"

"Nothing... I was just thinking that the Saegusa have surprisingly paternalistic traditions."

"Oh, well then, how is it with your family?"

Either she was embarrassed or angered—Tatsuya couldn't quite make out Mayumi's true intent.

But he'd still said something he hadn't needed to. Reflecting on that a little, Tatsuya decided to answer her question with a playful jab. "My father pretty much doesn't have any authority at all. He's too busy spending all his time at his new wife's apartment for that."

Mayumi's gaze flickered across his.

Whenever he saw her react in such a purely disheveled way at something so minor, he thought to himself that she was still a girl, even though she was older than him. She appeared mature some-times, but he still couldn't call her an adult woman.

"I think I made it clear at least that she's not his lover."

"How grown-up of you."

"No, I've just given up," answered Tatsuya in a completely resigned tone of voice. "Though I...don't really want to consider growing up to mean giving up."

Sometimes ill omens turned out to be nothing.

Tatsuya's prediction that the JGDF's intelligence bureau was try-ing to do something bad using the parasites never became a reality.

But it was difficult to call it fortunate.

Because the next morning...

A spy asylum facility belonging to counterintelligence Section Three has been attacked, and everyone was killed by the captured parasites.

So read the message he received from Mayumi.

[16]

——The intelligence bureau has been attacked and the people killed by the parasites detained there——

Struggling to suppress the desire to get in contact right away and ask for details, Tatsuya steered himself to the bathroom. As he washed away the sweat from training in a hot shower, he summarized his thoughts and considered what to do next.

He hadn't told Miyuki yet.

Coming home from Yakumo's temple and taking a shower. That was his usual pattern, and just because she'd seen that he got a message before he hopped in the water, she wouldn't assume anything had happened.

Well...I probably can't hide it from her, he thought, immediately rejecting the idea of not telling her at all.

His sister was sharp, and she'd have to figure it out at some point. It would be one thing if she hadn't been involved at all, but after all, she was just as deeply connected to this incident as Tatsuya was.

Deciding to be straight with her instead of tiptoeing around the subject so she wouldn't realize it, Tatsuya got out of the shower.

Tatsuya's fingers danced over the console at his workstation set up in the basement. Although if one was to describe how he did it, something along the lines of "swiftly" or "accurately" would be more fitting for his personality than "beautifully."

Even though it was morning on a Saturday, they had classes. But if it looked like his investigation would take more time, he was ready to play hooky for the day.

But if he did, his sister, who was always at his side as though that were natural (and in fact, it was unarguably natural for her), would take a mandatory day off for herself as well (and this time, it would be less natural and more *necessary for her clarity of mind*), so he planned to put off his decision of whether to play hooky until the last possible moment.

Fortunately, he quickly found the data he was looking for.

He'd been illegally accessing the JGDF intelligence department's distributed server, but the division's local systems, despite belonging to the intelligence department, seemed quite ill-equipped to oppose a quality hacking program made by the Electron Sorceress Kyouko Fujibayashi. Still, the segmentation of information systems was a form of risk prevention, stopping one division's vulnerability from leaking all their information, so perhaps it had both advantages and disadvantages.

Anyway, it meant Tatsuya got some expedient results, so he wasn't in a position to gripe.

The video recorded there was a shocking one.

Not in the sense that it delivered a physiological impact like cruelty or coldness.

No, it was the thing performed there and the person who carried it out, which gave the siblings no small shock.

A small figure blending in with the darkness as it broke in.

Illuminated by the lights coming on with the alarms—a girl with crimson hair and a mask.

With one glare from her golden eyes, she sent the civilian-clothed soldiers flying out of her way, then headed for a door engraved from top to bottom in complex patterns and gave four wide swings of her knife. As she stepped aside, the door fell into the hallway.

Beyond the door was a small room. It was about wide enough to fit two single beds and had a low ceiling of about two meters. In the room were three beds, one on top of another, placed along the wall.

A man, his hands' freedom stripped by a straitjacket and his legs bound together with shackles, lay on the second bed of the three-level bunk. He had a different impression since every last bit of the color had drained from him, but his face was, without a doubt, the parasite who had called himself Marte.

A white puff of air escaped the girl's mouth. The temperature in the room must have been quite low.

The redhead's hand now gripped an automatic pistol instead of a knife.

A bullet fired from her hand, boring a hole in Marte's chest.

Suddenly, the man's body went up in flames.

The only plausible source was the bullet shot into him. It probably had a combustion spell on it that would trigger when the bullet stopped inside its target body.

The girl with the crimson hair, Angie Sirius, fired another bullet into the upper bunk and the lower bunk. A homicidal act, clearly without any thought given to the "substance." The goal was only to burn the "containers" to cinders. It had been an execution.

As Tatsuya watched the video of the girl leaving calmly, he unconsciously let out a sigh.

He'd known the Sirius's mission had included the execution of rebellious and deserter magicians. He was also keenly aware that the "humane treatment of magicians" were no more than empty words, but he still couldn't stop himself from feeling like sighing.

They do cruel things, thought Tatsuya.

Saddling a sixteen-year-old girl with the role of a killer—what were the USNA military brass thinking? Even the mafia probably took a little more consideration when choosing people. Was this any different from religious idealists driving children to terrorism in the name of a holy war?

"Brother, was that...Lina?"

He'd let Miyuki know about Parade, Sirius's secret.

She seemed to have realized the killer in the rough image was Sirius—Lina.

"Probably."

Miyuki also seemed to have taken quite a shock, but Tatsuya couldn't find the right words to soothe it.

He wasn't about to nitpick about the mere act of killing at this point. He didn't think he had the right to anyway. There were plenty of missions that couldn't go public. When it came to the dirty jobs, one might actually put assassinations into the cleaner category.

But at the same time, it was a lonely, cheerless one.

Without a high degree of affinity personality-wise, it was too heavy for a teenage girl. So heavy she wouldn't be able to endure—it would crush her heart, little by little.

And as far as Tatsuya could see, Lina didn't have the affinity to be an assassin.

He understood from Miyuki's voice and expression that she had the same opinion.

The way things were going, they might have spent the entire day in a gloom.

Fortunately (?), though, an even more shocking event occurred a moment later to drive away the melancholy. Suddenly, the onscreen image, which Tatsuya had hacked into Section Three's video server to get, changed over to a completely different one.

Blonde hair and blue eyes—the bust of a boy who appeared to be Anglo-Saxon. He looked childish, but he was probably around Tatsuya's age.

Miyuki covered her mouth before a confused squeak could get out, but Tatsuya was calm.

This workstation was meant for hacking to begin with, so it was cut off from other systems. It used a dedicated line, too. The room was free of any sort of microphones or cameras. He knew that they were the only ones looking through and that the person on the other end of the line had no way of knowing what it was like on this one.

"Hello? Can you hear me? I'm going to assume you can, if that's all right."

As expected, the boy on the monitor didn't attempt communication. Instead, he started talking by himself.

"I'll start with an introduction. My name is Raymond Sage Clark. One of the Seven Sages."

At some point, Miyuki had tightened her grip on her brother's shoulders.

The sensation caused him to realize that he, too, was tense.

"I heard about you from Tia—or rather, Shizuku. Pleased to meet you, Tatsuya."

I see. The boy seemed to be a student at the school Shizuku was studying abroad at.

And probably her information source.

If Shizuku's information was coming from one of the Seven Sages Lina had talked about, it wasn't strange that he could gather intel off-the-record.

But what did the Seven Sages want? And so much that one would expose himself to Tatsuya?

It wasn't impossible that this video was a dummy, but Tatsuya's instincts told him this was Raymond Sage Clark's real face.

"I'll cut to the chase… Oh, I like that expression."

Incidentally, Raymond was speaking Japanese. His pronunciation of "cut to the chase" had a little awkwardness left in it, but he otherwise sounded fluent. Of course, the way he went on like that was clearly not cutting to the chase.

"I'm the one who told Angie Sirius about what's happening here."

Tatsuya reflexively thought, *You used the expression wrong.* Unfortunately, he didn't have any way to point that out.

And he didn't have to think about what "here" meant—it was obviously Section Three.

"Although, it seems like she somehow learned of this before I informed her."

What does that mean? Tatsuya wondered. If she already knew, then he wouldn't have been *informing* her of anything.

But there was no point making quick retorts to a recorded video. Tatsuya decided to watch the message through to the end.

"And I also wanted to give you the scoop, too."

He seemed to know quite a bit of slang Japanese with the "scoop" bit. Maybe he'd learned the word from the media?

"I think you'll find it highly beneficial. I'd like to say 'watch now, pay later,' but I'll give it to you for free this time, as a symbol of our acquaintance."

"Nobody asked you for it," Tatsuya muttered reflexively, even knowing he wouldn't be heard. But that was the last he could remain so calm.

"The magician boycott movements raging fiercely in the States right now—the ones starting to gain traction in Japan—were set up by one of the Seven Sages: Gide Sage Hague."

It was so sudden that even Tatsuya couldn't help being surprised.

"Gide Hague—also known as Gu Jie. A stateless overseas Chinese person and supreme leader of the international terrorist organization Blanche. He's the boss of Hajime Tsukasa, leader of Blanche's Japanese branch, who you caught."

As the familiar names listed out one by one…

"And also a senior member of Richard Sun's group—the previous leader of the international crime syndicate No-Head Dragon. In No-Head Dragon, they called Gu Jie 'the Black Elder' or 'the Great Hague.'"

…Tatsuya stared fixedly at the monitor.

"Oh, and just to be sure, just because he's one of the Seven Sages doesn't

mean I'm in conspiracy with him. Seven Sages isn't the name of a single group—it refers to the seven operators with access privileges to Hlidskjalf."

The fact that he couldn't converse—couldn't question—was, for once, tantalizing.

Hlidskjalf... He'd heard a rumor about it once before. It existed on the level of an urban legend. Did this mean it actually existed? And furthermore, was it just like the rumors said or different...?

"You see, Hlidskjalf..."

With timing as though Raymond had predicted Tatsuya's train of thought, he began to explain.

"It's one of the additional expansion systems for Echelon III, the global monitoring system. Maybe calling it a hacking system lurking within the system would be better, since it uses a backdoor in Echelon III? What do you think, Tatsuya?"

Ask he did, but of course there was no way to answer. Raymond knew that and continued his prerecorded explanation without leaving time for response.

"Even the operators don't know where the physical Hlidskjalf is. It might just be pure programming code, without any hardware setup at all."

Raymond shrugged his shoulders on the screen. The gesture was somehow cartoonlike.

"Anyway, Hlidskjalf collects information from throughout the world with even better efficiency than the main system, Echelon III, and gives information along with search matches to the operators. The system itself decides who the operators will be, and we haven't found any logic to how it chooses people. Ostensibly it's completely random."

Raymond pantomimed swinging a pipe around. He was probably quite disappointed he'd forgotten to get a small item to use.

"If there's any commonality, I guess it's that you need capital to use an advanced information system on your own. But you don't need to be filthy rich, either. You can just be an average middle-class citizen in the States or Japan."

This was insane.

That was Tatsuya's impression of what Raymond had explained so far.

What the hell could Hlidskjalf's creator been thinking? They seemed like a hacker purely out for the momentary thrill of committing crimes.

"Anyway, it's not actually that great a system. Hardware-wise, Hlidskjalf depends wholly on Echelon III. It's not doing anything except optimizing information search results. And since it's a monitoring system to begin with, we can't fish around for data saved to its storage. Plus, there's a system guard in place that prevents you from saving search results to external storage. The only place the info it gives you can stay is in your head. The Seven Sages are really just people who have the ability to gather that information internally."

Well, just that made them a huge threat. At this point, virtually all data of relevance moved through networks. How much of it sat localized, having never been transmitted even once?

"And using Hlidskjalf is a risk to the operators, too. In order to optimize its searches, it uses two types of agents called Huginn and Muninn. And the operator's search history is saved to Muninn. Whatever one operator looks up, the other operators will know about. Muninn's records are how I learned about Gide Hague."

That struck Tatsuya as odd. By that logic, wouldn't Gide Hague now know Raymond Clark's identity, too?

"When Blanche's Japanese branch went under and No-Head Dragon lost its Japanese headquarters, Hague lost all his ways to influence Japan. Hague was the one who set up the parasites to come to Japan, too. His goal is to rebuild his spy base in Japan by taking advantage of the chaos."

On the screen, Raymond had stopped his little performance. He seemed to be serious about this story as well.

"I've deciphered that his goal is to destroy magic through social means. If he can get rid of it, the Great Asian Alliance, which is behind the curve

when it comes to magic, will immediately see its military might improve compared to Japan. To reign over a world without magic—I think that's what Hague and the people behind him are after."

Tatsuya felt like the logic had leaps in it, but as a whole, it made sense. And the GAA wanting to eliminate magical proficiency was something he himself had already felt.

"And that isn't what I want... You can laugh at me, because this is going to seem romantic, but I think magic is a way toward a reformation of humankind."

He only did it because he knew Raymond couldn't hear, but Tatsuya actually did burst out laughing. It seemed like their views were misaligned on a fundamental level.

"Anyway, I'd like to keep on providing you with necessary information in the future. Tatsuya Shiba—the strategic-class magician, Shiva the Destroyer."

At the nickname, Tatsuya's face fully transformed into a scowl.

——That was the kind of name you'd expect a boss character in a cheap video game to have, wasn't it? Was this kid an otaku—a word that, by this point in history, had become common in all languages?

"Sorry, this all got a little long-winded. Basically, I'm proposing to help you get rid of the parasites."

A little? thought Tatsuya, but he didn't switch off the monitor.

"The info on Gide Hague was free. Believe that or not—it's your choice. And I'll leave it up to you whether to trust what I tell you in the future. But if you do trust me, then I'd like you to compensate me for my work."

Raymond paused for a moment. Not to put on airs—Tatsuya could tell over the screen from his expression that he was tense.

"Tomorrow, at nine PM on February twenty-ninth your time, lure all active parasites to the outdoor training area behind First High. Then I want you to annihilate them."

He had given no proof whatsoever, but at this stage, Tatsuya was ready even now to accept Raymond's proposal.

being polite, the miffed level showing from Aoki's neck up increased by another stage.

The man probably made his own feelings so blatantly clear because it was Tatsuya who he was talking to. He'd protected the Yotsuba vaults for over ten years from the hordes of evil spirits nesting in the underground economy. He would never *not* have worn one or two layers of masks, nor would he *not* employ three or four different ways of talking for different purposes.

There was no way Aoki didn't realize that making his emotions clear was making his job difficult. However, his thoughts were bound by the Yotsuba family's pecking order, by the organization's internal ranks he treated as authoritative.

And class consciousness invited folly.

"...I am currently in class, so if there is nothing you need, I should really excuse myself."

"Wait."

When Tatsuya presented Aoki with his final notice, the man opened his mouth—albeit reluctantly.

"You purchased a 3H P-94 the other day, right?"

The way he talked made it abundantly clear that he was struggling to maintain a businesslike tone. *What a farce*, thought Tatsuya, but he wasn't smiling. Exacting payback in such a dull way probably wouldn't even make him feel better.

"The day before yesterday, to be precise."

Tatsuya decided to match his professional tone. Unfortunately for him, his determination to do so would come crumbling down in a moment.

"The mistress desires it. We'll give you double what you paid for it, so hand it over at once."

With swift motions, Tatsuya rose, then glanced around for bugs or hidden cameras.

With devices that measured the usage of magical powers constantly active in magic high schools, he couldn't use his "eyes" on a whim. But his physical eyes were trained in their own right. For now, it didn't appear as though anyone had overheard their conversation.

Tatsuya took a portable terminal from his inside pocket, hooked a cable into it, and pushed the other end out at Aoki's face.

Thinking about it more closely—well, it didn't need to be that close to know that the behavior lacked courtesy. The light in Tatsuya's eyes gave no room for objection. Scowling, Aoki took out his own terminal and plugged the cable into it.

"Mr. Aoki, do you have a fever or something?"

From out of the blue, that was the first message he was sent.

Aoki nearly shouted out of reflex, but the immense pressure emanating from across him unexpectedly caused him to restrain himself.

"Today is Saturday. Four more hours, and you could have called me somewhere people weren't watching. Why would you run the risk of talking about family matters *in my school's reception room? You should know that Aunt Maya has ordered me to refrain from anything that would lead others to discover my* family ties.*"*

Sizable cracks began to appear in Aoki's mask of calm. The corners of his lips trembled. His face went rather white, too.

He understood Aoki's underlying motives for committing such a careless act. He'd probably tried to avoid Miyuki and use the Yotsuba pecking order as a shield to ram his proposition through.

And now, he would be realizing that Tatsuya had seen through him. Impressively, though, the pen writing a response didn't falter.

"I simply obeyed the mistress's orders that I act with haste. More importantly, hand over the 3H right now. If you do, I'll leave you to your business at once."

"You know I can't do that, don't you? Its ownership rights may have transferred to me, but the rental agreement I have with First High is still in effect. The reason I bought that 3H P-94 was to prevent a third party from making off with it. I will take responsibility for that 3H's administration. Please tell that to Aunt Maya."

The white in Aoki's face changed to red. He moved to castigate Tatsuya in his usual manner.

"Do you plan to disobey her command?"

But with those words and the stare from Tatsuya, the force of Aoki's wrath began to wither visibly.

After seeing the man's reaction, Tatsuya stood, deciding there was no reason to be held up here any longer.

"Wait. Please wait."

But Aoki didn't seem to want to leave yet.

The air of imperiousness covering his face—his whole *body*—had disappeared. But Tatsuya was sure he hadn't sincerely fixed his mind-set. Even from that point of view, his attitude had been renewed.

"I apologize for being impolite. Please," he said, bowing deeply. The bow still seemed sloppy, since he was still sitting on the sofa, but there was no way to misunderstand the apology he was giving.

"Please raise your head, Mr. Aoki," he said, returning to the sofa. But not in response to any sincerity from the man; he felt nothing like that from him to begin with. Tatsuya had simply gained an interest in what he had to say, now that he'd gotten somewhat *more serious*.

"Tatsuya— No, Mr. Tatsuya. Your objection is reasonable. If you made the purchase under the conditions that it was an ongoing rental, then you have every right not to let someone else take it away. I'm sorry for asking the impossible."

"Don't be."

Tatsuya bowed a little himself to match Aoki's second dip. He'd answered with only a couple of words, barely a sentence, assuming that since Aoki's remark had been so reasonable, any other response would have come off as sarcastic. For now, the fact that he wasn't worried about it anymore seemed to have gotten through. This time, Aoki immediately raised his head without Tatsuya having to prompt him to.

"But I want you to understand. The mistress isn't after *your* 3H out of pure curiosity. She probably believes she needs it for some sort of research."

"I can understand that."

"I won't force you into doing anything. You probably feel just as strongly about needing to keep it at hand. But if you ever decide you'd be willing to let it go, would you be able to give it to her? We'd prepare suitable compensation in that case, of course."

It wasn't difficult to read between the lines of Aoki's proposal. Tatsuya figured his aunt didn't want Pixie passing into the hands of a third party.

"If you approved of this, then as collateral, we would make a yearly payment for ten percent of your purchase cost of 3H."

"Every year?"

But he hadn't predicted *this* proposal. It might not have been very much money for the Yotsuba, but it was a very generous offer from a regular societal perspective.

"Yes, every year. To be more specific, we would officially form a contract with you regarding a conditional purchase reservation that will automatically renew at a designated time each year."

And it wasn't just an oral promise—he was suggesting an official contract. For both Tatsuya and the Yotsuba, one-tenth of the purchasing expense wasn't that much money. His goal in forming an official contract was probably to stress ownership rights in case Tatsuya tried to renege on his promise. The offer gave a glimpse into how serious the Yotsuba—how serious Maya—could get.

"But as you're aware, I'm a minor."

"I'll make the necessary preparations with your father."

In other words, Aoki was saying he'd take on all the troublesome responsibilities if and when Tatsuya agreed to enter into this legally binding contract.

"I understand. I wouldn't mind it if it's just that."

There was nothing disadvantageous to Tatsuya in Aoki's proposition. So for now, he decided it would be better to compromise than push through with stubbornness and further harm his reputation with his aunt.

After seeing Aoki to the entrance, Tatsuya headed to the practice room. Second period was already half over, but he figured he'd at least be able to put in a record of attendance.

But he stopped right before entering the staircase near the door.

"Lina?"

He hadn't seen the transfer student in a while, and her face looked a lot more worn. Not that her cheeks were hollow or that she had rings under her eyes—there were no visible abnormalities. He couldn't detect anything that would have been harming her health.

But she lacked vitality. She seemed to be pretending to be the same as always, and someone who didn't know her very well would have been fooled by her gorgeous looks. But anyone who knew her even somewhat—including only so much as Tatsuya did—would see that something was wrong. They wouldn't be able to sense the overflowing energy that had once shone even more brightly than her radiant appearance.

She looked very mentally taxed.

She seemed like she was at her wit's end, driven into a corner.

Of course, that only gave her a more shadowy, more transient type of beauty, a charm that was the exact opposite of the kind she usually had. Tatsuya didn't have too much interest in what women looked like—or rather, he'd gotten completely accustomed to it—but even he had to think to himself that being beautiful had its perks.

"Tatsuya."

But that didn't mean the situation developed in a clichéd way, with his eyes being stolen and being late to react.

His name called, he made direct eye contact with her sapphire-blue orbs.

"Did you hear?"

"Yeah."

They were both referring to the information they'd gotten from one of the Seven Sages, Raymond. The one-sided message telling them to lure the parasites to the outdoor proving ground behind the school tomorrow night. They omitted quite a few words in their conversation, but neither doubted their intent was getting through just fine.

"Did you find out who?"

"No."

I suppose he didn't show his face to Lina, thought Tatsuya after hearing the answer. And that made sense in a way. If the USNA military found out one of the Sages' identity, they'd be sure to aggressively pursue him and his fountain of knowledge.

"Oh. That's too bad."

"I guess. But this time, it's okay," said Lina, pausing, directing a confrontational stare at Tatsuya.

"Tatsuya."

Her eyes shone.

Her gaze was strong. More purposeful than even that night they'd been trying to kill each other.

"I'm not going to be your friend."

He knew this already, but it really drove the point home for him. It wasn't about whether they wanted it or not. They never had the option of fighting alongside each other to begin with.

"I know. We live in different worlds, after all."

Tatsuya's answer was right out of a parting scene in a classic (read: stale) romance novel.

He'd purposely chosen a roundabout way of saying it that would be easily misunderstood just in case there were people eavesdropping.

He watched as Lina swallowed the abuse she was about to hurl at him. It had taken a moment, but she seemed to realize what Tatsuya was going for.

Still, her face had blood in it. Tatsuya sensed, for whatever reason, that the reason for her red cheeks was different from a moment ago.

"You're an idiot!" she spat, wheeling around on her heel.

Had she spoken those words to match Tatsuya's acting?

Or were they her true feelings?

Right now, Tatsuya only knew one thing. A sense of the situation alone, which brought with it resignation.

——He'd be staying late after school today for practice.

The main Yotsuba residence.

As Hayama was serving his master her afternoon tea, a soft electronic sound in his inside pocket told him he had a call. Seeing Maya nod, Hayama took out a classic flip phone–like audio terminal, unfolded it, and put it to his ear.

"Aoki? …Hmm. In other words, you've fumbled your job… It is true that you couldn't fulfill the mistress's command. Still, in those circumstances, I suppose you couldn't help it… I don't think it's that much to panic about. Mr. Tatsuya wouldn't break his promise over something like this… All right. I'll tell the mistress that… Yes, work hard."

"…What did Aoki say?" asked Maya after Hayama put his phone back in his pocket.

Hayama bowed his head to her, his expression implying something troubling had happened. "I'm terribly sorry, mistress. We have failed to acquire the 3H."

It was Aoki who had failed in his role. But Hayama was the chief steward—and, one might say, Aoki's direct superior. He felt sincerely ashamed at his subordinate's botched job.

Maya, though, didn't give an answer that stated clearly whether she forgave it or not. "I heard Tatsuya's name come up," she said, her interest instead on that point.

"He has informed me that the 3H in question has been purchased by Mr. Tatsuya," answered Hayama, trying to suppress a dry grin. "It seems Mr. Tatsuya has devised his own plan to keep the puppet from falling into the hands of others. Apparently, he has purchased its ownership rights while a rental agreement with First High is still in effect."

This was the exact same arrangement Maya had pointed out as the second-best thing in case she couldn't obtain Pixie.

"…I wonder if he's doing this on purpose. Or was it a coincidence?"

"I would not be able to say, madam."

Confusion rose to Maya's face, but she seemed to clear things up in her head within an instant. "…Yes. If Tatsuya will take responsibility for managing it, that's fine."

"Aoki seems to plan on forming a purchase contract should Mr. Tatsuya decide to let it go."

"Yes, that is quite fine."

Hayama bowed again to Maya, this time lightly. She probably had no intention of incriminating Aoki, to say nothing of Hayama, from the start, but he wanted to express his gratitude that she'd forgiven their carelessness.

"But I would still like to obtain a sample…" muttered Maya to herself.

With an *I can't leave this alone any longer* expression, Hayama offered his advice. "Mistress, I know I may not need to suggest this, but would it not be wise to refrain from aggressively pursuing connections with malefactors?"

A sardonic expression came across Maya's pretty features, which still had yet to wane with age.

"Because it wouldn't be pleasant to them?"

"Yes, madam."

"Well, they are important sponsors." Maya's lips curled in a mean grin, and Hayama gave a modest frown. "I know what you're trying to say, Hayama. I'm certainly not about to incite discord for no reason. I believe acquiring a parasite is necessary for the Yotsuba."

"Do you believe researching these demons, these parasites, will bring you closer to the mysteries of mental interference?"

"Yes. The Yotsuba have always been searching for the answer to the mystery: What is the mind? They say parasites are actually independent mental information bodies. The mind's makeup, its construction, its location… Will it not give us a hint in elucidating the mind's characteristics, even if only a small part of them?"

Understanding Maya's idea, Hayama bowed respectfully.

Maya nodded magnanimously and got back to the topic. "By the way, what have the demons been up to?"

"According to Mr. Kuroba's earlier report, the demons he *dealt with* at midnight the other day have evidently already come back to life."

"Already? That was very fast."

"They must have had a reason to hurry. Mr. Kuroba believes they may be preparing for war."

"I see… I suppose I don't need to ask who they're preparing for war *against*, do I?" asked Maya, a suppressed smile on her face.

"Considering their style, I would guess they can't leave a comrade imprisoned inside a puppet."

"At this point, I have to wonder if it's trouble that loves him—or if it's he who loves trouble."

It went without saying that Maya was referring to her nephew. Said nephew would doubtlessly deny that idea fiercely, but there was nobody present here, at least, who would voice an objection.

"Do we know when it will be?"

"Mr. Kuroba predicted that it will be in the First High environs tomorrow evening."

"*Environs* is certainly a careful word choice and very like Mitsugu to pick it… In that case, please tell Mitsugu to assign people there. As for the leader... Yes, Ayako should do nicely. Their goal isn't to fight, after all."

"Of course, madam."

Hayama clapped his hands to call for the maid assigned to serving Maya in his place, then headed for the telephone room to convey his mistress's words to Mitsugu.

It didn't bear repeating after all this time, but Mayumi Saegusa was preparing for exams.

Today was Saturday, February 18—one week until the Magic University's entrance exams. Her chance of not getting accepted was virtually zero, but it still meant this wasn't a period where she could worry about other things. It was fortunate, mainly for her mental state, that the vampire incidents had, at least on the surface, settled down.

After refreshing herself on her weak subjects in the school library, she returned home as the sun was about to set. When the young servant who came out to greet her seemed a little nervous, Mayumi figured things out immediately.

"Is Father back home?"

"Yes, my lady."

Mayumi showed the maid a smile and then headed for her own room.

At that time, in the study, the current head, Kouichi Saegusa, was looking at his confidant Nakura's face with an expression that didn't hide his displeasure.

"...Then what you're saying is the Stars' Sirius was the one who infiltrated counterintelligence Section Three and killed the parasites they had captive?"

"There is almost no doubt about it."

Even with his master's anger upon him, Nakura showed no signs of fear. His attitude was a polite one, but unlike the one Hayama assumed with Maya, Nakura's appeared somehow businesslike. Nakura was the man's confidant, but he wasn't a member of the Saegusa family; instead, he held what one would call a mercenary-like position. After all, he didn't serve Kouichi by being at his side at all times. He sometimes served as a bodyguard to the children, including Mayumi, and sometimes had orders to engage in not-quite-legal activities for information gathering and the like. That was how Kouichi treated the man of the Extra Numbers.

"I can't believe it," Kouichi spat. "She may be the Sirius of the Stars, but they let her break in that easily and then let their captives be killed? What a bad excuse for an intelligence department. Have we been relying on the wrong people?"

Nakura responded with a calm counterpoint. "The JGDF's intelligence department is by no means incompetent. They had set up a security system in the Section Three building that I predict even we would have had considerable trouble breaking into. The Stars simply had the upper hand last night. They don't call themselves the world's strongest magician unit for nothing."

Nakura *sounded* as though he were admonishing Kouichi, which made his expression grow even more displeased. Still, he hadn't lost his calm enough to shout at Nakura for it.

"Master, if you would allow me to speak out of turn, I believe this business has run its course. I do not think there any merit in the Saegusa continuing its involvement."

"...You're right." Kouichi was still calm enough to give due consideration to his associate's advice. "It seems the Kudou are active in this incident as well. I figured we might be able to recoup some of our lost forces, but it seems it's time to pull out."

"Yes, master."

"Order all mobilized members to return to normal duties. Nakura, you may leave now."

"Yes. Excuse me, master."

After a bow to Kouichi, who had picked up an encoded communicator, Nakura left the study behind.

Sunday, February 29, 2096 AD.

Lure out the parasites tonight. This information, which he'd gotten from across the sea, wasn't something Tatsuya trusted fully.

A boy named Raymond Clark being enrolled at the school Shizuku was studying abroad at was proven to be fact, after some investigation. His photographed picture saved on their high school's server matched the videomail caster's features.

But that alone wasn't a guarantee Raymond Clark was speaking the truth. In the same way anonymous tips weren't always just rumors, information with a name behind it wasn't always trustworthy.

However, Tatsuya had come here to First High's outdoor training area as indicated. He didn't have any other convincing clues.

He'd wait for them to come out. Or hope for a coincidence. With no other measures to take in the situation, it wasn't much different from wasting a day on bogus intel.

A man-made forest spread out behind the high school's exceptionally large property. Actually, this was technically part of First High's campus, but you couldn't tell it apart from a natural mountain forest. Even if you knew it was part of the school, it was hard to really feel it. Especially late at night when even visible outlines were dubious.

It was only just after 7:00 PM. The term *late at night* might not have actually been appropriate. But unlike the heart of the city, which suppressed the darkness with lights, there wasn't a single streetlamp in this forest. It had sunken into true darkness, making words like *nightfall* more appropriate.

There was a tall fence around the training grounds so that no outsiders would mistakenly enter. If a normal person—meaning, a civilian who couldn't use magic—wandered in while a magic shoot-out was happening, there was no telling what sort of tragedy could occur.

Still, even without the fence, there was almost no worry of townspeople setting foot in the proving grounds. Everyone, at least those living around here, knew it was First High's practice area.

Besides, none of the houses in the region were unrelated to magic. When First High was built here, the people with no connection to magic, those who couldn't use it, and those who didn't want anything to do with it, while not altogether forced to by the government, exchanged their homes for suitable compensation and moved themselves elsewhere. Those who remained were well aware of the dangers setting foot in a magic high school's outdoor practice grounds could bring.

That was part of why there were no security systems in particular here. They called it a proving ground, but it was really just a man-made forest. Nobody would be stealing anything from it, so they didn't need to spend the budget on preventing intruders.

"Can you all get over this?" Tatsuya asked his companions, looking up at the fence, which was about three meters high. The only entrance was a direct road from First High's back door, so since they'd left school already, they'd have to get over the fence. It was a simple matter to sneak into the training grounds from school, but it would have been hard to fool the surveillance systems monitoring the grounds from inside the building. They'd been put in place out of concern for burglars breaking into the campus through the practice area, but the systems watched not only for people getting *in* but also suspicious students escaping out of the school, onto it.

"Of course, Brother."

"I'm okay, too."

"This much is nothing."

Miyuki, Erika, and Leo answered Tatsuya's question.

"Yes."

At the end came Pixie's telepathy—as she'd been the one he'd actually asked.

His companions tonight included those three and the robot. ——Tatsuya hadn't originally planned to bring Miyuki along. Even Erika, with what had transpired previously—he'd intended to just tell her what happened later.

But as soon as they got wind of what was happening tonight, he realized it would be impossible to have them wait patiently for him. He hadn't really fought it, either, when Miyuki followed him when he'd left or when Erika had taken it upon herself to decide their meeting time. He knew his efforts would be in vain and that his time arguing would be wasted. After giving up, he actually went on the offensive and worked his friends into his strategy instead.

After turning his attention back to the proving grounds, he felt a stir in the forest air. It seemed the other actors had already gone up onto the stage.

Pretending to use his CAD—he hadn't forgotten his duty to secrecy, even at this stage—he called up the Jump spell from his memories, then went ahead and leaped over the fence first.

The four plus one proceeded through the vast artificial woods as one. They did not adopt the method of splitting up to search for their targets. In this vastness and this darkness, having just four people look around separately had no merits. It just increased the risk of them getting taken down one by one.

And they already had a guarantee from back at Aoyama that they didn't need to go out and search—*they* would come to them. There was a chance they would be more cautious this time and not appear, but there was no point thinking about that. If he didn't find the parasites today, he'd just go back to his routine search again tomorrow.

And Tatsuya had a premonition they'd show up.

It wasn't precognition.

Nor was it a logical deduction.

It was close to groundless, but Tatsuya went through the trees and foliage with a sort of conviction. His flashlight only illuminated a small portion of the ground, but nobody tripped over tree roots, alive or dead. For about fifteen minutes, the group went ever deeper into the forest at a normal pace, eyes peeled, looking to see if there were any new footprints. Until—

"Tatsuya, please wait."

Mizuki's voice came through the hands-free communicator hooked onto one of his ears. It was a conference call, so it was going out to everyone's receivers.

"I can see a parasite aura thirty degrees to the right of the direction you're moving."

Instead of going with Tatsuya and the others, Mizuki was using her "eyes" to navigate the four from the rooftop, where she had a good outlook on the training grounds.

"I see them, too! Three of them—two men, one woman."

With the aura light Mizuki had sensed as a guide, Honoka's spell took in an image from a camera. The image, acquired via her optical magic, sent a picture of them, clear as a photo snapped in the daytime from up close, into the camera lens, after which it wirelessly reached the information terminals of Tatsuya's group.

This search scheme would have been impossible without Mizuki and Honoka, who each had a singular talent even among magicians. Tatsuya had decided their usefulness was indispensable for tonight's mission, which is why he'd dedicated Mikihiko, a valuable part of their combat force, to guard them. Mikihiko didn't voice any complaints about the assignment, either. He knew it was a crucial role, and he was convinced he was the right person for the job.

"Oh! A girl in a mask is approaching the parasites from the opposite direction as you."

Another report came in from Honoka. The parasites' auras energizing must have been a result of trying to engage Lina.

Tatsuya used his hands to instruct his group to move. Miyuki, Erika, Leo, and Pixie nodded.

A moment later, Tatsuya was a wind rushing through the forest.

Erika followed hot on his heels, while Leo matched his running pace to Pixie's, his eyes darting right and left.

Tatsuya's group, the parasite party, and Lina plus her backup team.

Both Tatsuya and Lina thought that those were the three factions gathered here.

Tatsuya had known there was a group within the JGDF with their eyes on capturing the parasites, but he considered that group under the Saegusa family's influence. Because of the warning delivered through Mayumi, the Yotsuba's containment that was surely happening, and the devastating blow from Angie Sirius, Tatsuya had judged their ambitions shattered. He thought, at least, that they didn't have the time to get involved barely days after the fact.

However, in reality, there was a group moving in the shadows of the trees and scrub, closing in on both Tatsuya and Lina from the flank.

It was nicknamed the *Batto-tai*, a commando infantry platoon belonging to the JGDF's First Division and comprised solely of magicians specializing in hand-to-hand combat. As the nickname would imply, they didn't use any firearms, instead sticking only to sword device–based surprise attacks.

They'd been mobilized tonight because Tokyo was the First Division's jurisdiction and because the mission demanded stealth operations—and in addition to those points, they were also under the Kudou family's influence. In fact, that last reason might have been the biggest.

Tatsuya wasn't clairvoyant. There was no way for him to factor the unknown into his calculations, and as a result, it only made sense that he'd arrived at the wrong answer. He had no way of knowing that the Kudou elder had taken an interest in the parasites' value as weapons and sent in forces within just three days.

And then there was one more. One more person, to be exact.

A figure trailing the *Batto-tai* on their own.

Tonight, in the First High outdoor training grounds, five factions awaited an inevitable clash.

If nothing else, she would fulfill Sirius's mission as the Stars commander.

That was the only source of self-worth holding Lina up anymore.

It wasn't as though she'd never experienced setbacks before coming to Japan. During the Pentagon-operated educational programs for young officers, she'd only been able to get a C in algebra and biology. Furthermore, she was desperately behind the monstrous physical abilities of some of the other female soldiers her age, in the same group as her. And bluntly, she'd been awful during her training to operate vehicular devices.

But she'd never lost at magic.

The Stars commander, Angie Sirius.

One of the strongest magicians in the world.

That was how everyone praised her. She, too, had unfaltering confidence in her magical abilities.

But now, here in Japan…

She'd lost to those siblings.

Their first match had been at her pace.

Her retreat had been a planned action; in fact, she'd gotten away incredibly cleanly.

In their second match, despite being pinned down by Tatsuya's "kamikaze," she'd ultimately lost to an ambush. She'd lost in terms of the mission, but she hadn't lost in terms of magic.

But her one-on-one with Miyuki after that had ended in her defeat.

She'd had a disadvantage, sure, but even she knew she couldn't use that as an excuse. It had been a fair fight, and Miyuki had beaten her.

The defeat had kindled a renewed fighting spirit within Lina. She vowed not to let the defeat break her and swore to get even.

However—

When given the chance to do so...

She'd suffered a total defeat to Tatsuya.

She'd dragged him into a one-on-one and even used the Brionac. And she'd still lost.

She may have felt frustration toward him but not resentment or hatred. Tatsuya hadn't disgraced her—he hadn't even tied her up.

The fight itself had been a fair one, too. Actually, the conditions had been in her favor.

Tatsuya's magical abilities, and more than that his mental prowess, outclassed her own... Lina was convinced of that.

But that defeat had, without a doubt, also rocked her very raison d'être.

The world's strongest combat magician: Sirius. It was an indispensable billboard for the Stars to call themselves the world's strongest. Because of that, they selected the USNA's strongest magician, regardless of age or gender, to be the commander. If that magician wasn't in the military, they would devise a way to get them there and sit them in the seat.

There was virtually no possibility of her defeats getting out. Besides, Tatsuya, Miyuki, and whoever backed them were all avoiding it. Nobody related to that battle desired any damage to the Sirius "billboard."

But even though no third parties would find out about it, the hard facts were that she'd lost. In order to recover from that blunder, Lina needed to prove her ability to carry out the role of Sirius.

So that she could keep on being it.

For the girl who had gone away when she'd become Sirius, for the self that, once upon a time, could have been—for Angelina Shields.

By the time Tatsuya secured the site in his physical vision, Lina, her hair crimson, eyes golden, and face masked, was already facing off against the three parasites alone.

While the parasites repeatedly attacked with magic purely by willing it, without needing activation programs, Lina hadn't withdrawn even a step. She was 70 percent on the offensive and the parasites only 30 percent. But one of the parasites had a troublesome ability that seemed to be preventing her from landing a finishing blow.

The ability was pseudo-teleportation.

Magically speaking, it was categorized as a compound inertial-dampening/high-speed-movement spell.

Using its mobility and the nearby trees in the man-made woods, he would move in a three-dimensional manner, then immediately shower her in bullets and magic wherever he reappeared. The magic he used for his attacks had a low degree of influence, so they didn't present a threat to Lina considering her magic power. But that didn't mean she could let the enemy's attacks strike her defenselessly, either. Each time she deployed a defensive spell, her attack against another enemy would cut off—such was the situation she seemed to be in to Tatsuya at a glance.

He didn't intend to back Lina up, but Tatsuya stopped, then aligned his Dismantle with the parasite using the quasi-teleportation.

Most magicians took aim using their physical senses. Even when they used perception beyond them, they would aim for the target's coordinates.

That was normal. But Tatsuya could target their very *information*. Even if they changed their coordinate information at a dizzying pace, it wouldn't present an obstacle to him taking aim as long as he could perceive the values themselves.

To Tatsuya, quasi-teleportation didn't qualify as "dizzying."

"Leave this to me!"

But that didn't apply to just Tatsuya. Erika, who had caught up to him when he'd stopped, overtook him and triggered inertia control.

Quasi-teleportation was a threat when someone's hands, feet, or most importantly their eyes, couldn't catch up. Therefore, if the caster had greater speed than an opponent, the three-dimensional mobility granted by quasi-teleportation was nothing but pointless acrobatics.

With an integrated armament CAD in hand called Mizuchi-Maru, a downsized version of the Orochi-Maru she'd asked the Isori family to build and made (not asked) Tatsuya adjust, she accelerated in a straight line.

Her destination was the point the parasite, after kicking off trunks and branches, was about to land.

A rare level of kinetic vision, enough body control to stay balanced even when under the effects of an inertial-dampening spell, footwork that kept her feet on the ground without letting her float too much, and the insight to pinpoint the instant her opponent would land: that was her ability.

But as far as power level, the parasite probably had more magic.

But Erika's skills as a martial artist overthrew that difference.

The Mizuchi-Maru flashed.

There was no hesitation as she sliced her honed blade across the parasite's torso.

Tatsuya altered his partial dismantling spell, then shot through the parasite's limbs as it tried to ram a psychokinetic attack at Erika,

forcing it into a crawl. The swordswoman delivered the finishing blow with a backswing, and Tatsuya thrust his left hand out at the remains of the parasite's host.

Mikihiko had already laid down a barrier to block the parasite from escaping its host, from a simplified altar he'd constructed on the school rooftop. He had remained there not just to guard Mizuki and Honoka but so that he could use a long-distance barrier spell.

Still, the barrier's effects weren't perfect. It wasn't an issue of Mikihiko's skill but one of the spell's properties. Barriers were never spells meant to be constructed on the fly like this.

As long as the host didn't die, the parasite couldn't escape and flee. In other words, if the host died, the parasite would be able to escape his or her body. This meant they could put a corpse under their control but not capture the parasite. Now that Erika had killed the parasite, they had to deal with it before that happened.

A clump of pure psions fired from Tatsuya's palm, ripping psions off the parasite's main body. Actually, visually speaking, it was more like "blasting apart" than "ripping off."

After going over the results of the last battle, Tatsuya, Miyuki, and Mikihiko had reached a hypothesis. The parasites' core was a psycheon information body, held together by slender psion information bodies on the outside—like fibers, in a physical sense—that wove together with the psycheon core, meaning that each time one used magic, it consumed some of those psions.

It was too difficult for Tatsuya to destroy the main body's psycheons themselves. They'd verified that over the two battles.

But at the same time, he'd felt he'd been able to weaken them.

Likewise, Mikihiko couldn't seal a parasite in that state with his own strength, but he gave his word that he could as long as it was weakened, its magical power of resistance lost.

"Mikihiko!" Tatsuya called into the hands-free transmitter, part of the set with the receiver. But the act wasn't actually necessary.

Mikihiko knew the state of the battlefield thanks to Honoka's optical magic and Mizuki's "eyes."

As proof that Mikihiko was "watching" the place, the thin bolt of lightning jolted out of the sky at about the same time Tatsuya shouted. The lightning bolt struck the host body's remains, burning its skin to a crisp. The burn marks left on its skin depicted a regular pattern—a geometric one, with characters.

"That makes one!" cried Erika in exhilaration. And she may have been right—Tatsuya's vision hadn't given him a sight of an information body escaping the host. But he didn't have the time to celebrate with her.

He fired a farstrike at the parasite whose movement he'd stolen. The host body, its vital signs lingering, jerked and jolted.

A sealing bolt fell once more from the heavens. The body, writhing at Tatsuya's psion strike, stopped moving. That made two sealed demons.

Out of the corner of his eye, a different electric light sparked. It wasn't an ancient lightning spell but an electric attack from modern magic.

Lina's spell had burned the parasite's host body to black. That one was already an empty shell.

"One got away. Mizuki, can you see it?"

"I'm sorry, but I can't make out individual movements from here…"

His question, asked reflexively into his communicator, garnered a mournful response. It made sense, upon thinking about it a little: Mizuki was expanding her physical senses to see the invisible. It was no wonder she couldn't enlarge distant objects to see them.

"Oh. Sorry, that's okay. Don't worry about it," he offered in a supportive tone before turning a bitter face on Lina and Erika. "Angie Sirius."

Tatsuya could see the dismay behind the mask, and it probably wasn't an illusion.

"What?"

But it seemed she'd still talk to him. Her voice was different— probably another effect from Parade.

"Could you not kill them before we finish sealing them? The cleanup is going to be a *pain*."

He briefly sensed that she was dumbstruck. He didn't call it a "pain" because he liked putting himself in a bad light. He literally thought nothing more of a human's—well, things that used to be human—life or death. Lina probably sensed that instinctively. Still, her answer didn't change.

"Nothing to do with me. I just need to deal with the deserters."

She seemed to be carefully managing her tone. *But you still give everything away*, thought Tatsuya.

"Sirius's mission?" Tatsuya asked, changing subjects. "What I mean is, I want you to do that after we seal the parasites' main bodies. One of them already got away."

"That isn't part of my mission."

Lina was being more stubborn than ever before. Tatsuya hated having to negotiate with people who didn't want to listen to him. He was more the type of person who would tell someone to do whatever they wanted and, in turn, let *him* do whatever he wanted, but that still required them to listen in the first place. And this time was crucial. He continued his persuasion, stifling the urge to sigh.

"Your mission? That one you just killed looked like a pure-blooded Northeast Asian. Was he actually one of the deserters?"

Tatsuya wasn't convinced he was wrong. This was a bluff—he was trying to trick her into answering. But Lina was clearly disturbed. His guesswork seemed to be on the mark.

"…If they're assisting the deserters, they're just as guilty."

So Lina's stubborn attitude still didn't change.

"And also, these parasites are none of my concern. I only need to complete my mission—*and do the Sirius's duty*."

Leaving him with that, Lina disappeared into the forest.

Suppressing the impulse to shrug his shoulders, Tatsuya turned back to face Erika.

"Quite a star, eh?" Erika quipped. From the grin on her face, he realized it wasn't out of a grudge from what had happened three days ago, so Tatsuya responded with a chagrined smile.

After changing her smile to an elated one, Erika wiped it from her face altogether. "That... That was Lina, right? She looks like a completely different person."

"If she looks like a completely different person, why would you think it was her?"

"Her gestures, I guess. The way she carries her arms and legs, the way she shakes her head. And you can tell a lot from the eyes."

"I'm impressed..."

Tatsuya couldn't help but marvel at Erika's insight. Parade had changed all of Lina's features, from her facial shape to her build, but Erika had still identified tiny little characteristics. A person's skills, honed over many years, could be more magical, more miraculous than actual magic.

But he had to put his admiration aside at some point. "I'm sure you know this, but this is a secret, too. And I'd like to say the same thing I said to her to you."

"Not to kill them?"

"Exactly. You heard my explanation, right? As long as the host body doesn't die, the parasite can't get out of it. We can put up a barrier to block their escape, but nonlethally disabling them is more certain to do the trick."

Tatsuya's request was logical. Erika knew that, too.

"Sorry, Tatsuya. I just can't do that."

But now she was shaking her head, too.

"I've been prepared for my opponent to kill me ever since I decided I'd kill others with my sword. So when I think about me being killed... Well, I can't leave them alive on purpose and draw out their pain."

Her reason, though, was quite different from Lina's. It was personal and thus sincere.

"If we were rescuing them instead of killing them, that would be one thing. But sealing them is the same as killing them, isn't it? Even if they're not human, I don't want to make them suffer for long. I want to give them a swift death."

Her face, her eyes, showed no sign of eagerness. But she was certainly displaying a different sort of resolve.

"Well, can't argue with that."

Tatsuya considered killing an absolute form of theft and didn't think there was any difference between making them suffer before killing them and killing them before they suffered, given that they had the same end result.

But that didn't mean he was about to try to convince Erika.

Everyone had their own set of values. And some of them would never be up for discussion.

"I guess I'll just have to put in more work, then."

This parasite hunt wasn't worth him breaking that taboo.

As Leo was chasing after Tatsuya with lightning bolts and psionic lights flashing by, he stopped a moment before setting foot onto the battlefield. Almost at the same time, Miyuki stopped as well. It was such a sudden stop that Pixie, who had a robot body, stumbled a step or two forward.

"Saijou, be careful."

"That's my line."

One might have called his tone joking, but his eyes were darting left and right without cease.

"We're not exactly surrounded. Just feels like it, I think. My right hand's open. What do you think, Miyuki?"

It wasn't X-ray vision, infrared perception, or anything like that. Despite never having gone through this sort of training, Leo realized their opponent's trick just by sensing their presence—they were half-encircled.

"Let's go out to meet them."

Miyuki's answer was short and clear.

"…You're pretty gung ho about this."

It was firm enough that even Leo had to pause before responding.

"Am I? Still, there's no reason to be scared, is there? If this is too much for me, Brother will come to my rescue."

"Uhh, yeah, sure."

But secrets aside, it was a cute thing indeed.

Enough so that his eyes narrowed and he sighed.

"But I wouldn't want to bother Brother with too much…" she continued, as if to herself. Turning to face the brush to her left, Miyuki gave out instructions. "Pixie, stay behind me, all right?"

"Understood." The robot, which Tatsuya had ordered to obey Miyuki's commands, gave the minimum required response and moved to the position stated.

Miyuki held a portable terminal-type CAD in standby mode in her left hand. Despite having been next to her this entire time, Leo hadn't realized she'd ever gotten it ready. He looked at her with admiration and praise anew.

Unfortunately for Leo, his gaze never even entered Miyuki's mind. She completely ignored it actually, but right now, anyone other than her brother looking at her would automatically just slide off.

Her mind was on her enemies.

Miyuki's fingers moved smoothly. With her left hand holding the CAD, her thumb danced swiftly over the force-feedback panel.

She gave no warning of any sort. And then:

Small flashes of light melted into the forest air. Tiny droplets of ice fell onto trunks, branches, and the ground. It was a phenomenon called diamond dust. February, inland, nighttime, a mountain forest—it wasn't totally unfeasible considering the environmental conditions.

But nobody, friend or foe alike, misunderstood this as a natural occurrence.

The spell instantly created diamond dust in an area one hundred meters in radius. But this was neither an offensive spell nor a defensive one. Miyuki had simply placed the surrounding space into her sphere of perception just in case someone without clear hostility was to attack her.

Just by spreading a thin layer of event-influencing force, she could alter the weather conditions. Once before, during the Yokohama Incident in October, Mari had praised Miyuki's magic as possibly even strategic-class.

Part of that assessment was correct and part wasn't. Miyuki's magic wasn't *possibly* strategic-class—it *was*.

For Miyuki, skill in magic wasn't for increasing effectiveness. It was more for limiting and suppressing a range of influence.

——A power that, if unleashed with abandon, would bury the world in white for as far as the eye could see——

That was Miyuki's magic.

Presented with it, Leo actually started to panic.

For him, fights were a way to get your point across; for situations like Yokohama, when the opponent had no intention of listening to you, he'd use force to ask them to leave. Should the opponent come along trying to humiliate him and butt into his business, he would use his fists to let them know he wasn't cheap or easy. If someone he knew was being subjected to trouble, he'd get a little bit rough and make them go away.

It might have been a somewhat (?) violent way of talking things out, but fights were nothing more than a way to negotiate.

But this power Miyuki had wouldn't only blow off whatever it was the opponent was saying—it could blow off their very existence.

She wasn't a cat tormenting mice. She was an elephant stepping on ants.

It made him feel really sorry for their opponents. After all, it went against how Leo did things.

"Miyuki, I'll take these guys. Back me up until Tatsuya gets here."

In a world where thin fragments of ice piled up, a will to fight, pointing in a specific direction, sprang forth.

Not hostility but will. A sense of purpose with no negative emotion.

He was up against pros, incomparably better than street punks. But they would be a piece of cake for Miyuki. It probably wouldn't ever be a "conversation" in the first place.

"Oh? I'll leave it to you, then."

Miyuki readily took a step back at Leo's words, but the chill blanketing the forest stayed put.

Can't pull back now, thought Leo, pumping himself up.

From the shadows of the foliage, from inside the brush, men holding large knives and wearing field uniforms appeared, one after the other. After their numbers reached ten, the increase stopped.

At some point, the flashes in the direction of their travel had stopped and, with it, the sounds of fighting. The other group seemed to have finished up for now.

"Panzer," intoned Leo, the voice command for expanding an activation sequence.

You better get here soon, Tatsuya.

Ironically, that was the signal to go.

Without a word, without a sound, one of the soldiers charged in at him from the front.

The knife was thrusting at Leo before he had a chance to think how fast he was.

He repelled it with his left arm—

And that was when both Leo and the soldier gave each other astonished looks.

But that didn't lead to a delay of game. The soldier's left hand, the one not holding the knife, reached toward Leo's face.

Despite all the distance they still had between them, Leo obeyed his instincts and threw himself to the right.

A shock wave crashed by his face.

Eardrums—normal. Balance organs—slight damage.

Confirming the damage he'd taken, Leo rolled once on the ground and immediately stood. He'd wanted to get a little more distance first, but the opponent wouldn't make that easy.

Right after rising, the knife thrust at him again. If he'd kept rolling, the soldier would have leaned over him from above and that would have been checkmate.

As the blade's tip came toward the base of his shoulder—the soldier didn't seem to want to kill a civilian from his own country—Leo lifted an arm and caught it.

The piercing spell cast on the knife clashed with the hardening spell cast on his faux-leather sleeve.

The knife didn't reach Leo's skin, and Leo's fist rammed into the soldier's jaw.

It was a superb left hook.

His power defied logic, a result of genetic enhancement combined with assiduous training, and it did the illogical and knocked out a trained soldier in one hit. However, the other nine people didn't stop in awe.

Without skipping a beat, they came at him from the sides, knives drawn. He felt like he had his hands full with just one, but now it was two at once. To make matters worse, their weapons all sported blades of different lengths.

Even a famed swordsman would have had trouble parrying this combination. His reflexes might have been incredible and his motor nerves superhuman, but Leo was far from a master of the blade. To learn the *Usuba Kagerou*, he'd trained at the Chiba dojo, if only for a short period of time, and as a result, he had sword combat power that would rival some lower-ranked black belts. However, it was still only like forcing vegetables. He was being whipped around by a storm, and the abundant soil of his physical abilities wasn't enough. He could only do so much.

Believing in his own magic, he focused on the left-hand enemy.

He ejected the incoming blade on the right from his vision.

As the slender straight sword went for a spot under his clavicle, he threw his left hand up and bent it.

The flicker punch struck the opponent in the nose at about the same time the right-hand blade met with a hard-sounding *clang*.

"——Thanks for that."

Leo's flicker punch hadn't landed very heavily on the opponent's face. It was far from a decisive blow.

The two soldiers who had attacked him withdrew to a safe distance.

One of them was now unarmed. The knife he'd been holding lay at Leo's feet.

"Looks like they're a handful even for you, huh?"

Erika's katana had been the thing to knock his knife down.

"Well, looks like Miyuki had things covered even if I didn't butt in."

Leo's eyes swiveled around. Miyuki responded with a slight smile. It looked like if Erika's support hadn't made it in time, she would have frozen the enemy soldier's arm.

Leo secretly trembled.

"What happened to Tatsuya?" he asked, changing the topic to get rid of his weakness.

"He's taking the ones who went around to flank us," answered Erika in a purposely loud voice.

Sure enough, just as she'd ordered, a tremor rolled through the soldiers.

"Miyuki, Tatsuya says to go meet up with him."

"What about Pixie?"

Erika, who had been playing the observer from behind, responded to Erika's message with a slightly restless tone.

——It wasn't the time to be laughing, but the impulse still made it to Erika's throat.

"Pixie will help us. Pixie, you got an order from Tatsuya, right?"

"Confirmed an order from master, along with permission to use psychic power."

"There you have it. Miyuki, you can just leave this one to us!"

Despite the situation, Erika decided to goof off, feigning total relaxation.

"I will, then. Thank you," answered Miyuki shortly, running off without turning back around.

"Huh... Does she know where he is? Thought she had a brain in there."

"Well, you know how those two are," said Leo, a fearless grin on his face, completely unlike before—though he'd have vehemently denied as much given the chance. "Anyway... Gotta keep up our end of the bargain. Let's get this over with, eh?"

Without noticing the change in Leo, or maybe just not pointing it out, Erika repositioned the Mizuchi-Maru, and then—

"No, that's enough, Erika. Lower your sword."

A new actor came onstage.

Erika sucked in her breath.

A tall figure came out of the web of darkness in the man-made woods.

"Brother Tsugu..."

It was Erika's older brother—Naotsugu Chiba.

◇ ◇ ◇

Tatsuya hadn't called Miyuki to his side because he was worried about her. It wasn't necessarily wholly without such a factor, but the reason he was conscious of, at least, was different. He'd detected a situation occurring that Erika's and Leo's abilities wouldn't be able to deal with. And his thought was that he needed Miyuki's power to respond.

And a situation exactly like what he'd predicted had, in fact, happened.

Right behind him, Miyuki gasped—at the carnage spread out before her brother.

In front of him lay groups of JGDF soldiers in groups of twos and threes. Tatsuya and the others weren't aware, but these combat personnel were from a team under the Kudou family's influence. Eight of their ten were corpses, and the other two were heavily wounded to the point where they couldn't stand. In other words, they'd been wiped out.

Tatsuya hadn't been the one responsible for these results.

It had been the parasites Lina was now engaging.

"Lina, get back!"

"Nobody asked you!"

Tatsuya hadn't simply been viewing the fight, either. Far from it—he was in the middle of the engagement, too.

Lina charged at the group. The parasites stood six strong. Given the number they'd already finished off, they'd increased beyond what Pixie had told him.

With just six normal opponents, one could have made the case. The name Sirius wasn't for nothing, and the Sirius's central mission was to *handle* deserted magicians. Anti-magician combat was practically the Sirius's specialty. Normally, the Sirius having trouble against this few people would have been impossible.

And yet Lina was struggling. If not for Tatsuya continuously dismantling all the spells attacking her, they might have gotten her already.

Lina's greatest weapon was her spell activation speed.

It was so overwhelming that even if she started late, she'd still take down her opponents without letting them do anything. That was Lina's specialty and her style. She favored a handgun armament device because it matched this style.

But the parasites could literally use magic just by thinking it.

Just envisioning something turned it into magic.

The fact that they didn't need activation sequences or other trigger mediums meant they had the same characteristics as psychics.

It wasn't only the parasites' strong points that matched—their weaknesses were similar to those people as well. It was the lack of variation in the abilities they could use. There must have been a limitation on the images these monsters could manifest but for a different reason than humans.

The system of modern magic was advanced on the concept of increased variety being a merit. By sacrificing the speed psychics had, it granted versatility and stability. Many experiments and tests had proven this to be a beneficial change. That was why they'd pressed onward in that direction.

But the benefits applied to small groups and individuals being able to react to a myriad of situations. In cases where one had to focus on a restricted response, such as "defeating detected enemies," speed still had great meaning.

CADs had unquestionably been developed as tools to allow both speed and versatility. But the mere fact that a subtype existed called "specialized CADs," which sacrificed versatility to prioritize speed, spoke to how much of an advantage speed was.

These parasites already excelled in speed—and now, instead of three of them, there were six.

One couldn't call that simply twice the threat.

According to Lanchester's second law, the difference in combat strength in a ranged firearms battle occurring within a visual space (the perceivable area) was proportional to the square of the number of soldiers (weapons, or discrete units of combat power). If you applied this law to magical battles, if the number of possible magic activations at a discrete time was one to three, the combat power would be one to nine, a difference of eight. If the number of possible magic activations was two to six, the combat power would be four to thirty-six, a difference of thirty-two.

It was a very large difference in the number of people.

Tatsuya and Lina could take on multiple opponents because they could overcome the numerical difference with a higher number of possible magic activations at a discrete time. With this option unable to put them at an advantage, both of them were forced to prioritize defense. Tatsuya in particular had been completely shut down, only able to dismantle the spells flying at him and Lina.

He'd called Miyuki here because he'd predicted a situation like this beforehand.

"Miyuki!"

"Yes, Brother!"

Those were the only words they exchanged.

Miyuki fully understood what her brother wanted from her just from him calling her name.

A high-pressure, event-influencing force shot out from Miyuki's body—more specifically, from the coordinates that her body inhabited.

Area Interference.

An anti-magic spell that, rather than defining the result of an event alteration, simply applied a force of influence to a specific region.

In other words, a spell that wouldn't let *others* alter events. A trick to disable all spells *except her own.*

Lanchester's second law worked when you could quantify attack power against interspersed targets. You couldn't apply it to overwhelming surface suppression, since you couldn't measure that on the same scale.

Miyuki's Area Interference created a zone that was empty of

magic, whereas Tatsuya and Lina built narrowed, thin spells with high density.

They possessed enough influence to overcome Miyuki's Area Interference. They would have had trouble launching a direct attack on her while under the effects of it, but otherwise, they could still go through the activation process for spells, even if their number and speed was low and their effects were dampened.

But the parasites didn't have the event influence to rival the two of them—no, the three of them.

Tatsuya and Lina fired a volley of spells.

Lina's had six targets. Tatsuya's spell had twelve. Half of his were to dismantle Lina's spells, since she was trying to kill the parasites' host bodies, but his Program Dispersion only made it in time for half of the magic programs Lina fired.

As a result...

Three of the parasites were killed by Lina's magic, and three of the parasites self-destructed after Tatsuya's magic pierced them.

Sword magicians.

This nickname was given to the Chiba family when they'd established close combat techniques that mixed swords and magic together before anyone else could.

Close combat techniques using magic wasn't exactly a Chiba family patent, though.

Chronologically, magic martial arts were created earlier, by the Stars before they'd split from the Marines. Even the New Soviet Union had developed a melee-magic combat style colloquially called Command Sambo, based on military hand-to-hand combat techniques. (This quickly died out, however.) Areas around Delhi in the north of the Indo-Persian Federation during its period of formative upheavals saw the birth of a set of melee weapon techniques that used traditional short swords called jamadhar, improved in a modern style.

However, these magic-combined close combat techniques created outside of Japan were all, as far as was known, developed as a way to supplement firearms or spells used as projectile weapons. Their chief form came in close-quarters situations, where they could exhibit attack power rivaling that of firearms or defensive power to nullify them.

In contrast, the Chiba family's systematized *kenjutsu* was a set of techniques with its main emphasis on close combat using swords. You would cast magic on yourself to jump from firearm range into sword range, then use a sword, which had more offensive power than bare hands or a knife, to quietly and swiftly slay the enemy. The techniques were excellent in terms of surprise and stealth, and they gave Japan's military and police force a large advantage during urban guerrilla warfare and anti-terrorist operations.

Kenjutsu by itself wasn't something the Chiba family had developed. At about the same time Japan began researching military applications for magic, various magicians had tested the idea of linking it with sword techniques to varying degrees of success. The Chiba family had just systematized everything to make it easier to learn.

However, the act of systematizing something so that it was easier to pass down elevated "techniques" into "technology." For technological proliferation, this meant something revolutionary. The previous head of the Chiba family was praised as a modern Kamiizumi Nobutsuna, and out of respect for his deeds, the family became known as the sword magicians.

With that historical background, they said that 70 to 80 percent of all magicians now foot soldiers in the army or working as riot police had once studied the Chiba's *kenjutsu*.

The JGDF's First Division's commando infantry platoon, nicknamed the *Batto-tai*: They belonged to the Kudou family's faction, but they were also a close combat team that used swords and close combat magic. Some of them had been trained in the Chiba style for an exceptionally long time.

For them, the Chiba family was their collective sword master. They might not have known about Erika, since she'd never appeared at a public function, but they sure did know of Naotsugu, famous as the Kirin Child of the Chiba. In fact, they more than knew of him—this team's commander had experienced sword fundamentals training from Naotsugu himself.

Thus…

"The acting master…"

When Naotsugu appeared from nowhere, they froze, and they had a good reason for it.

Since Naotsugu was still a student, the official officer in charge of this team held rank over him.

But right now, it was the ranking of a martial family that held sway over this place.

With the team stopped, Naotsugu passed beside them, coming to face his stepsister.

Erika winced.

But she immediately met Naotsugu's gaze with a strong one of her own.

It might have been an empty display, but for Erika, and more so for Naotsugu, this was epoch making.

Erika pitted against Naotsugu.

They weren't actually pointing their swords at each other. Both had their weapons aimed at the ground.

Nevertheless, emotionally, their blades were pointed at each other.

Naotsugu had realized his stepsister sometimes depended on him. And he knew he couldn't blame her for it.

The way he saw it, children weren't strong enough creatures to live without anyone to lean on. He was the same. That was why he knew he didn't have the right to tell anyone else to grow up, to stop relying on others so much. At least, that was how he thought of it.

Normally, you had parents. Children could depend on their parents unconditionally.

But that didn't apply in Erika's case. Her mother was frail, and her father never wanted to play the role of parent in the first place.

Naotsugu actually hated his father in his own right, too. When he'd worked himself heart and soul over what Erika would call "cheap tricks," it was partly to get back at his father. For some reason, his older brother and older sister didn't see their father's abdication of his parental responsibilities as anything strange. In fact, Naotsugu had reason to believe they considered it rightful as a leader of one of the Hundred.

Maybe Naotsugu had felt a sense of camaraderie with this younger stepsister of his. That was why he, and nobody else in the family, treated her kindly, sometimes spoiling her, sometimes encouraging her, and letting her depend on him.

But, thought Naotsugu, it seemed the time had come for her, too, to grow up.

As a test, Naotsugu let out a burst of sword *ki*. It was a technique called *ki-atari*, but when a high-leveled magician did it, an opponent could, if they thought they'd been cut, actually experience line-shaped bruises or literally have their skin sliced.

Erika repelled Naotsugu's *ki* with *ki* of her own. She hadn't dodged it or diverted it—she'd fought back directly.

A smile appeared on Naotsugu's lips despite himself.

His right arm rose.

By the time it was visible that he'd lifted his weapon, the blade was already swinging down at Erika.

It wasn't so fast the eye couldn't even see it.

It was a speed born of skill, of having only the bare minimum amount of windup, so little that the borderline between windup and the actual motion was imperceptible. A technique that lied to your face and plunged into a blind spot in the opponent's perception. The sword of a genius, which itself became a technique through the mere movement of hands and feet.

Erika's katana caught Naotsugu's slash.

He had planned to stop right before landing the strike, but he hadn't held back. Erika had blocked his early attack with superb reaction speed and swiftness of blade.

The smile that came to Naotsugu's lips had now changed into a very clearly ferocious grin.

The tension apparent in Erika's eyes grew thicker.

She held her ground, pushing Naotsugu's single-handed katana back with both her hands.

Suddenly, the pressure disappeared.

Without wasting a moment, Erika pulled back.

Brother and sister faced each other once more, neither even needing to regroup.

Naotsugu whirled around, showing his back to her.

Caught off guard, an "empty gap" appeared in Erika's stance.

But no attack came to take advantage of it.

"Brother Tsugu…?"

Without answering her dubiousness, Naotsugu directed his *ki* at the *Batto-tai*.

He could sense their consternation. They'd adopted stances of their own, but as far as Naotsugu could tell, their reactions were slower than Erika's had been.

——There was nothing appealing about them.

The smile vanished from Naotsugu's face.

"I am Naotsugu Chiba, second lieutenant in reserve, from the Academy of Defense's special combat techniques graduate course."

With his katana still lifted in front of him, Naotsugu announced only his attachment, his rank, and his name. (As for why he'd been given the rank of second lieutenant despite still being in school, and a second year, and in the reserves: It was an exceptional treatment even considering he was a magician and spoke fully to the fact that he had the achievements to back it up.)

"I am currently on a mission to protect civilians targeted by terrorists. I ask for your attachment, your ranks, your names, and your objective!"

Erika and Leo exchanged glances. Naotsugu's attitude seemed to have turned on a dime.

"If you have been mobilized with the objective of harming civilians, I warn you that this is an act of treason against our democracy, and I will stand my ground and stop you from doing so."

Someone from the Ten Master Clans or Hundred Families bringing up the democracy like this was deceitful, in a way. They pursued benefits for magicians more than benefits for the nation.

That was what Erika thought of his speech. To be honest, Naotsugu himself didn't exactly believe what he said, either.

But the spirit and energy he was emitting hadn't even the slightest disturbance.

With his sword thrust toward them, the situation entered a state of deadlock.

The stare down between Naotsugu and the *Batto-tai* broke down after an explosive psion emission happened a short distance away.

"Erika, Leo, be careful!"

"The parasite's main body is over there!"

Voices, speaking quickly and slightly tangled up, betraying panic, came to them from their communicators.

The voices belonged to Mikihiko and Mizuki.

For a report, it was imperfect.

"Brother Tsugu! It looks like the parasite's main body is heading this way!"

But Erika accurately deduced what they wanted to say. In turn, the *Batto-tai* actually showed more caution than Naotsugu when she said that.

On second thought, it was highly possible Naotsugu hadn't been briefed on the parasites in detail. Erika faltered, then panicked, trying to think of how to explain the threat they presented.

Her mind, having spread a net of caution out in all directions, even under her feet, now turned to Naotsugu.

It struck at that very moment. Had it precisely timed it like this, or was it a coincidence?

Behind Erika, the ground suddenly erupted. A figure leaped out from underground with a spray of dirt.

"Doton?!"

That shout had come from Leo. Aside from the five *tonjutsu* techniques, which were known as being *commonplace*, *ninjutsu* as an ancient magic style handed down reconnaissance, escape, and surprise attack spells that used the five elements—wood (*moku*), fire (*ka*), earth (*do*), metal (*kin*), and water (*sui*)—as a medium. This five-elemental idea had come from mainland China, from the *main family*, and it passed down a plethora of many kinds of ancient magic spells using those elements as a medium. It had more variations than *ninjutsu* and Japan's *onmyou-jutsu* (yin-yang techniques), but because of how famous *ninjutsu*'s five *tonjutsu* techniques had become, the spell using those five elements as mediums tended to be called by their Japanese names internationally: *mokuton*, *katon*, *doton*, *kinton*, and *suiton*.

The important thing was that this spell, which you could use to spring an ambush from underground, wasn't restricted to *ninjutsu*. It was perfectly possible that it was some ancient magic from mainland China. But now wasn't the time to figure out which it was, nor was there any time to do so.

The man's target as he fluttered up from underneath the ground wasn't Erika, but Pixie, who was on the opposite side of her.

The assailant from underground swung his blade, which was like a thick billhook, at Pixie.

"Schild!"

Leo jumped out before he could hit. With his left hand, he caught the man's billhook perfectly on his hardened CAD protector.

"Leo, that's a parasite!" Mikihiko warned.

Leo swung his left arm around, knocking back both the billhook and the parasite holding it.

He hadn't directly touched the opponent's body—he knew better from his bitter experience of having his spirit energy taken. But even Leo's physical strength couldn't put enough distance between them just by knocking the weapon away.

The parasite swung its billhook again.

But the demon never got started running.

Instead, a katana tip appeared, protruding from its chest.

Having pierced the parasite's chest with the Mizuchi-Maru, Erika made an *oh, crap* expression. She'd probably just remembered how Tatsuya had cautioned her not to kill them. She'd snubbed his words at the time but now seemed to have taken them to heart.

Underground wasn't the only possible attack route. The very instant Naotsugu had turned his gaze on the pillar of earth that sprang up behind Erika, one of the soldiers *jumped* out from behind the rest of the *Batto-tai* with an unsheathed sword in hand.

He'd looked like a soldier, but that had been an illusion. The man, dressed in deep blue garments to blend into the dark, stole one of the *Batto-tai*'s katanas and shot toward Pixie. His leap was enhanced with a weighting-type spell. Instead of going through an arc, his body fell with acceleration exceeding gravity.

But his uplifted blade never reached its target. Naotsugu had kicked him away during his descent. It was a splendid flying kick, not at all what one would expect from a *kenjutsu* practitioner. His form was beautiful, the kind you'd want to adapt for a karate dojo poster.

In the past, Erika had criticized Naotsugu for wasting his time with "cheap tricks," but he was experienced in many things, not just magic but martial arts as well.

A murmur came from the *Batto-tai*. The soldier whose katana had been stolen was down. This man had probably hit him with an attack.

Naotsugu felt that his kick had done enough, so with careful steps, he walked toward the man on the ground. The man was skilled enough not to let even Naotsugu realize his intent until a moment before the attack landed. There was no being too careful here.

His caution, his deliberation, was immediately rewarded.

Once Naotsugu had drawn within three steps, the man's body suddenly burst apart. Naotsugu quickly jumped back, but he couldn't avoid the spraying blood.

It was such an unexpected development that even Naotsugu was at a loss. Behind him, Erika and Leo were grimacing as well. The *Batto-tai* was dumbstruck. Everyone present missed how clumps of psycheons wrapped in psions escaped, one each, from the man whose chest had been pierced and the body that had blown up.

"Pixie, get over here!"

Tatsuya's harsh voice, audible through their transmitters, broke the spell.

"At once, sir."

Pixie began to run toward Tatsuya—in the direction of the psionic wave explosion and the direction Miyuki had run off in.

"Honoka, you back up Pixie."

Tatsuya's voice sounded again from the voice communication unit, which was set to conference call mode.

"Right!" came Honoka not a breath later.

"Erika, Leo, stay where you are. Tell the others there, too."

"Huh…? Okay."

"R-right."

Erika and Leo responded with shaky voices.

Above them, the two clumps of psycheons and psions began to move like a cloud, drifting after Pixie as she ran.

"Honoka, you back up Pixie."

"Right!"

When Tatsuya's instructions came flying through her receiver, Honoka agreed without skipping a beat. ——Then, after replying that she'd do it, she realized she had no idea what, in this case, "backing up" meant.

It was a very Honoka-like problem to have, as was the way she dealt with it. To back Pixie up, she had to get a good read on her situation first, so she connected a visual pathway to the robot using optical magic.

Attempts sometimes go easier than expected.

Bad choices occasionally brought good results.

There were a lot of expressions and interpretations, but her choice coincidentally opened a psion circuit from her to Pixie.

A total of twelve parasites had been drawn into this world.

One of them had possessed a human-shaped chore-assistance robot, a Humanoid Home Helper 3H type P-94 nicknamed Pixie.

Two of them had been sealed during today's battle.

During the battle, Lina had killed four of their hosts and Erika one, releasing their main bodies.

The remaining four had self-destructed to release themselves.

Nine—that was the number of parasites that had lost their host bodies and were now assembled here. The number of demons drawn together to Pixie, exposing their main bodies.

They were psycheon information bodies summoned to this dimension from another one.

Originally, they were twelve in one "consciousness." Now that their main bodies were exposed, they tried to return to their singular state.

Nine parasites had already combined.

A protean information body with one consciousness but nine wills.

The structure was like nine branches coming from one trunk. If one had the ability to "see" psycheons, one would have seen something akin to an orochi, this nation's most famous monster, with one extra head.

And now it was trying to absorb one more fragment of itself.

A huge serpent, rearing its nine long necks, trying to devour Pixie.

Pixie resisted with a barrier from her own "will."

This will had been shared with her by the one who had molded her, the human known as her "mother." Even now, things were flowing into her through a psion circuit, mixed in with the psions.

A will: that the self was not part of "that thing."

A will: that she didn't belong only to herself.

A will: that she belonged to "him."

Any will derived from an individual would not normally have been able to oppose "that thing."

But Pixie's "mother" Honoka was not normal.

She was a descendant of Elements. The inheritor of the "light" Element's blood.

The Elements were the first magicians this country had tried to create, even before developing the Numbers. At the time, the classification and systematization of four families and eight types hadn't yet been established. At the time, people instead thought an approached based on more traditional elements—earth, water, fire, wind, light, lightning—would be more effective. They advanced the Elements' development based on this concept.

However, when the system of four families and eight types was established, magician development based on traditional elements was deemed inefficient, and development on the Elements stopped.

One may say that alone was a story seen all over the world in the hidden histories of magician development. But in the Elements' case, there was something aside from magical talent they gave them, something innate—or, at least, had tried to give them.

The dawn of magician development research. An age where those in power were so fearful of magic as to be superstitious.

Those in power who had decided to develop the Elements wanted a guarantee that these artificial "wizards and witches" would never turn against them. They ordered the scientists to program into their genetic code a factor of absolute submission to their master.

Did personalities get passed down?

This was still a subject of debate that worried geneticists and psychologists, one for which no answer had been found.

Even identical twins could grow up with completely different personalities. Given this fact, many would be willing to conclude that personalities must not be genetic.

On the other hand, if one looked at vertical bloodlines such as parent and child, grandparent and grandchild, great-grandparent and great-grandchild, there would be a trend of similarity that one's environment couldn't merely account for, and that couldn't be ignored.

The genetic engineers went along with the task set forth by those in power and took whatever measures they'd been able to.

As a result—though it wasn't even certain that it was a result—a certain tendency could be found at a high percentage among descendants of the Elements.

Dependency.

One could observe at a large probability a trend in which the person would aggressively depend on a specific other person, in most cases of the opposite gender.

The descendants of the Elements themselves considered it their destiny, engraved into their DNA.

Perhaps they could use that excuse to forgive themselves for depending on others.

But their "dependency" was not a "weak" emotion seen in the rest of the world.

It was, in other terms, "loyalty."

An unbending belief that one belonged to another.

And it was strong enough to repel the collective will of these combined demons.

This was the point at which Tatsuya was engaging the parasites and the point at which Erika had confronted Naotsugu.

Pixie was fighting "the thing," withstanding it, at a point exactly halfway between those two.

When Tatsuya arrived at that point, he saw the nine-headed dragon, heads reared and trying to devour Pixie.

He didn't understand the psycheon information body's structure. But he knew it was *there*. And he could *see* anything that existed.

Nine psycheon information bodies were combined into one at the base, trying to absorb Pixie with its nine-branched interface. In Tatsuya's head, that matched up with his image of a nine-headed dragon.

"What is *that*?!" cried Lina in surprise, who for some reason had followed him.

"You can see that?"

"I can't…really, but I just know. There's a giant power pressing down on that doll. Tatsuya, what on earth is that?"

"The result of you not listening to what Brother told you."

It was Miyuki, not Tatsuya, who answered Lina. Her voice was brusque and below freezing. Lina kept her mouth shut for now, even though it riled her up.

"Brother told you not to kill them, but you went around killing every parasite host body in sight without a second thought. Now they're free—and on a rampage. How exactly do you plan on making amends for this mismanagement?"

But this time, she couldn't stay quiet. "What do you mean *mismanagement*? I was just carrying out my mission!"

"Then the least you could do is clean up after yourself. Can you do that? Even Brother is stuck with having to seal them—a passive method."

Ever since the previous battle in this outdoor training ground, an air of storm itself had been drifting between these two beautiful girls.

And into that storm now came words of provocation.

"Just watch, I'll do it!" she shouted, accepting the impossible task.

"Wait, Lina!"

This was too much—he had to stop her. It was far too reckless to dive into the fray when you didn't have a good countermeasure for the opponent.

That was what Tatsuya thought when he tried to soothe her.

"Shut up! You be quiet, Tatsuya!"

But he was thrown upon his own resources.

"I need to finish this mission successfully! If I don't, then what am I even doing here?!"

Lina's fit of anger wasn't only directed at Tatsuya. He understood that, too, after hearing her shout.

When she said "here," she wasn't just referring to this location. No, she was referring to the fact that she—Angie Sirius, not Angelina Shields—was here now, in this situation, in this position.

Before he knew it, the gold had returned to her hair and the blue to her eyes. Even exposure to Miyuki's Area Interference hadn't canceled it, and now she did so on her own.

She was giving everything she had as Angelina Shields to carry out Angie Sirius's duty. She was trying to remain the Sirius.

After getting a glimpse of the burdens she bore, Tatsuya faltered over his next words. During the time, Lina unleashed every spell she had at her disposal.

A rainbow of magic, each one firing after the other, all ending in vain.

It was to be expected.

Lina's magic was for altering physical events. She didn't have spells that could affect mental bodies.

The thing's consciousness pointed toward Lina. Tatsuya immediately "saw" it, as though its nine heads had turned upon her.

Instantly, a magical storm was upon them.

Tatsuya had to rally every last bit of his power to shoot it down.

When he'd fought the parasite in its information body form at First High, he'd only been up against one, which had possessed a single human.

And he'd struggled that much against it.

This time, there were nine times as many.

It gave him no time to use his farstrike.

Not only that—Tatsuya wasn't the only one bearing out against the thing's vehement assault. Behind him, Miyuki was maintaining a spherical Area Interference field where the thing likely existed. But though she may have had the sense of touch to detect psycheon information bodies, she didn't have the sense of *vision* to get a bird's-eye view. Because of that, the area of interference was necessarily slipping out of position. But if she created a field to cover the entire area, she'd end up blocking Tatsuya's Program Dispersion, too.

With the desperate conflict continuing, it would be too much of a risk to go for any plan that had even a slight chance of whittling down their combat power.

He felt a firm tug on the back of his blouson. Miyuki was feeling anxious, too.

They knew that if the parasites "consumed" all their magic now that they were outside their host bodies, they would eventually lose their strength. But it was extremely taxing to think about holding out in a situation you didn't know how long you'd have to hold out for.

At this rate, Miyuki and Lina might give in before the thing did.

Because of her earlier recklessness, Lina was already holing up inside an Information Boost shell and staying there.

None of them could make an effective attack. The handicap was too high.

Magic that interfered with physical events wouldn't work.

Physical attacks were out of the question.

If they had any chance, it was magic that affected the mind...

...*It's the only way left.*

Tatsuya gritted his teeth, then resolved himself on a gamble.

"Mikihiko, can you see what's happening here?"

"Yeah. I'm in the middle of really quickly making a sealing circle, so wait just a little longer."

There was more panic in the voice coming over his voice communication unit than in Tatsuya's. "How likely is it that the sealing circle will suppress all this?"

In response, a short silence.

"...To be honest, probably less than fifty-fifty."

And a bitter confession.

Hearing this answer didn't make Tatsuya think of Mikihiko as weak. Tatsuya would know better than him that they couldn't make rash promises against something like this, since he was the one confronting it directly.

"Mikihiko, it only needs to be for a moment. Ten seconds—please just suppress it for ten seconds!"

It was Tatsuya's first-ever plea to someone.

So not only Mikihiko gasped but everyone else listening to the call.

He gave nothing to explain himself—just a request to "do it." One could call it reliance on others, in a bad way.

But it could only be done when one trusted the other.

"...*All right.*"

Mikihiko, at least, felt that way.

"I'll suppress that thing for ten seconds, no matter what it takes. I'll give a countdown, so you do whatever you need to do."

He knew Tatsuya must have had some sort of plan, and he needed ten seconds for it.

He knew his power was necessary to secure that time.

The trust Tatsuya had placed in him was rousing.

"Tatsuya, I'll help, too!"

Honoka's earnest voice followed after Mikihiko's. She wasn't trying to one-up him. She was of one emotion: the desire to help.

"Great. Mikihiko, start the countdown."

"Okay... Three, two, one, now!"

As he called out "now," Mikihiko fired his anti-demon spell, Garudaflame.

Its "flames," independent information bodies, coiled around the thing, the nine-headed parasite amalgamation. It was as though two draconic serpents were trying to devour each other.

From below, Pixie put more strength into her thoughts, trying to push the thing away. Psions came in to replenish her own expended ones at the same rate they left. Honoka seemed to have mastered the art of supplying psions to Pixie.

Tatsuya didn't just sit there watching, of course.

As Mikihiko gave the signal, he reached behind his back with his left arm, the one not gripping a CAD.

With that arm,

* * *

he took Miyuki's waist,

and pulled her in tight.

"...!"

A silent yelp. Maybe it was actually a cry of joy.

In that moment, Miyuki's Area Interference and Tatsuya's Program Dispersion both ended, but Mikihiko and Honoka were suppressing the thing just like they'd promised Tatsuya.

Miyuki, now hugged in Tatsuya's arm, looked up at him with a blank, utterly surprised face.

As she stood on her tiptoes, looking at him at point-blank range, he drew closer still to her face.

Their foreheads touched,

their gazes melted into each other,

and with their noses close enough to graze each other, their lips almost about to meet...

"Miyuki, *look!*"

Tatsuya whispered firmly into his sister's ear.

An invisible light flowed into Miyuki from Tatsuya.

An invisible light flowed into Tatsuya from Miyuki.

Two auras revolved between them.

"*I can see it*, Brother!"

Those words may not have been from her lips—her mind may have spoken them.

Their communication lasted but a moment.

Half the ten seconds they'd been given were still left.

Tatsuya's left hand pulled Miyuki's head to his chest.

Miyuki's hands pressed against it, too.

Tatsuya's right hand showed her the way.

And that thing was now displayed in Miyuki's mind.

Tatsuya's power to "see" information bodies.

Miyuki had used Tatsuya's "eyes" to perceive the creature—

—and now that the seal had been undone, she unleashed her natural magic.

The exotyped mental interference spell Cocytus.

A spell to freeze minds.

Miyuki's spell applied directly to the mind, and it froze the psycheon information bodies...

...and the vessel-less thing shattered and scattered into the void.

[17]

Even Lina, who didn't have the senses to perceive a demon's main body, sensed the thing in its destruction. The ball of "information" stopped, frozen, and then shattered. If controlling psion information bodies in the information dimension was what made a magician, then the Sirius, one of the highest-level magicians, would have certainly noticed the huge amount of psions spraying everywhere during the main body's collapse.

"Lunar magic…?"

And even if she couldn't personally use mind-interfering magic, she had enough magical sensibility to make a guess as to what had been used from the result it had brought about.

Lunar magic was the name in the English-speaking sphere for certain mental interference spells, especially ones that attacked the mind or dealt direct damage for it. It came from the name of one of the most famous mental interference spells in the exotyped group called Luna Strike.

Unusually for mental interference exotyped magic, Luna Strike's process had been formularized. The first-magnitude Stars learned about the Luna Strike spell in case they needed to protect themselves against it.

Lina had seen Luna Strike many times as well, of course. Therefore, even though she didn't understand the mechanism behind Cocytus the first time seeing it, she correctly deduced that the spell had done direct and lethal damage to the mind.

And that Miyuki had been the one who had used it.

"Such powerful lunar magic... Miyuki, you... No, you and Tatsuya both... What are you?" muttered Lina in a daze, still slumped on the ground.

The idea of what might have happened if she'd used this spell in their duel didn't coalesce into a clear form in her head. The surprise racking her mind was still too great.

Miyuki was actually in a similar state at the moment.

She leaned against Tatsuya's chest, half her body awash in the ecstasy. It was both because it had been a long time since she'd used every ounce of her power for a spell and because she'd been intoxicated by the sheer quantity of information she saw for the first time through her brother's vision.

Now that the stormy pair had lost their sobriety (?), this was his chance. Tatsuya removed the communicator from his ear and turned it off.

"Lina, tell nobody what you saw just now."

His gaze was downturned, his voice low, and his tone overpowering.

"Wh-what the hell...?"

Normally, such a high-pressure warning would have had the opposite effect on her. But as Tatsuya predicted, Lina wasn't her normal self.

Exposed to a large amount of stress, her nerves strained to their limits, she had lost sight of her main objective and fallen into a state of absolute bewilderment. It was the perfect chance to "persuade" her.

"In exchange, I swear to keep quiet about your identity as Angie Sirius. This applies to not only Miyuki and I but to everyone on our end involved in this."

Lina had a hard time coming up with a reply. She stared with her blue eyes at Tatsuya as he looked down at her.

He made out the light of thought steadily returning to them.

A sense of duty.

Suspicion.

Self-preservation.

Self-justification.

Many an emotion flitted through her eyes, trying to (psychologically) rationalize themselves in her head. Tatsuya didn't have any psychoanalysis know-how or mind-sensing skills, so he didn't clearly understand it to that point, but he instinctively knew Lina was desperately trying to convince herself of something.

Her internal chaos didn't last for very long.

"...I don't have any right to refuse, do I?" she said, words dripping with resignation.

"That's not true," denied Tatsuya. But he didn't tell her what would happen if she did.

Suspicion bred unease. Words unspoken—or rather, the act of not speaking them—was the last push Lina needed.

"Fine... If you'll stay quiet, it's a good deal for me, too. I'll keep you and Miyuki a secret... Nobody would believe me anyway, I bet."

Tatsuya couldn't make out the last sentence, since she'd said it to herself. He didn't ask her to repeat it.

He picked up his sister under the arm—she still couldn't walk—and then, when she suddenly came to and started flailing under his grip, he ordered her to calm down and turned his back to Lina.

But that was all he did—he didn't start walking.

Lina, dubious, went to say something to him, but a moment before that—

"Lina."

—he said her name.

"Something else?"

Those words could have been interpreted as irritation on their own, but her voice wasn't as angry as that.

The cornered air around her had disappeared as though a spirit possessing her had left.

"Lina, if you ever want to leave the Stars…"

"Huh?"

"If you ever want to quit being a soldier, I think I can help. I mean, I don't have much to offer myself, but I have acquaintances who do."

"Tatsuya? What are you talking about?"

Lina didn't blow up and say, "None of your business," or laugh it off and say, "That's absurd."

"I never… I don't want to leave the Stars or stop being the Sirius." She simply answered him, mystified.

"I see," Tatsuya noted shortly, without turning around. He started to walk.

"Wait, Tatsuya! Why would you ask me that?!" shouted Lina after him.

Still not turning around, though, he only offered, "Sorry, that was a weird thing to ask," and continued on his way.

The mechanical doll that obeyed him, of course, didn't turn to face her at all.

Only Miyuki, held in her brother's arm as they departed, looked over his shoulder at her apprehensively.

When Tatsuya disappeared into the shadows of the trees, Lina suddenly snapped out of it.

Realizing she'd been staring at him leave, she hastily rose from her kneeling position.

Why had her eyes been chasing after him like that…? When the question came to mind, Lina shook her head violently.

It's because he said that weird stuff. Obviously.

As far as she'd been aware, she really had only been watching him leave.

The moment she was aware she'd done it, though, she sensed her pulse accelerate and her cheeks warm.

In actuality, this was all just a "misunderstanding" that had been dragged into her thoughts. But since she had, in a way, fallen for her own trap, there was no way for her to coolly analyze herself from an objective viewpoint. She was caught in a psychological state similar to the suspension bridge effect.

To divert her thoughts away from her nonexistent "love," Lina decided to think about something else, anything else. As a result, her mind was naturally drawn to her most recent question.

Tatsuya's inexplicable proposition.

She thought again about why he'd said such a thing.

Had she looked like she was suffering through eliminating her countrymen who had been violated by a monster—had it been in her face or in her features?

If that was how it looked to him, he'd made a grave mistake.

Sure, it pained her to point a gun at one of her own.

...But giving them a peaceful sleep is better than letting them live as a monster.

Lina thought it was the more merciful option. She believed she was saving them.

Because she'd been taught that the dignity of a human, of a soul, was just that precious.

——It was a difficult job, to be sure. But somebody had to do it.

——She wasn't about to flee from it.

——If a magician with strong magic power fell to the demon road, the strongest magician, the Sirius, had to be the one to hunt him. In other words, only she could do it...

...Only me?

But her thoughts stumbled over something unexpected.

To eliminate magicians who had lost their mind without creating more victims. The mission was definitely most applicable to her, the strongest magician.

She'd never doubted that point—until now.

Now she knew that wasn't necessarily true.

Even if she didn't do it, those two would.

She didn't have to go through this suffering, the bitter experience of guilt at killing her own countrymen—those two, from another nation, they could…

I see… That was why I was lost and impatient.

She felt like the haze lurking in her mind for close to a month now had suddenly cleared up.

Even if she didn't do it, someone else would.

The discovery was unexpected for Lina.

She'd thought the future was set in stone, that she couldn't change it. But now she knew she could choose. The path, which she'd always thought was straight, had suddenly branched out in front of her—and both hopes and anxieties came with it.

She'd finally made it out of one maze, and now her mind was in chaos.

Tatsuya was headed for where they'd left the two specimens, the parasites sealed successfully inside. But someone had beaten them there.

Two groups were staring each other down.

One wore all black, led by a man standing up straight, his face creased with wrinkles gained over many years.

The other was also in all black, but this one was led by a pretty girl wearing an extravagant dress.

They may have been staring each other down, but it wasn't hostile. At least, the group the girl led wasn't. That was probably because she didn't have any hostile intent against the old man.

In fact, the girl looked upon him with a respectful gaze—on the surface anyway.

"Your Excellency Kudou, I consider it a great honor to meet you," said the girl, walking out in front of the old man, bending at the waist in a refined curtsy. But while it may have been refined, it didn't come off as chaste. The light in her eyes was too strong to call it that.

"My name is Ayako Kuroba. I am a member of the Yotsuba's lowest ranks, charged with serving our family head, Maya."

She lifted her head and smiled sweetly.

But that, of course, wasn't enough to move Retsu Kudou. "A representative of Lady Yotsuba? No wonder you're so levelheaded despite your age. You seem to know who I am. Or should I introduce myself?"

In front of associates he was close to, Kudou called her "Maya," but officially, they were of equal rank, each the head of a family in the Ten Master Clans. Calling her Lady Yotsuba served to show that right now, he considered Ayako, young enough to be his granddaughter, an enemy of equal standing.

"No, I would never think to suggest something so rude."

A light that could only be called deliberate shone in Kudou's eyes. But even before that, Ayako's sweet-but-fearless attitude didn't crumble.

"Incidentally, Your Excellency, we don't have very much time to spare, so there is one thing I would like to ask you about."

One might call that attitude impetuous, but the Kudou elder didn't show any signs of displeasure in particular. He didn't necessarily think they didn't have time, but he felt the same way in wanting to get this over with quickly.

"Go ahead."

"Thank you."

After the elder nodded magnanimously, Ayako gave another theatrical curtsy, then looked up directly at him.

"With all due respect, I am given to understand that Your Excellency's intent is to bring back these sealed monsters called parasites. But to tell you the truth, the errand I have been sent on by my family head is to also collect the sealed parasites."

"Is it?"

The intensity and sharpness of the light in Kudou's eyes increased.

Ayako, facing its full brunt, winced for just a moment before painting her expression over with a firm smile.

"...Fortunately, there are two sealed vessels here. Shall we each take one, Your Excellency?"

Maintaining her firm smile, Ayako looked right back at the glow in the elder's eyes and waited for his answer.

Suddenly, Kudou broke out laughing.

Loudly, in amusement.

"Well, well... This really is something. I thought you were still only in middle school."

Ayako had never told Kudou her age. With this statement, he was implying he'd investigated her before she'd even named herself.

But this time, Ayako showed no sign of disturbance. She, too, was of the mind-set that there was nothing strange about Retsu Kudou investigating the Yotsuba's playing pieces, herself included.

She'd known the woman would appear here in person, so it would actually be stranger if he hadn't learned at least that much.

"Very well. We'll take the friendly approach and share the spoils evenly."

"Thank you very much, Your Excellency."

Ayako breathed a sigh of relief behind her poker face.

She didn't overrate her own magic power. She wasn't restricted to specific magic like Tatsuya was, but she wasn't an all-around type like Miyuki, either. No, she was the kind of magician with very clear strengths and weaknesses. And her strengths didn't really include direct close combat magic. She knew a fair match with a magician once called the trickiest in the world would leave her with little chance at victory.

She offered up a silent word of thanks for the coincidence that there were two prey.

And...

Thanks to you, Tatsuya, I'll be able to finish this mission safely.

She'd never gotten Tatsuya's word that he'd help, and she'd never even requested his help in the first place. But that didn't stop her from thinking that on the sly.

In Tatsuya's arms, Miyuki was curled up and stiff.

Today, for once, no matter how much she pleaded, Tatsuya wouldn't let her out of his arms. She wasn't particularly petite for a woman, so she wasn't a featherweight. No matter how much Tatsuya had built his body, she'd have to feel heavy after all this time. But his arms never twitched. In fact, he carried her so smoothly he never even rocked her, despite all the dips and bumps in the forest ground.

Given their normal behavior, maybe it would seem more natural for Miyuki to be the one who aggressively pursued physical affection. However, Miyuki wasn't even clinging to Tatsuya's neck—she had her hands balled into fists in front of her chest, trying to hold in the embarrassment.

The silence was painful.

It wasn't just difficult, it was hurting her chest.

At this rate, she thought her breathing might stop and her heart might burst—someone else would definitely have sighed and said "you're exaggerating," but Miyuki herself was at a significant loss, desperately racking her heated-up brain over something to talk about.

"Brother, about Lina…"

And that was the topic that came out as a result.

Tatsuya put a lot of thought into Lina. More so than, at least, the kind of consideration one would show a friend.

She understood that, so deep down, Miyuki didn't really want to bring up the topic of Lina in front of her brother.

But that was the only topic she could think of at the moment.

"Yeah?"

"Do you think…she'll take what you said to heart?"

Besides, Miyuki had Lina on her mind now, too.

"Who knows? I certainly don't. I mean, I'm not her."

Miyuki caught a glimpse of self-deprecation somewhere in his tone of voice. Maybe he felt like he was meddling in someone else's business.

Of course, Miyuki knew that her brother's words had been more than meddling. Even from her point of view, the kindhearted and impulsive Lina wasn't cut out to be a soldier. Perhaps it wasn't her place to mind that, but when she looked at Lina, she seemed incredibly endangered.

"I'm sure Lina has her own things to deal with. She's certainly not the only one who can't get herself to the place she wants."

"But you still offered to help her anyway... Why?"

"What do you mean?"

Miyuki was aware that the conversation had suddenly taken an unexpected turn. And that now was her only chance to stop.

But she didn't stop.

"Brother... Why do you try to help Lina? Do you...have special feelings for her?"

Tatsuya's eyes widened at his sister's words but really only for a moment.

"You seem to be misunderstanding a few things..."

There was an air about him, as though he was smiling painfully. But his actual expression was a serious one. He seemed, at least, to be faithfully trying to answer his sister's question.

"You make it sound like it's only her. But this is the first time I've had any connection to someone in a position like Lina's. Before now, anyone from the military has been a lot older than me, and they were all people who had chosen it as a life path."

He neatly unraveled each misunderstanding, one by one.

"The feelings I have for Lina aren't the kind you're thinking. To put it bluntly, I just thought leaving the Stars would be better for her future.

Not just leaving the military, either, but getting her to move here. The best option would be to have her naturalize as a Japanese citizen."

She couldn't sense any lies from his words. They could sense each other from this distance of zero. If there had been the slightest falsehood in what her brother was saying, she was confident she'd have noticed it.

"But that doesn't mean I don't sympathize with her. In a way, we're a lot alike. Or maybe I should say we belong to the same category of person."

Tatsuya's eyes gazed into the distance.

"Neither one of us had any real choice in where we ended up today. You could call me enrolling at First High a choice I forced them to let me have, but I don't think Lina even had a little choice like that."

His eyes were still directed at Miyuki, but he was focusing on a point farther away.

"I was never given a choice, but one day, I'll make one and choose for myself. I'll throw away the role assigned to me and jump off the stage I was placed on. I figured I'd offer help out of friendship if Lina wanted the same thing, but..."

Tatsuya stumbled over his words, then returned his focus to Miyuki and gave a harsh smile.

"I guess it was none of my...business?"

There was a good reason he stammered there.

Miyuki, who had until now been making herself small in his arms, had wrapped her arms around his neck and hugged him so tightly he was having trouble breathing.

Without thinking, he let her go. But he didn't just drop her there; he let her gently down to the ground, an unconscious display of skill that had been trained into him.

Even after her feet reached the ground, her arms remained wrapped around his neck.

"That isn't true... I'm sure that one day—no, in the near future, your consideration will reach her heart."

Tatsuya felt his sister's words seeping directly into his chest.

"Because this incident must have made Lina *doubt her current self.* She may be a little simple, but she's smart. It is simply not possible that after such close dealings with you she wouldn't have any doubts at all."

"Simple? That's pretty mean."

Miyuki lifted her face, and Tatsuya moved his hands to her shoulders.

The siblings grinned, then began to walk, side by side.

——Pixie, who had read the mood (?) and turned into a literal decoration, silently followed after them.

When they saw it, even the siblings' heartwarming mood was forced to change.

The spot where they'd first sealed the parasites was an empty husk. Someone had taken the two away.

"I'm sorry, Tatsuya... I didn't mean to take my eyes off them."

"...Tatsuya, I'm really sorry."

"Tatsuya, please don't blame Shibata or Mitsui. I can vouch for them—they weren't being careless. Even I didn't notice the sealed 'vessels' being taken away. They were my seals, too..."

"All three of you, stop blaming yourselves. I don't mind at all."

From the communicator, he heard a despondent voice, a voice seething with self-loathing and a voice that sounded frustrated, respectively. Tatsuya made an effort to respond cheerfully.

"Tatsuya..."

The voice of admiration he got in return, for some reason, was probably due to a misunderstanding. Tatsuya's attitude wasn't an act out of consideration for them. He really didn't mind it much at all.

...He did feel like sighing, though.

"They may have been snatched away from right under our noses, but that only means whoever did it was one step better than us. I actually hadn't thought much about what to do with them after we caught them, and it's not worth obsessing over it anyway."

Like Tatsuya said, they hadn't made a concrete plan for what to do after capturing them. They'd just figured they'd leave the sealed parasites to Mikihiko's family without thinking at all about how to use them.

In that sense, it seemed more efficient that the parasites had been taken away. *They* wouldn't do anything careless like letting the parasites accidentally escape.

Still, though... Was this what they were after all along?

"Brother?"

She'd probably misunderstood why he'd fallen silent. When Miyuki questioned him out of consideration, Tatsuya waved his hand to indicate it didn't matter.

Miyuki understood from the way he was acting that he had an idea who the culprits were. She figured he'd used his information-tracing power to identify the culprits.

——And to be sure, Tatsuya had used his "vision." As a result, he now had a general idea of what had happened here.

But more importantly, there was a message left here for him from one of the "culprits." That was the main thing mentally exhausting him.

A gust of wind blew through, whipping up dead leaves that hadn't yet decomposed.

Within it, Tatsuya, who had good eyesight in the dark, caught a glimpse of black wings, probably belonging to a crow.

By the time Tatsuya met up with the "Leorika" pair, Naotsugu and the *Batto-tai* had both finished withdrawing.

They thanked each other for their hard work and, neither of them prying very deeply into the other's affairs, set back on the road home.

He left Pixie as she was in the school garage.

To enter the building, they had to take the time to jump back over the fence first, then go around to the front gate. Neither Erika nor Leo backed out, though.

The four of them met up with Mikihiko's group, and in a cluster of seven they left the school behind them.

Considering their group's size and the time, they were obviously stopped at the gates when they went to leave. But with an excuse they'd prepared beforehand—an experiment for a ritual magic that needed to be carried out at this time—and the power in the girls' radiant eyes, they successfully escaped without much questioning.

And that was how this long night came to a close.

At the time, Tatsuya had no way of knowing that tonight's events would be the opening of a new history of a battle between man, demon, and monster fought in the shadows of society.

[Epilogue]

Merry noises came, riding the wind. First High's campus was filled with delighted voices.

If you listened closely, you might hear crying mixed with it but certainly not because anything terrible had happened.

In contrast, the cafeteria was dull. You could count what few figures were here on both hands.

They weren't exactly students cutting classes. Graduation was today.

Tatsuya took a sip of his coffee—in a proper ceramic cup, not a paper one—then placed it directly on the table, without using a saucer. (It hadn't come with a saucer to begin with.)

His gaze fell to his multi-faced wristwatch, a thing magicians didn't often use. The ceremony itself would just about be over now; the voices must have belonged to the graduates going out in the courtyard.

They would be having a party in the two small gymnasiums after this. It felt awful to have Course 1 and Course 2 students still separated, but everyone involved would probably be more comfortable with the arrangement.

What was right wasn't always the best option. If Course 2 students were with Course 1 students, they might get weirdly passive, and the Course 1 students would be too preoccupied with the Course

2 students (mainly with the rate of advancement to Magic University) and unable to party to their hearts' content. There was no difference in food or drinks or anything else between the two venues, so Tatsuya figured it wasn't the time to get hung up on what was right.

Still, because they were separate, some people were having to do more work than necessary. The workers setting up and the meal staff providing the food would be getting paid extra for there being two venues, so it wasn't *unrewarded* extra work. But the student council, for example, which was hosting the graduation party, immediately came to mind as candidates who *were* being forced to do unrewarded extra work.

Things might be clear at this point, but Tatsuya was waiting for Miyuki, who was more than fully occupied with running the graduation party today.

Just to clear up any misconceptions, he'd offered to help set up and run it, too. Many times over.

Some—for example, Azusa—clearly wanted him to help. But Miyuki had stubbornly refused any of his assistance.

"I cannot allow a job like this to bother you, Brother!" she'd said, not budging an inch. Azusa had no choice but to dejectedly back off.

Well, even ignoring his sister's excessive thoughtfulness (?), Tatsuya was in an odd and complex position with many of the Course 1 students and more than a few Course 2 students.

For seniors, he was a seed of trouble suddenly thrown in during their last year. It was probably the correct choice not to show his face.

Of course, when it was ultimately decided that he wouldn't be helping and he had casually said something like, "It's better this way," Mayumi, who just happened (?) to be there, too, got indignant for some reason.

Mayumi, for her part, had passed the exam to get into Magic University. It seemed only natural given her abilities and grades, but doubtless the fact that the "vampire" victims immediately stopped appearing after that night worked in her favor, letting her devote her full concentration on the exam.

She would be a student at Magic University come this April with Suzune and Katsuto, who had also passed quite reasonably.

Mari hadn't taken the exam for Magic University. She'd been accepted to the Academy of Defense. The reason went without saying, but Mayumi apparently hadn't known about it until moments before, and Tatsuya had seen Mayumi teasing her to no end—probably with some loneliness under the surface.

The Magic University and the Academy of Defense weren't very far apart, so they could see each other whenever they wanted. But two close friends—they might dislike being called good friends, but at this point, everyone else thought as much—were going to different schools when one had thought they were going to the same one. She was understandably a little upset.

Speaking of people going to the A.D....

"Shiba."

Just as he thought about it, a voice addressed him.

"Kobayakawa? Hasn't the party already started?"

The exact person he'd just been thinking of appeared.

"Well, yes, but Mari told me you were here."

After the accident during the Nine School Competition, Kobayakawa's magic faculties had never returned, despite a lengthy rehab period. Her sensitivity to magic was undamaged, but she'd never cleared away her jealousy of magic and the idea of being able to use it.

Kobayakawa had apparently decided to drop out at the time, in October.

But even if she transferred to a liberal arts or science high school, she'd never have enough time to prepare for advancement. She seemed to want to transfer, then take a year off to look for a new life course.

"What did you need me for?"

"Well, how do I put this...? Man, this is hard to say to your face… What I mean is, I…I wanted to thank you." Kobayakawa's face blushed red in embarrassment.

Tatsuya was pretty seriously confused. "I didn't do anything for you that warrants thanks."

"Yes you did!"

Kobayakawa's raised voice rang out clearly in the sparsely populated cafeteria. She evidently hadn't meant to do that, since she hunched up her shoulders and her face flushed even brighter. She continued to mumble, "You were the one who gave that advice that there are ways I can put my magic knowledge and sensitivity to good use even if I can't use magic, weren't you?"

For a moment, Tatsuya almost frowned, but in consideration of her feelings, he stopped himself from doing so.

"I see Watanabe couldn't keep quiet…"

Still, he couldn't keep his voice from sounding appalled.

"Don't blame her. I forced Mari to tell me."

"I thought I told her to make it sound like it was her own idea."

Mari, Mayumi, and all the other senior girls picked as reps at the Nines had been worried about Kobayakawa. For Mari, who barely managed to scrape by after a similar accident had happened to her, the issue must have felt deeply personal. And the incident Chiaki Hirakawa had caused because of Kobayakawa's accident had only made her more worried.

Mari had complained to Tatsuya once after that incident. She'd prefaced it by saying it wasn't his fault, but to sum up her complaint, she had wanted to know if there was really nothing he could have done to prevent her accident.

Tatsuya had an answer for that.

He couldn't have stopped it.

He wasn't all-knowing or all-powerful. Well, leaving the all-powerful bit aside, he was far from omniscient. His attention was completely dedicated to Miyuki, himself, and the scope of his own support role. He didn't have the time to mind anything else. That went for the other members, too. Even Koharu Hirakawa (Chiaki's older sister), who had been in charge of Kobayakawa and her CAD, hadn't spotted the tampering, so obviously nobody else would have.

But in that situation, he hesitated to coldly cut her down. Instead, he'd hypothetically suggested an alternate path.

Fujibayashi was always telling him that they didn't have enough support staff who understood magic for when they integrated magic into their operations. The reality was that the incredibly few people with magical talents were always sent to the front lines, meaning the staff behind them in charge of directing missions were all non-magicians who only knew of magic in theory.

As someone forced to handle both the front lines and the rear support, she'd complained to him that if a talented magician happened to lose the ability to use magic for whatever reason and joined their operational staff, it would be infinitely easier for frontline magicians to act. He'd told this all to Mari, leaving out the names.

"That's what it seemed like. But she wasn't very private about it."

"I swear…"

"And I'm happy she told me," interrupted Kobayakawa earnestly as Tatsuya bitterly mumbled. "I wasn't aware of it at the time, but until I heard those words, I'd given up on myself. I was bragging to everyone that I wouldn't lose, but the fact that I thought it was bragging was just a way to fool myself into believing I hadn't already lost."

Kobayakawa's eyes were watering—maybe she was remembering what she was like at the time. But it showed no weakness or self-criticism.

"But when I heard all that from Mari, I really felt like everything in front of me opened up. I knew it was the path I had to take. And not just for me. Any magic high school student with the road ahead of them cut off—it applied to them, too. I think that's why I could get out of my funk, change course, and work hard enough to get accepted in just half a year."

Kobayakawa's face reddened again, doubtlessly because she considered this all embarrassing to say.

None of it sounded embarrassing to Tatsuya, though.

"Shiba, thank you."

Kobayakawa bowed deeply to him, her attitude changing to a polite one.

Even Tatsuya wasn't dense enough to remain seated after something like that.

He rose from his seat, clapped his heels down, and put his feet together.

The sudden clap of his soles not only surprised Kobayakawa, it also drew gazes from the few student council members also in the cafeteria. But Tatsuya ignored them, without being particularly conscious of it, and gave Kobayakawa the salute drilled into him by the Independent Magic Battalion.

"Shiba…"

"Kobayakawa, it may sound clichéd, but do your best," said Tatsuya, finishing the salute, without being embarrassed or smiling.

Tears nearly rose to Kobayakawa's eyes again, but instead of starting to cry, she smiled and nodded.

"The party has already started."

"Yeah. That's true… Well, goodbye, then. You do your best, too."

Kobayakawa trotted away. Tatsuya saw her off, then sat back down.

His coffee was lukewarm now, but strangely enough, it didn't taste bad.

"I'm all finished, Brother," came a voice speaking between animated breaths.

Tatsuya looked up from the document he was in the middle of writing on his portable information terminal.

"What were you writing, Tatsuya?"

That was Mayumi, not Miyuki, smiling and clutching a diploma-filled tube—they still used paper for these sorts of things—to her chest.

"Just a few notes about system-level assistance that could lengthen spell duration."

Mari looked at him, a little appalled. "I don't think that's the sort of topic you can just brush off like that."

Tatsuya was about to ask what this was all about, but he stopped, only shrugging a little. He also, out of reflex, considered making a mean remark to her about the business with Kobayakawa. But he changed his mind. Today was a joyous day where they were the main characters, so he stopped himself from doing anything dull like that.

"Anyway, what are you all here for? I'm sure both of you have gotten more than a few after-party invitations."

The two female students exchanged glances before Katsuto abruptly appeared from behind them.

"We wanted to say hello to you first," he said.

"...That's very kind of you. You didn't have to come all the way here—I was planning to come say my hellos later on."

"Oh, you did? You were cooped up in here during the party, so we thought you pretended not to notice and went home," remarked Mayumi snidely, now in full-throttle sulking mode.

Tatsuya knew it was an act but couldn't help feeling like he had to excuse himself. "I can't exactly turn up at a graduation party when I'm not even on the student council. Especially not the Course 1 party," he said, pulling out a reasonable-but-fake argument as his justification.

"Why not?!" came another voice flying at him, this one serious.

A brilliantly blonde head appeared before him, parting through the graduates.

"Why did they make me help with the party when I'm not even an official student council member, and someone on the disciplinary committee doesn't have to do anything?!"

It was Lina, whom the others had shrewdly included among the helpers.

"...Disciplinary committee members aren't on the student council," said Tatsuya. "And you are technically still on the student council, even though it's temporary, aren't you?"

"You'll need more than that to convince me!" said Lina, erupting just like she always did, troubling Mayumi and the others. She didn't care much about the fact that graduates were watching.

"Wait, Lina, don't be rude to my brother."

Then came Miyuki, standing up to her just like she always did, her words considerate of her older brother—though that was fairly standard.

"We decided before we started setting up for the graduation party that you were a temporary student council member and that Brother was a disciplinary committee member. Besides, why are you suddenly so unhappy about it? You were so keen on the idea before."

Tatsuya didn't know what she'd been keen on exactly, but judging by how red her face got, a lot of people had definitely seen her doing something.

"Miyuki, what do you mean?"

Right now, Tatsuya didn't have the choice of purposely not asking what happened.

"It's nothing, Tatsuya!"

"Since Lina is a temporary officer, we would have felt bad putting her on a task that demanded very much work. Instead, we put her in charge of the day's entertainment, but—"

"Miyuki!"

"—when I said 'entertainment,' I didn't mean she had to do something, just to round up students and graduates who wanted to. But—"

"Miyuki, don't say it!"

"Lina seems to have misunderstood, and—"

"Miyuki, please! Don't tell him!"

Lina desperately tried to interrupt her, but Mayumi and Mari, who found this amusing, deftly blocked the action.

"And?"

Lina's incredibly desperate voice had earned a glance from the

Shiba sister, but as soon as Tatsuya urged her on, her gaze quickly returned to him.

"She got up onstage in front of the band," explained Miyuki. "Then she sung about ten songs in a row. Everyone was very excited."

"Yeah, that was a pretty good live performance," Mari said, nodding several times. "Better than some professional ones."

"It's true. You're very good at singing, Ms. Shields. You have a wonderful voice," Mayumi praised honestly.

"Ugh..." Lina looked down, her face red.

Not out of anger but clearly out of embarrassment.

Seeing that warmed Tatsuya's heart. "I see... You made a good memory today, Lina."

"...Buzz off."

When she turned her cheek up at him, everyone else present raised their voices in warm laughter.

That was the last time we saw Lina.

The graduation ceremony was the final time Lina had come to school.

When he'd asked Miyuki about it, she said that she'd explained to 1-A that she was too busy getting ready to return home.

But presumably, she'd had orders to withdraw since before then. She'd still attended until that day, though. Maybe it was to help set up for the graduation party and carry out the last task assigned to her as a high school student.

If that was true, he expected that she'd been able to enjoy being in high school, if only for a little while.

——These were the things on Tatsuya's mind as he watched the arrival information.

The day before yesterday had been the end of their third term. That meant his first year in high school had come to an end.

Tatsuya's grades hadn't changed. His marks in theoretical subjects were extremely high, while his marks in practical subjects were pretty low.

He was middle bottom in terms of overall ranking.

But that didn't worry him, either.

He'd gotten involved in all sorts of trouble this year, but he was getting closer to his goal, slowly but surely.

He'd unexpectedly been able to forge strong friendships. Even when considering the negatives—the string of incidents—he'd probably say it had been an excellent year.

Today, he'd come to the Tokyo Bay Maritime International Airport.

Not alone, of course.

Miyuki and Honoka sat to his left and right, as Leo, Erika, Mikihiko, and Mizuki sat in front of him.

The plane with Shizuku on it was planned to arrive in less than an hour.

"Well, it really does take a long time to get here from the American mainland," said Miyuki to him from his left.

"Military planes can cross the Pacific in less than one-fourth of that time. How come civilian planes take so long?" asked Honoka.

"They've got different engines," Leo put in from the front. "Military planes go up to the outer atmosphere. They focus on safety and economy for civilian ones."

"Gee, you seem to know a lot about this for a barbarian who got kicked by a horse," Erika teased.

"What'd you say?!"

"Leo, give it a rest."

"You too, Erika. Don't tease him over everything."

Mikihiko and Mizuki took the job of mediating, which was pretty much the usual fare.

Then Tatsuya spotted a familiar golden glow inside the crowd in the lobby.

He quickly stood up, and his friends looked up at him wondering why.

Miyuki was the next quickest one to stand up.

She'd seen the same thing as Tatsuya, just a moment later.

Tatsuya excused himself with a simple "Be right back," then started to walk. Miyuki followed him.

Honoka sprang to her feet, too, but for some reason, Erika, who was sitting in front of her, grabbed the sleeve of her spring jacket.

"Honoka, no getting in the way. They need to say goodbye to a rival," Erika whispered, turning around to lean against her seat.

She watched as, instead of seeing Tatsuya and running away, Lina actually walked up to the siblings of her own accord.

"Tatsuya, Miyuki, did you come to see me off?"

Once they'd gotten close enough that normal voices would reach, Lina was the first one to open her mouth.

"Something like that. Though actually, running into you was a coincidence."

The air of tormented obsession that had clung to Lina for a while was gone, replaced by an austere, casual smile. But she didn't seem perfectly back to normal, either. A shadow of doubt lingered in the back of her eyes, one that hadn't been there right after she'd arrived in Japan. It made her look quite a bit more mature for the short time she'd spent here.

"Wait, didn't I tell you what day I was leaving?" joked Lina, pretending to feign innocence.

"I don't think so," replied Miyuki, cutting her down with a single stroke. Nevertheless, it hadn't offended her, either. She had a pained grin on her face.

"Well, jokes aside. Thanks for everything," said Lina, her smile changing to a more brazen one.

"Don't you mean *sorry for the trouble*?" asked Tatsuya, smooth and sarcastic.

"You're the ones who caused trouble for me," Lina shot back. "...You really don't have any mercy even at the end, Tatsuya."

"I expect holding back wouldn't make you any happier... And this isn't the end, right?"

Lina shrugged. "Who knows? I'm pretty sure I wouldn't just leave my home country on a dime."

There was a feeling of resignation in her voice.

But then, as if to erase that, Miyuki piped in, a strong intent in her voice. "But no, this isn't the end."

"Miyuki?" said Lina.

"So I'm not going to say goodbye, Lina."

"...You know that sounds kind of like a confession, right?" Lina's eyes widened at first, then her expression shifted into a mischievous smile.

"Yes, maybe it is a kind of confession. You are my rival, Lina," declared Miyuki, unaffected, voice unwavering. "I'm sure you'll take the help Brother offered you. I know you'll join him. That will be when our real competition begins. That's why I won't say goodbye. We'll see you again, Lina."

Lina's eyes widened a second time. And this time, she gave a soft smile, a smile like the sun that suited the color of her hair and eyes.

"I don't really understand what you're talking about, but...I have a feeling that you're going to be right. In that case, Miyuki, Tatsuya—until we meet again."

"I'm home."

An hour after Lina disappeared through the gate, Shizuku appeared, and that was the first thing out of her mouth.

"Welcome home!"

As a teary-eyed Honoka hugged her, Shizuku patted her on the back and then looked toward Tatsuya.

"Welcome back, Shizuku. I'm happy you had a safe flight."

"Yep."

Her curt responses hadn't changed since before she studied abroad, but...

"Shizuku, you seem kind of different."

"Yeah. More mature-like."

...Like Miyuki and Erika said, the aura around her seemed quite a bit more adult.

"Had any experiences you weren't supposed to over there?" grinned Erika.

"Erika?!"

Mizuki was the one who reacted to that, while Shizuku just tilted her head a little in confusion.

The behavior itself was a similar sight as before, but it felt strongly like she was more relaxed, more composed.

"Tatsuya?"

"Yes?"

After Honoka finally released her from the embrace, Shizuku walked up to Tatsuya and looked up at him. "There's a lot I want to talk to you about. A lot of messages from Ray, too. Do you want to hear it now?"

"Sure. Let me hear it."

It was probably because she'd acquired a lot of knowledge in America.

That was what Tatsuya thought.

Shizuku's story was quite a long one.

Nevertheless, she couldn't talk about everything.

The message from Ray—Raymond Clark—wasn't something she could talk about in front of their other friends.

No choice but to accept the invitation...

To tell them the rest of the story, Shizuku invited Tatsuya and

Miyuki to her house. To the private residence of tycoon Ushio Kitayama, without mixing her other friends in.

That was something with no lack of meaning for the Yotsuba as well.

However, they didn't have the option of not accepting her invitation. The information she'd brought back with her would be necessary to decide a course of action for the future.

In his house's living room, Tatsuya reaffirmed the conclusion, which was a foregone one to begin with.

Then the doorbell rang.

The surprised voice Miyuki gave upon going to check the intercom reached Tatsuya's ears.

On Miyuki's face as she appeared before Tatsuya was a tinge of surprise and panic.

"Excuse me, Brother, we have a guest…"

"Should I take it?"

Thinking some sort of unwelcome visitor had come, Tatsuya was about to stand up, but…

"No, it's nothing that important… The visitor is Minami Sakurai, whom we met at the Yotsuba main house."

"What…?"

Tatsuya remembered the young maid girl as well.

Honami Sakurai. A former member of the Tokyo Metropolitan Police Department's security police who had been their late mother's Guardian. A woman who had been like an older sister—good-hearted, comfortable to be around—who had showered the siblings with love. The engineered magician who lost her life protecting Tatsuya during *that* battle on Okinawa three summers ago. The siblings would never forget her—and this girl looked just like her.

She was a completely unforeseen visitor even for Tatsuya.

To Tatsuya's side was his sister, and in front of him was a girl in a springlike, pastel-colored dress.

After she, Minami Sakurai, gave a polite bow, she handed an envelope to Tatsuya.

Tatsuya encouraged Minami to sit down, then took a seat on the sofa himself. With Minami watching him, he took the cue from her gaze and broke the envelope's seal before reading over the letter inside.

The further along he read, the more he felt an illusory bitterness spreading through his mouth.

The letter's sender was Maya Yotsuba.

After the set-in-stone seasonal greetings at the top, the letter read:

"Minami will be enrolling in First High this spring.
Tatsuya, please let her live at your house, okay?
She already has the requisite skills to be a full-fledged housekeeper.
If you purchased a maid robot, you must need help doing the chores.
After all, I'm sure you and Miyuki will both get very busy once you enter your second year of high school.
I've instructed her to do her work as a live-in maid, so please don't hesitate to get her to do whatever you need around the house.
Also, I plan to have Minami learn to do a Guardian's job.
As her senior in this regard, please teach her everything you know."

Tatsuya could almost hear his aunt loudly laughing from the paper.

He folded the letter up, returned it to the envelope, and placed it on the table. Sensing something from the motion, Miyuki considerately inquired, "Brother?"

Tatsuya took a deep breath, then handed the letter to her.

A few moments later, the sound of a gasp came from Miyuki's throat.

As though waiting for her eyes to leave the letter, Minami stood up across from them.

"I may be inexperienced, but I will be in your care. I will devote myself to this job as the mistress has instructed."

She bowed her head deeply.

Tatsuya knew Maya had sent her as a wedge to drive between them, but neither he nor Miyuki could refuse someone with the same face as Honami.

The only thing he could do was put on his poker face and nod to the sarcastic, all-too-troubling "gift" his aunt had given.

A premonition sat in Tatsuya's chest, one he wasn't thankful for in the slightest and didn't seem to want to go away.

Starting in April, this new school year would be rife with even more commotion.

First Year Fin

A Young Lady's Splendid (?) Day Off

November 2, AD 2095. The whole nation was in a good mood from its victory in battle.

The night before last, the news had reported that the Japan Ground Defense Force had wiped out the Great Asian Alliance fleet, along with its base, using a secret weapon. And late last night, the scoop that Beijing had sounded out Washington for peace mediation was revealed. Some doubted the scoop's credibility given the extremely swift developments, but only a select few citizens had maintained such calm reasoning ability.

Many Japanese turned into impromptu military commentators; boys normally uninterested in politics spoke loudly at school about diplomacy and realistic power politics.

This time, annoyed and troubled stares from the girls weren't enough of a damper.

It wasn't only inside school, of course. Sighing at the entertainers on the screen and their irresponsible *merriment*, Mayumi Saegusa switched off the TV.

* * *

It was currently 10:00 AM. Considering today was a weekday, it would normally be a time to be at school. But like yesterday, every magic high school, each an involved party in the Yokohama Incident, had the day off, and First High was no exception.

As someone waiting to take the university exam early next year, she had complex feelings about getting the day off from study. But as someone not only present during the incident but also very much central to the whole thing, she would take rest where she could get it.

…Unfortunately, she couldn't bring herself to unwind.

"Madam, I apologize for interrupting you while you're relaxing."

Did she know I turned off the TV? thought Mayumi when she heard their housekeeper's well-timed voice over the intercom.

"I'll be right there," she replied, getting out of her seat. She really only had to order their HAR's voice-recognition interface to unlock the door, but for whatever reason, she decided to walk over and open it herself.

On the other side was the housekeeper assigned to catering to her personal needs. Certain subcultures, still widely supported today, might describe her by the clothing she wore by something starting with an *m*, ending with a *d*, and followed by the honorific *san*… Still, it was a practical uniform, whose skirt reached down to her calves and collar covered up to the base of her neck and without any large opening in the back.

And anyway, in this house, the presence of housekeepers wearing this sort of clothing wasn't unusual in the slightest.

"What is it?" asked Mayumi of the housekeeper in her midtwenties, with no reason to think the outfit was strange at this point.

"The master has called for you."

Upon hearing that, Mayumi frowned slightly. *Again?* she grumbled to herself. *He already asked me about every little tiny detail yesterday.*

The housekeeper's next words, though, confused her.

"He is waiting for you in the reception room."

Despite that, she kept any indication of her confusion to herself.

...The reception room? Not his study?

That was the question Mayumi now had.

"Is it a guest?"

"It appears so."

She couldn't call their time together a long one, but this house-keeper was essentially assigned specifically to her. Through this short exchange, Mayumi gleaned that the housekeeper didn't know who the guest was.

"Please tell him I'll get changed right away."

"Will you require assistance?"

Mayumi thought for a moment, and then it hit her. With today's fashion world, there weren't many opportunities to try on dresses you couldn't don yourself.

"I'll be okay. I'll make sure to be formal enough."

Which meant the helper unit had been ordered to suggest it. As expected, the housekeeper bowed respectfully to her reply and left.

After lifting her dress's ankle-length skirt around her thighs and adjusting its lace-edged hem, Mayumi knocked on the door to the reception room.

"Come in."

The voice sounded like it was coming from inside the room, but it was actually a flat-surface speaker built into the door panel playing a recording of her father's voice, reproduced with a level of precision that made it almost impossible to tell it apart from his physical voice. As part of his family, she knew he was being formal with her.

Evidently, today's guest was not the sort one could speak too can-didly around.

"Please excuse me."

Assuming a mask 20 percent more ladylike than usual, she lowered her tone and quietly entered the room.

Eyes still down, she glanced at her visitor's face.

The man and woman sitting across from her father were both familiar to her. And not the kind of familiar where she wanted to give them much of a welcome. Still, she didn't exactly *hate* them.

But without breathing a word of it, Mayumi set a benign smile on her face and walked over next to her father before giving an elegant bow to their two visitors.

"Welcome, Mr. Hirofumi. It has been a long time since I last saw you, Ms. Mio."

The young man had stood before she'd addressed him. The woman, though, who had the appearance of a young girl, remained seated. Nobody here frowned at that, either.

After all, Mio Itsuwa wasn't sitting on the sofa but in a wheelchair.

However, her brother Hirofumi Itsuwa seemed to feel guilty about it, though not so much that he thought it was rude. His greeting in return was a little ambiguous.

"Yes, thank you, Ms. Mayumi."

"Please take your seat. And you may feel free to remain seated, Ms. Mio."

"Thank you very much, Ms. Mayumi. And yes, it has been quite some time."

In fact, it seemed like Mio was the one who had taken the offensive suddenly. She returned Mayumi's words with a cherubic smile.

Like every time they saw each other, as she timed taking her own seat with Hirofumi sitting back down, she had to wonder if the woman was really older than her.

Mio Itsuwa had turned twenty-six this year. That was an undeniable fact. But the facts paled when seeing her in the flesh like this.

She was only one or two centimeters shorter than Mayumi, but that was where their physical similarities ended. In a word, she was immature. She had a distinct lack of femininity.

In truth, her legs could still move. But because of her incredibly weak constitution, her body couldn't endure long periods of walking.

She'd started using a wheelchair after turning twenty, but she'd always been frail, never able to do much exercise. That meant she didn't eat much, which in turn implied she was never able to get healthy. It was a vicious cycle. Her stunted figure was a result of that.

As far as anyone could see from her clothing, she had very little chest, too. So little that calling it nonexistent wouldn't have been an exaggeration. Her waist was slender like a young girl's as well. Her body was close to that of a girl in her low teens, judging purely on her size.

Her facial features were just as childish as her physique. Her looks combined with her figure to somehow give an impression of someone who wasn't quite fully a "woman."

Still, regardless of her youthful appearance, she couldn't go out much after graduating from university, and she had apparently taken most of her postgraduate classes online. What could someone like her be here for?

I'm pretty sure she's not here just because Mr. Hirofumi is, she wondered to herself.

"We came today to say our goodbyes," began Mio, probably having detected the doubts in Mayumi's eyes and preempting them.

"Are you returning home?" asked Mayumi, clamping down on the slight panic she felt at being read like a book—despite having zero reason to feel that way.

The main Itsuwa family house was in Ehime Prefecture, but ever since Mio had to go to Tokyo in order to commute to university, she'd been living in a separate residence. After she'd finished postgrad, her younger brother Hirofumi had just advanced to it, so they'd still been living together.

"Yes, we will be, but before that..." Mio paused, then gave the classic *I'm hiding something* smile. An unhappy scowl, though a very slight one, came over Hirofumi's face as well. "I'm being deployed."

"Deployed... You're going to war?!" cried Mayumi in spite of herself after putting together what the word meant. "I'm sorry. But may I ask why...?"

Quickly apologizing for her bad manners, Mayumi turned confused eyes on Mio and her father.

"The public announcement will be next week, but this is an official decision." The answer came from her father. "Ms. Mio is headed to the base in Sasebo first, and then they'll go with the JMDF west over a sea route. Even we haven't been told of their destination, but their objective by doing this is to convince the GAA to form a peace treaty... I know I don't need to say this, but don't tell anyone until the official announcement."

"Yes, I understand," nodded Mayumi immediately to her father's reminder. Still, the only part that convinced her was the "no telling anyone" part.

Mayumi knew the reason the military had brought in Mio. She was one of only thirteen publicly recognized strategic-class magicians in the world, who probably numbered less than fifty in total including those who were in hiding or who were being hidden. She was the one and only user of strategic-class magic in Japan that the Japanese government had officially recognized.

Her strategic spell, Abyss, was mainly for intercepting maritime powers, but it had more than enough destructive potential as a means to attack surface positions. The simple fact that she'd be with the military was sure to place immense pressure on the enemy.

But this time, Mayumi got the feeling even that reason wasn't logical enough. The previous military action had begun with an invasion onto the Yokohama shoreline and had ended with the complete destruction of the Korean Peninsula's southern tip. In point of fact, that matter had ended on October 31. As long as Japan wasn't looking for greater results, like gaining cessions in return, a counterinvasion was no longer strategically necessary. Without the intent to pursue things so aggressively, Mayumi had to say that having Mio accompany them for weeks when her health was so uncertain brought more demerits than merits.

Mayumi wasn't thinking about it clearly enough to explain it in words, but this was generally the sense of oddness she was feeling now.

"I'll be going with my sister."

He must have nursed similar dissatisfaction. But now that the government had made its decision and the Itsuwa's head approved, Hirofumi couldn't overturn it. The Itsuwa family had determined he'd be the next family head, but he still wasn't the *actual* head, so objecting at this stage wouldn't change the situation. Instead, the determination to at least go with his sister and help her was clear from his face.

"Actually, though…"

As a grimness drifted from her brother, Mio, perhaps wanting to cheer him up, shifted her tone into a lighthearted, jovial one.

"I just wanted to see Ms. Mayumi become my brother's wife."

It was more than effective at changing the mood. Just in the exact opposite direction than she'd intended.

They couldn't laugh at it—bringing this topic up given what they'd just been talking about was commonly called a "death flag."

"Mio…"

"…I'm sorry."

As the severity in the air strengthened, Mio, cautioned by his grave voice, wilted, crestfallen.

"A-anyway, we can talk about that again once Hirofumi comes back," put in Kouichi quickly, maybe out of a sense of responsibility as their host.

Mio's smile returned, albeit a weak one, while Hirofumi and Mayumi, struggling to decide what kind of face to make, ended up without any expression at all.

This was the reason Mayumi said it had been a while since seeing Mio but not Hirofumi. The reason she'd randomly thought to herself was that Mio simply hadn't come along with him.

Hirofumi was one of her marriage candidates. Actually, since

Hirofumi was the leader of the Itsuwa family, it might be better to say that Mayumi was one of *his* marriage candidates. Both of direct Ten Master Clans descent, both a similar age, with him being a successor and her the eldest daughter with an older brother who would succeed. The conditions were favorable.

To tell the truth, Katsuto from the Juumonji family met the same conditions, and Kouichi was of the mind to have Mayumi marry either Hirofumi or Katsuto. (Masaki of the Ichijou family had been excluded due to being younger.)

She had her own ideas, of course. There would be other marriage talks in the way that she wouldn't be able to get out of, so things hadn't yet progressed to betrothal. However, Hirofumi and Mayumi had eaten together several times at one of their family's homes and gone to the theater a few times. Contrary to the adults' ideas, though, neither of them really cared for it, which was why they now both wore poker faces.

Still, Mayumi was sensible enough to know that this silent ritual would only drag the mood down. "So when do you depart?" she asked, trying to arouse their interest.

Hirofumi couldn't completely hide the relief he felt—Mayumi didn't like his weak defenses in this regard—when he answered, "We leave for Sasebo this weekend. I hear we'll be departing from land next Friday."

Mayumi, for her part, didn't let so much as a split-second expression let him on to her dissatisfaction. "My, that is sudden... Please do be careful. I'll be waiting for your safe return."

Armed with a catlike, impeccable mask, she bowed deeply while still seated.

"Thank you."

As she stared down at her fingernails, she thought to herself that she was free to go now.

"Actually, we wished to ask for your aid in advance of this campaign..."

So when she heard Hirofumi suggest that, she had to try a little to control the speed at which she rose.

"Me, you mean?" she asked, purposely tilting her head a little childishly, implying that there was nothing she could do for him. The act wouldn't have bothered her boulder-like classmate in the slightest, and her mature—read: *cheeky*—underclassman would have seen through it and given her a chilly stare. Hirofumi, however, let his eyes wander, unable to conceal his unrest.

"Well, when he says *assistance*, he means that we'd like to borrow your knowledge."

But it didn't work on Mio. Either it was ineffectual against members of the same sex, or despite her childlike looks, she was still a big sister.

"After all, this is, as you said, very sudden. We haven't had enough time to prepare for it."

"I understand what you mean."

Mio put a hand to her cheek as though sincerely troubled. It made her seem *a little* more like an adult, but it also felt like a child overreaching herself, and so it ended up looking much more heartwarming than attractive. But Mayumi, not about to let down her guard, hid a sense of caution and nodded.

"Fight magic with magic and magicians with magicians. It's a commonality."

Hirofumi continued, having gotten backup (?) from his sister and recovered his calm. By "commonality," he probably meant it was the same for both Japan and the GAA and any other country. Interpreting it as such, Mayumi awaited his next words.

"They likely know full well that my sister will be with us."

Mayumi noted her agreement. Japan had no intention of keeping Mio's participation under wraps anyway. Their plan was to register Mio and Hirofumi to the roster of high-ranking officers as possessing the right to engage in hostilities.

The deterrent would only work if the enemy knew about them.

Secret weapons, in the truest sense, couldn't be used as negotiation tools for coaxing an enemy into compromise.

"They should understand as well as we do that marine forces are ineffectual against her Abyss. Therefore, we predict they'll use air power and magic as the backbone of their interception force."

The movement-type, strategic-class spell Abyss caused the sea's surface to collapse into a spherical shape anywhere from a few dozen meters to several kilometers in radius. Warships engulfed in Abyss's zone of activation on the water would slide down the steep ocean slope or simply fall, as well as capsize or drown in the giant waves caused by the water's surface reverting upon the spell's cancellation. An Abyss one kilometer in radius would create a hemisphere one kilometer deep at its lowest point, easily enough to engulf submarines.

With too little distance, the displaced water would surge before the spell ended, causing damage to allies as well. Despite that flaw, though, Mio's strategic magic, with its firing range of dozens of kilometers, was considered the archenemy of any naval forces, above or below the water.

At the same time, however, Mio's Abyss was completely ineffective against airpower. She could only activate it on a continuous surface of water, and in order to attack a ground facility with it, they'd have to inject enough underground water ahead of time. It had many restrictions on its usage.

Hirofumi knew the enemy force's composition because they didn't have any other choice.

"We can leave their airpower to the JDF, but we'll have to think about magician countermeasures on our own."

That, too, was an unobjectionable fact.

Whatever the formalities, at the heart of things, it didn't matter whether you belonged to the government, the military, or were a civilian. All Japan's magicians, whether modern or ancient, belonged to a community that had the Ten Master Clans at the top, and they held to autonomy. JDF magicians would be with them, too, of course, but they would belong to the same category.

"Ms. Mayumi, in Yokohama, you witnessed the enemy's magic, and our allies' magic that defeated them, right? We'd like you to tell us what you know about any tendencies the enemies had in their spells and about effective magic to use against them."

It was a truly difficult, troubling question. There was no reason to doubt the necessity of providing information. She couldn't refuse, nor was it anything she had to refuse—but still.

"...I didn't see very much of the enemy's magic, since I was very far in the rear. The only time we actually crossed swords was during the sniper attack from above our helicopter."

There had actually been a second time—when she destroyed the upright tank—but she hadn't lied on purpose. It simply hadn't left much of an impression on her.

Hirofumi certainly didn't doubt her words, but he wasn't satisfied with the answer. "I heard you strove to get ordinary people out until the very end, though."

"Ordinary people" meant non-magicians. It was a bias, seeing magicians as something special and those who weren't magicians as powerless. Mayumi had always felt that view only made things worse for both sides. But now wasn't the time to point that out.

"You misunderstand. It wasn't until the very end... And it was my classmates and underclassmen who held the enemies off while we were waiting for the helicopter."

"Then would you be able to introduce us to those people? Especially to the freshman who actually fought against the GAA's magicians?"

The first thing that came to Mayumi's mind was a certain mature, cheeky, but still dependable upperclassman. A freshman who had turned a large truck to dust, been surrounded by brilliantly glowing psions, and used a healing technique that was nothing short of a miracle.

But a moment later, almost at the same time, the simple term *state secret* came back to her, paralyzing her from speaking.

"Ms. Mayumi?"

Mio gave the clammed-up girl a dubious look. She wasn't the only one with suspicion on her face, though. Hirofumi, obviously, too—but Mayumi started to panic at her father having doubts.

"Oh, well… If you visit the Juumonji family, I think they'll be able to tell you the details."

"Katsuto, right…"

Hirofumi was by no means a mean-spirited person. In fact, he was a quite agreeable young man. But for a while now, Mayumi had considered him, in a normal way, too *good* of a person.

She knew he felt a sense of competition and inferiority toward the boy two years younger than him, and she understood that she couldn't blame him. But given the context, showing jealousy wasn't very commendable of him. Especially showing it to the point that a much younger girl would notice.

Mayumi stamped her mental report card with a "pass," then feigned innocence once again.

"As for others who might help… Mari Watanabe, Kei Isori, and Kanon Chiyoda, all from the Hundred. I can contact them if you wish."

"Yes, please do."

Well, commenting only on his flaws just made her feel less cheerful.

In a businesslike manner, Mayumi counted off the names, then promised to set up a meeting for them.

After that, Mayumi called Mari, Kei, and Kanon straightaway (Katsuto wasn't home). After making appointments with all of them, she and her father saw the Itsuwa siblings out.

Her real intentions now were to take a short break. But judging from her father's expression, it looked like it would be a little longer before she was released.

"Mayumi, I'd like to talk to you for a moment, if you have time."

As expected, after they left the hotel-sized porte cochere and came back to the entrance hall, which was big enough to host a ball, Kouichi stopped her.

"Let's talk in my study."

Without waiting for an answer, he immediately started walking.

Kouichi's appearance strongly resembled that of an elite business-man from the latter part of the last century. If forced to explain in detail, his physique's most distinct detail were the slender lines, and his facial features came off as amiable rather than dignified. His tone of voice was soft to match, but his way of being the family head by not giving his family choices in matters like this was much like the other Ten Master Clans heads.

Adopting a pointlessly rebellious attitude wasn't Mayumi's style, either. Still clothed in her long, stifling dress she wouldn't normally wear, she followed after her father.

The study only had classic bookshelves, an imposing desk, and a single high-backed leather chair. Kouichi sat in the chair right away, meaning Mayumi would have to listen to his words while standing. This was the usual fare, so at this point she didn't mind it.

"I didn't hear the freshmen's names in the list you provided," began Kouichi without any preface to his daughter standing about two meters away. "I heard the young Chiba lady and the second son of the Yoshida family played quite a role, too."

My tanuki of a father, thought Mayumi. His appearance was more like a fox than a tanuki and more like a wolf than a fox, but she was convinced that when it came to her father, what was on the outside didn't match what was on the inside.

"As you know, they are still freshmen, so I thought it would be difficult to explain that part well to Hirofumi and Mio."

And you got a detailed report from Nakura anyway, didn't you? she thought as she watched her father say "ah." Just yesterday, she'd had to go through a questioning that started in much the same way. He was stubborn, more like a hunter than a raccoon sprite.

"But they apparently fought incredibly well for freshmen, didn't they? Especially her, the one who was all over the Nines—"

"Miyuki, you mean?"

"Yes, yes. Miyuki Shiba, wasn't it?"

She thought she saw his lightly tinted, false-glass frames glinting. The glasses were for hiding his fake right eye, but she'd had suspicions that there was some kind of special gimmick built into them as well.

"She seems like a very talented girl. Top of her class this year, vice president of the student council—and if all goes well, she'll be student president just like you."

"Yes, she is an extremely talented girl. And a very pretty one, too."

"Oh, so even you think so, Mayumi?"

"*Even* meaning as another girl? Well, in my opinion, her beauty transcends gender."

Kouichi's lips softened a little.

There was no muddled lust showing in his left eye behind his glasses.

And that only aroused Mayumi's caution further.

"Well, well... Not only can she master difficult spells like Inferno and Niflheim, she can even use incredibly powerful and unique exo-typed magic... I'd like to see it sometime. Can't we invite her here?"

"I don't know... I would have to ask her."

"Right. Would you mind asking if she has time? And Miyuki has an older brother, doesn't she? You said he helped you during the Nines, remember? This is a good opportunity, so I'd like to invite them here together, partly to thank him."

His amiable smile wouldn't clue others in to his inner thoughts. His tinted lenses wouldn't let them see the intention in his eyes.

However—they'd known each other her whole life. At eighteen years old, any one-sided relationship where only one could see through the other would change.

So that was his goal...!

In the helicopter, she'd made Nakura promise to keep it a secret. The episode concerning Tatsuya's singular spell shouldn't have made it to her father's ears.

But she didn't think none of it had gotten to him.

She wasn't optimistic.

Nakura was a crafty old fox; he would have implied the hidden truth to his employer in a way that wouldn't break his duty to secrecy. And her father was a battle-hardened veteran; he would have dug up whatever information he could from him.

Her father suspected him—Tatsuya Shiba.

Suspected him for something he didn't know, for something he hadn't figured out yet.

The desire to know smoldered within Mayumi as well, but her desire to let the secret sleep was still the stronger.

She was unconsciously afraid of revealing it and ruining their current relationship.

"I'd have to ask about that, too..."

That answer was all she could manage right now.

After staying shut in his study and looking at his desk for a short while, the Saegusa family head looked up at a soft knock at the door.

"Enter."

Unlike the reception room's door, his study's door didn't have a built-in speaker. His low voice, almost a mumble, couldn't logically have gotten through the thick door and into the hallway.

But with no repeated knocks, the study's door opened without a sound.

The one who entered was a middle-aged butler with neatly combed gray hair—Nakura.

"Any results?"

His question was fragmentary, but Nakura, after walking up to his master, respectfully held out a memory card to him.

Kouichi took the paper card printed with minute, microscopic patterns, set it on his scanner, and called a decrypted document up onto a display he unfolded on his desk.

"The 101st Brigade's Independent Magic Battalion... That's trouble. That was the unit the Yotsuba are so enthusiastically approaching, wasn't it?"

"They do appear to make contact from time to time, but their goals are unknown."

"I would think there is only one reason any of us would contact the military."

When Kouichi said "any of us" here, he didn't mean just the Saegusa family or just the Ten Master Clans but every magician in Japan.

Japanese magicians didn't desire government positions. They were forbidden by the Ten Master Clans from acquiring "public" influence endorsed by the state.

In exchange, they built their continued existence upon providing their magical skills to politicians, the military, the police force, and the economic world—to people with varied types of influence. By becoming a tool they'd continue to use rather than a disposable one—by becoming an indispensable *tool*—they had worked their way up to be servants controlled by a master. For that, they needed two things: to continue to be useful and to be seen as necessary. An ongoing, mutually beneficial relationship was required.

To acquire that, they needed more than just a quantity of strength.

The sharpest swords carried a fear for the user that their blades might turn upon him. An ongoing, mutually beneficial relationship needed to be built on trust that there would be no betrayal.

If a magician was in contact with the military, it was to acquire and maintain trust, to build a mutually beneficial relationship, or to solidify such a relationship. This idea was *common sense* to those with knowledge of magician affairs.

But Nakura didn't agree with what his master said.

"Major General Saeki created the Independent Magic Battalion with the goal of organizing the Ten Magic Clans' independent magical forces. Its leader, Major Kazama, is considered by the retired Major General Kudou and the Ten Master Clans to be a critical figure. The Yotsuba may be quite heterodox, but I'm given to believe even they couldn't use his unit for their own purposes."

Kouichi frowned. "...This is the first I've heard of this."

"The Independent Magic Battalion has never mattered to the Saegusa family's interests in the past."

Then why do you know about something like that? Kouichi wanted to ask, but he held the question in. If Nakura explained that he'd just found out now, that would be that. And even though he was of long service to the family, Kouichi didn't think of him as one of them. Nakura probably felt the same way.

"...Then why are the Yotsuba in contact with the Independent Magic Battalion?"

Instead, he asked after something else. And a moment later, he figured it out for himself.

"I believe your idea is correct."

Nakura had no mind-reading skills. Neither did Kouichi. But Kouichi was sure that Nakura had arrived at the same guess as he had.

Kouichi removed the card from the scanner and held it between his right index and middle fingers, then waved his hand nonchalantly. The thrown paper card shone in midair and burned up in the blink of an eye.

Nakura bowed and turned around before putting the ashes into the garbage bin.

◇ ◇ ◇

On a corner of the expansive Saegusa family residence, there was a building with a long, slender, rectangular motif. Simple but not boorish, it was the Saegusa private shooting range.

It belonged to the family, but it had been made primarily for Mayumi. It was built five years ago, when Mayumi had won her first trophy at a national competition.

With nervous strain building up, Mayumi had holed herself up in the shooting range right after lunch, and three hours had already passed. One by one, she raised her specialized CAD, which looked like a long staff with a grip attached, and fired at the targets.

She shot.

She destroyed.

Since she was shooting magic, not using real bullets, her hands wouldn't get tired, but the mental fatigue would have been even greater.

But Mayumi had a lot of pent-up gloom, and even that exhaustion felt good to her.

As she continued shooting one after the other with no regard for pacing herself, she ran through their entire target stock without realizing it. She glanced at the clock and was belatedly surprised at the time. After standing her CAD up on the rack, she started to clean up—but didn't get very far.

"Sis, we're home!"

Just as she removed her goggles, which were also an information terminal, someone suddenly hugged her from behind, forcing her to change her plans before getting to clean up.

"Kasumi, don't run up and hug her like that. You're bothering her."

"Come on, Izumi. Why do you have to be so whiny?"

"Because you're always impolite."

It wasn't really a bother—she'd just stumbled—but she was honestly grateful Kasumi let go right away (or rather, that she was peeled off).

"Kasu, Izu, welcome back."

Mayumi straightened herself while the twins were arguing like always and welcomed her younger sisters back for real.

"Thanks, Big Sister."

One of the girls bowed politely, hands at her sides: Izumi Sae-gusa, the younger of the two twins. She was an effeminate girl with a straight bob cut that reached her shoulders.

The one who had hugged her was the older of Mayumi's twin younger sisters, Kasumi Saegusa. In contrast to Izumi, she had a boy-ish look with her hair cut short.

They were identical twins, but since their style and moods were polar opposites, nobody would normally mistake one for the other.

"What were you practicing? Not live bullet movement magic, right? Virtual-region magic?"

"Was it piercing magic that extends a virtual region? Big Sister, you've been practicing that kind of spell a lot lately."

But they shared a sharp eye when it came to magic.

If Mayumi had to say, she'd call herself the type to prioritize the feel of using magic over its theory, and the twins emphasized the feel in the same way. Their instinctive insight into knowing what kind of magic was triggered might have been even better than Mayumi's. They'd figured it out again, too, from the bullet holes left in the targets.

Mayumi loved her younger sisters to the point where she pampered them too much, and they were both attached to her. Lately, though, she'd been seeing them get a little cheeky. She put it down to their age.

"You were doing a lot of shooting, Big Sister," sighed Izumi, sharply noting that there were no remaining targets.

"I bet Hirofumi came again!" grinned Kasumi. "He always puts Sis in a bad mood."

Mayumi had erased her expression right away to hide her sur-prise, but she didn't think it had fully worked. These two really had sharp intuition. *Or maybe I'm just too easy to read?* she thought, getting a little blue.

"Even though I don't think he's a bad guy," added Kasumi.

"He isn't a bad person, but that's all," stated Izumi. "He's not very reliable, which makes him a bad match for our sister."

"Your grading is too strict, Izumi. What kind of person *would* be good, then? Like Katsuto?"

"Wait, Kasu, Juumonji and I aren't—"

"Well, there's certainly nothing wrong with his looks, but he doesn't, shall I say, understand a maiden's heart. That part is a little unfortunate."

When Katsuto's name came up for no reason—which Mayumi truly believed—she quickly tried to untangle her sisters' "misunderstanding," but neither of them were listening.

"*Shall I say?* You don't need to pretend to be someone else around me, you know… And how is a man supposed to understand a maiden's heart anyway? We don't know what men think about, either."

"That won't do! Think harder, Kasumi! Maidens only need to understand a man's heart after they're already dating! The man has to be the one to win the girl's heart."

"Win her heart? …Well, whatever. So what besides looks would they need?"

"True love, I guess…but that's a really high hurdle to start with, so maybe just falling in love."

"I've known you ever since we were born, but I didn't know you were so romantic about stuff. I thought you were just a prude."

"I happen to take offense at that… But anyway, I'm not a romantic. You just don't pay enough attention to these things."

"Okay, okay. I'm not very girlie anyway. Anyway, who would fall in love with her? Hattori?"

"Kasu! How do you even know who Hanzou is?!"

Even Mayumi, who had been left in the dust at some point (since the beginning, actually), couldn't let that one go. She had literally no recollection of ever introducing Hattori to her sisters.

"Oh, we know all the dirty bugs flying around you, Big Sister."

"Izu— You two haven't been spying on me, have you?! Anyway, can we stop talking about who I'm dating?!"

"Come on, Sis. We have school, too. We can't *personally* go there to spy on you."

But you'd get other people to do it?! she screamed to herself, but nobody could hear her, of course. Actually, the twins might have heard it in one way or another, but they didn't show any signs of it.

"And we're worried about you," said Izumi. "You're so beautiful, but you're eighteen now and you've never dated… You're about to graduate from high school, too."

"It's not that I can't, but my position…" She trailed off, realizing that finishing the sentence would sound like an excuse. And a pathetic, sad excuse at that.

"Besides, neither of you have ever dated a boy, either!"

She tried to veer away from the topic but hadn't realized this was a pretty pathetic thing to say in its own right—at least, not until her sisters counterattacked.

"Well, we're only fifteen."

"But I had two people confess to me today. I politely turned them down, though. It is certainly difficult to meet the right person, isn't it?"

"That's because you're a prude, Izumi. You should just give it a shot."

"And *you're* just a big risk. None of the boys you're friends with think of you as just a friend, you know… If you keep being so carefree, you're going to get a painful reality check someday."

As her sisters' conversation faded into the background, Mayumi, now aware of how pathetic she was, felt depressed.

November 4.

The day classes's lunchtime finally continued:

"President—or rather, Mayumi. You seem very tired."

Mayumi, who had visited the student council room saying she'd help do ex post facto cleanup, was being watched by Azusa's worried eyes.

"Mm, I guess. But I'm fine."

"Maybe you should have rested until next week."

Today was Friday. There were classes on Saturday, too, but the seniors were essentially allowed free attendance now, so plenty of students were studying at home today and tomorrow.

"And sometimes you're more tired than you think you are."

"You're right. That's why I came to school."

Azusa looked at her in blank confusion.

Well, other people wouldn't be able to understand that she'd come to school because being at home wore her out even more.

She also kind of felt like explaining it would be embarrassing.

So instead of answering Azusa's doubts, she put a hand to her mouth and gave a little audible yawn.

She overlapped her hands on the table.

She put her cheek on top of them.

With her suddenly collapsing on the table and starting to take a nap, she sensed Azusa's eyes going wide, but she didn't care, and soon she was snoring away.

Afterword

First, I'd like to extend my heartfelt thanks to everyone who purchased this book. I hope you'll continue to support me in the future, whether this is our first meeting or not.

This volume is both the conclusion to the Visitor arc and the final episode in the Shiba siblings' freshman year. In that connection, I'd like to talk a little about how it was a little backstage feeling this time and how *The Irregular at Magic High School* is written.

My writing process has no sense of life. I've never had the god of novels descend to me or the characters ever act on their own even once. I'd like to experience that at least once, but unfortunately, it seems the god of novels is giving me the cold shoulder.

When I write a story, first I think about its structure, then I summarize it, then before I start each arc I piece together scenarios, and then I finally start writing the actual text. By accumulating smaller episodes and thinking about what a character would do in this situation, I build up to a larger story, like the Enrollment arc or the Visitor arc.

It doesn't always work this way, though. Exceptionally, sometimes I'll have an image of a scene I'd like to write first. When that happens, I add factors into the scene I imagined to work it into the rest of the story. There are three concrete examples of this:

the last dance scene in the Nine School Competition arc

the ability-unleashing scene in the Yokohama Disturbance arc

and the siblings' combination attack in this book

Looking at it this way, it's easy to understand that *The Irregular at Magic High School* owes its story to Tatsuya and Miyuki.

Since this was the last episode in Tatsuya and Miyuki's freshman year, that also means the seniors will graduate. But please don't worry—in this series, graduation doesn't mean leaving the stage. I can't say all the current senior characters will appear again, but there will be no shortage of opportunities for them to. And in this way, the number of characters will keep increasing. I apologize for the burden I'm placing on persons concerned.

Anyway, Tatsuya and the others will advance to their junior year next time. Tatsuya's position will change completely, too. I'll keep on presenting aspects that might turn the story into *The Revolutionary at Magic High School*, but rest assured that the actual title will remain *The Irregular at Magic High School*.

I look forward to your support in the next volume: *The Irregular at Magic High School: Double Sevens Arc.*

Tsutomu Sato

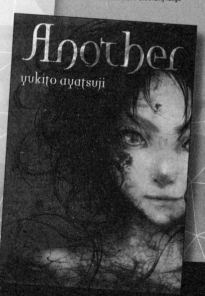